A WARDROBE FULL OF CLOTHES

PATER AVE AND GLORIA

She moved her knees which had dug through the carpet and had found the bare floorboards. Her back ached as she laid flat her palms to raise herself from the floor. She moved over to her bed and switched off the alarm set to go off at seven-thirty. She took a cigarette from the box sat on the marble ledge of the fireplace that had been boarded up with a large slice of plywood. She lit the cigarette with the matches she used to light the candles. She set the cigarette in the ashtray and went to the foot of her bed and slipped on her skirt and cardigan she had placed there the night before. He was right, she realised, as she buttoned the cardigan up to her throat, the room needed decorating, the walls and ceiling could do with a lick of paint, the curtains needed to be washed, not burnt as he had suggested. She would talk to him, get him to paint the room as he had promised, it would take his mind off things; God knows he needed it right now.

She took the cigarette down from the ashtray noticing from the naked light bulb from the beside table the blue veins snaking across the back of her hand. She examined both hands under the light and was reminded of her mother's hands clasped in prayer, prepared for her final rest. We come into the world as a child and we leave it as one, she could hear her say with a wry smile that encapsulated a lifetime of world-weary knowingness. She would get him to fix that lampshade too she thought standing up.

She felt sure the contract between sinner and Saint, made in devout silence to protect its sanctity, would be honoured. She came to believe her case would be strengthened by the same devotion to the same cause she had made before; and then as now, she knew that the sweet infant Jesus would hear her petition and act. Act too for her dearly departed mother and father. Act for John, her beloved husband, who would have more than a word to say about these latest shenanigans. Him, a pioneer from the age of eleven, when a family member, an uncle from the Glens, she recalled gave him a glass of clear liquid at a family wedding. Dr. Gibson, who was at the function, examined him in the hotel manager's private office prescribed plenty of strong tea and a good nights sleep. Works wonders for hangovers he diagnosed.

Alcohol never touched his lips from that day, nor tobacco. His disciplined lifestyle was something she admired, but fought his predilection into obsession from extending into all areas of their lives, particularly with the children. Children are supposed to get dirty, scabby knees, she would clean their clothes and tend to their scrapes and grazes. He would retreat into lengthy silences with a book or the paper and only broke that silence with withering remarks of such personal acerbity that was incinerating to her heart. The love she had, she administered with the same economy.

It was the 'trouble with his waterworks' that signalled the end and it came with an intolerable alacrity and cruelness that robbed him of his life's time regime of cleanliness and privacy. Not a sick day in eighteen years he would remark. His abnegation was all the more cruel and distressing as he lay amongst his own filth, tended by strangers. She prayed now he was at peace and that he had forgiven her as she had him.

Two million thoughts ago. Yet there it remained on the receipt for two pints of Guinness, one vodka (Smirnoff), a coke (diet). One written word, deliberately mis-spelt, a word , not within her emotional vocabulary. Perhaps it was a million thoughts ago.

Perhaps he was awake, perhaps he was dead, perhaps; because he felt the same.

A feeling brought to life within a dead body, one that summed up his whole being, his character, his soul. None of these were to take flight. His fate lay in the drudgery of a less than ordinary life, a life, like so many others; in place to serve as a back drop in which others would shine.

Woman! Take one more step and I'll choke out the last breath from your diseased lungs, he thought, his mind a co-conspirator to the savagery he felt. This is it, dragged into being to bear the bluntness of another day. He turned to look down on the cigarette box, empty, torn open, flattened out on the floor; the graffiti of hastily scribbled words lay without meaning or significance outside of the nowhere hours when sleep deserted and the awake proved unmerciful.

The voice again, straining under the weight of exhortation and effort, with every erratic, strangled breath forced from brown paper bag lungs laying the siege of artificial life.

Day had begun in earnest.

Oh dear, he yawned, determined not to rise to the sheer bloody-mindedness of it. Wandher she las' got 'er leg over, eh? *Not since you were right in the 'ead me ole china.*

Fuck off. he thought back. And you too, he thought towards the brown door and beyond it to the staircase. "Alright, I'm up. I'm getting' on me now. Go on back down. I'll be there in a minute." He allowed his raised head to fall back on the pillow. He lay motionless, rigid, hurting, listening to his breathing; listening for her listening for him to make getting up sounds. He could envisage the fine grey line of a moustache twitch in anticipation, preparing, before he heard the sound of a begrudging retreat.

"Aye well, hurry up, ye haven't all day."

There it was, the utterly unnecessary sweep of the coated tongue. A few moments of hot silence gathered in and around him. Moments he would use to summon the will to get up and get out of bed. With feigned difficulty, he released himself from the bed's anxious support, dragging his shattered legs over to the chair dressed in anarchic design of clothes. His movement severely restricted, his walk stilted and difficult, made virtually impossible by the replacement joints and harvested muscle lost in a machine gun attack on his holiday home in Donegal. The publication of his fourth, and certainly not his best novel, a scathing indictment of the bloody power struggle for the streets of Belfast had so enraged a certain power broker that the equivalent of a fatwa, an O'fatwa, he supposed, had been issued on his life.

He could only thank God that his Nobel prize-winning wife, his trilingual children, his incredibly talented and urbane friends, and as an assortment of literary alumni whom had gathered to celebrate his Pulitzer were all spared in the ghastly, cowardly attack.

He lifted his shirt from the chair and put it on as he crossed without difficulty to the wardrobe mirror, rubbing his eyes free of the honeycomb of sleep and used both hands to put down rebellious clumps of dirty fair hair that had been nailed into his head throughout a fitful, dreamless night. His teeth felt like sponge to the touch of his coated tongue; his armpits and crotch smelt of ripened vinegar. His palms gloried in sweat, his fingers cracked as they caressed the moist shroud of flesh constituting his face. His body ached at every effort and the relentless throbbing sub-dividing his brain made the intermittent, uncontrollable noise emanating from the stairs intolerable.

He was late. Hours late, if you were to believe that 'oul shites clamouring, creaking endeavour on the stairs. He scrutinised the imposter, cracked bloated lips remained unmoved as the stranger stared back in mute indifference. It probed for features the face denied him. Anonymous. If ever a face reflected the true character of its owner, his was it.

M. M, my subhuman friend is for mediocre. How right, my dear bogshite. Yet, d, d, is for dead. Born in bogland, dead in a boghome for bogbollockeses's. Sin è.

Ireland, he though savagely, buttoning up his shirt, with it's necrophilic landscape, dead heroes, poets and lovers, of heart-warming fires to keep out the chill of ghostly tales. A green, unspoilt land, abundant in deference and devilment, awash with well-meaning priests administering to thoughtful, faithful congregations who peered towards a European funded future and a whoring of its past. He returned to the bed to put on a fresh pair of socks. Oh begorragh! Greedy in rebellion, suppression and uprising with a good ole IRA to give it a bit of substance, armed with impotent subversiveness to soothe and assuage delicate southern dispositions and excite the limited imaginations of fourth and fifth generation Irish Americans. Ah to be sure, we shot up a few places, but there was no harm meant. T'was all poetry and very little blood. Not for them the meanness of the everyday, the banality of the evil, the personal proximity of the present. Ah, alliteration, where would won be without it, ha ha, good one.

"It's almost nine." She underlined the word nine with three red lines of disapproval. With shoulders hunched, chest withdrawn, eyes lowered he moved to the breakfast table in deliberate incongruity to the noise, movement and purpose of the room.

He dragged a chair out from beneath the table, sat down and buried his elbows into the surface of the table until it hurt.

Somewhere in the no-mans land between the table and the cooker her old slippers, left a slapping sound on the linoleum as she circled the room; an unspoken, undeclared enmity brooded in the vacuum that existed between them.

"Oh for Godsakes, get yourself a new pair of slippers and give those back to the museum." Entente not so cordial, he thought, the unintended loudness of his outburst forced the knitting needle lodged in his brain that bit further in. "And stop smoking over the food." He further complained, pushing aside the ashtray of drained cigarette ends piled up in formations only the dead could assume.

The breakfast plate hovered into view, with one large chapped thumb, the nail sketched in embedded dirt, perilously close to the scrambled egg. He left his stare where the thumb had rested on the plate. Irrespective of her total disregard for hygiene and health, the egg looked hard and dry with a protective skin covering it, the bacon in a state of petrifaction, which with one light prod of his fork snapped into several pieces. "I'm not eating this shite." He dropped the fork emphatically onto the plate as she returned to the table with a mug of tea. She placed it beside his plate and without a word parried his glare with one of her own. He would have left it at that, cut his losses, his disgust duly registered, if it were not for the noise she sucked out from her mouth. "And why don't you put your teeth in?" His retort followed her out of the kitchen and into the living room. He sat on at the table and tried a piece of toast that had been set out on a separate plate. Cold, soggy, with a buttery under felt that made him spit out the piece he had in his mouth onto the scrambled egg. He stood up, took the mug of tea, and went into the living room possessed by an urgent, unpleasant need for a fight. "That was lovely, but I can't for the life of me understand why you didn't wait until the food got cold before serving it?" He went to the mantelpiece to get one of her cigarettes. "And that fork," he said lighting up, "if you stabbed someone with that you'd be up for attempted poisoning." He sat down on the settee opposite her on her chair by the window. She continued to read her paper in complete silence, contemplating the word anachronism. She knew it meant something bad, as it was contained within a line in the letters page in relation to the Orange Order. 'The Orange Order and what it represents are at best an anachronism and at its worst an enemy to the democratic peoples of Ireland and beyond its shores.' Signed MH. True Democrat. Newry. She made a mental note to look it up in her dictionary and also try to find a word for what her grandson was doing, when he asked why she didn't spruce up her living room. It was rhetorical, she now knew as he continued.

"I mean, it's like a Clingon's view of somebody's arse." He laughed aloud at the analogy he drew with the room and its dominant colour, brown.

"You'd be better getting onto your work than coming out with that filth." She answered him, turning the page on the paper with an inordinate amount of flappy paper noise that grated on his nerves. He watched her, as she read undeterred, in her quest for some unfortunate creature that had found his or herself on the obituary page. Her winged glasses perched on the round tip of her fleshy nose made her face a portrait of concentration that made her appear almost scholarly and her endeavour all the more chilling.

"Well, I'll be going in on an empty stomach, thanks to that so-called breakfast you served up."

"It's nobody's fault but your own." She shot back, folding the paper down to a more manageable size. "If you'd got up when I called ye."

Jeezus. He knew the road they were on and the pointless destination that circumstance had mapped. If he were to point out that any sane person might have kept the food in the oven, her repudiation would have involved the cost of electricity, the rise in the Bank of England base rate, the collapse of the Iron Curtain, the Albanian grain crisis, Christ knows what else. He sat back on the settee having thoroughly defeated himself. "Anyone in the obits you know? Any bombings, shootings, knee-cappings, severe paper cuts? I'd love to know as I've a bet on." He got up and extinguished the cigarette in the ashtray placed on the dead electric fire. She made a humph sound to it all. "Here, turn the TV. up I want to hear the news." She leaned to one side, removed the remote from the side of the chair and lobbed it onto the settee. He picked it up and turned up the sound just in time for the local news. A bomb attack on a mobile police patrol in Tyrone had resulted in shock for its members. "Shock! Horror! Damn that ceasefire. there's no bloody news worth listening to, especially from that bunch of recidivists. The weather gets more coverage and even the most boring man this side of Christendom gets his bake on much too often. Who cares about ten jobs created in a factory making filters for some bloody lorry ." There were reports of shooting in East Antrim , early indications were that police thought there was no paramilitary involvement. "Nothing's going right. I'll never win my bet with this level of so-called terrorism." He muttered aloud. "Bloody newscasters , state-censored retards."

"It's no wonder there's no luck in this house." She sucked out her lament turning the page of her paper. He shushed her to be silent. Bomb scares were disrupting traffic in and around Lisburn. An elderly man had been knocked down and killed in the early hours of the morning. The car had failed to stop at the scene of the accident. And now the weather.

"Useless. Where's the indiscriminate acts of violence that the lefties can applaud, only if it's not in their back yard, oh they'll support lesbian car bombings in the name of vegetarianism in Guatemala, but , ah to hell with it. I can't be arsed. And you put your teeth in before spouting off." He told his granny, before placing the remote on the arm of her chair taking his mug he went into the kitchen.

"Christ of almighty." His exclaimed. "Can't you wash your drawers in the machine like a normal person?" He shouted.

"They're not drawers you." She told him, rushing into the kitchen and using her entire frame to edge him away from the sink. "It's the net curtains steeping." She explained, plunging both hands into the bowels of the sink. "The machines only for full loads."

"Like your drawers." He laughed and the laugh was made all the more genuine when he saw her smile.

"Away you to work before you're thrown out of that job." She told him, hoisting the drowned material up to inspect in the dim light lurking in the backyard.

"Alright, I'll get on." He submitted, suddenly gripped by the absorbing meanness of her life and the meanness absorbing his own. He glowed with a minor rage at the suppressing regime of indignities and injustices life made for them. He looked at her arms; the sleeves of her cardigan rolled up to the elbow, and felt a rush of sadness at the sight of those forearms cast in skin no longer required. Her once beautiful face carved up in wrinkles, her brittle grey hair thinning, exposing her flaky scalp. He could kill God all over again for what He had created, a life-time of enduring suffering and decline.

"Your lunch is over by the breadbin." She told him, squeezing the air trapped in the body of the material that let out in watery dripping gasps.

"See you later then," He said collecting the lunchbox. "I'll collect the washing after work. Ok?" There was a watery gasp to that. "Then back to the flat." He attempted brightly. There was one of her humph sounds to that. "I'll get on them." He added, forced by the jagged, tortured nature to his gratitude that compelled him to retreat from the kitchen.

"Oh, before I forget," he called back, " if that scoundrel Murray rings about the car. Get him to ring me at work. I'll call in after and see him anyway." He added, embodying his performance.

"Yes. Yes, if you ever get to work." She shouted back, blindly ushering him from the house with a vigorous sweep of one of her arms.

Aye and to hell with you too, he thought back, relieved that normal relations had been resumed.

Outside the sun dot lounged low in a cloudless sky, casting perfect shadow and giving the glare of a bedside lamp. He lowered his eyes to shield them from the stabbing light and lifting one deadened leg in front of another, he walked.

Instantly they came, coaxed from their expectant buds, sweat blossomed and reigned on his forehead. Accompanied by the unremitting intensity and constancy you found only in something extremely stupid. With the heat, he began to loathe. He found his aimless animosity his only source of comfort, it grew and developed as he swapped the punishing concrete for the muscled liquorice of the tarmacked road. He was confident by the time he reached the first set of traffic lights, he was being targeted by that glaring dot. He should have worn jeans instead of the cords that were proving unyielding in the integrity of their material. The material began to chafe at his upper thighs and crotch. The trousers seemed to trap the heat and in some hostile transmutation, he had become a walking barometer with the heated mercury blazing a trail from the epicentre of his balls, up through his chest and up into his head, threatening to crack open his skull.

He cursed that effulgent dot and it's sustaining of life, he cursed the howling, growling, dogs skulking in and around the foul smelling wheelie bins left out in the entries. He cursed the open theatre of the road, strewn with empty beer cans, the bottles, the food congealing in half-eaten takeaways, the spat out chewing gum pebble-dashing the ground. He cursed the people responsible, the people whom he passed and was passed by. He damned their ghetto mentality and clothing, their over-fed and under-nourished children, who looked like they had boxed for Chernobyl A.F.C. and lost. He damned them all for their diminished language and thought, they, who hated the Brits, but were in receipt of their benefit system that kept them in bed, babies and beer.

He waited for a gap in the traffic and without waiting for the lights to change, crossed to the other side of the road passing a tattooed thug in a tee-shirt sporting a giro sunburn on his arms and neck. Charles Darwin would have wept to see his life's work challenged and thoroughly discredited. He cursed the noise of the hot cars shitting out stench as they roared past containing their hot, fat, thin, bald, hairy, crumpled drivers. He damned to Hell the turnip-headed taxi drivers, who had never been introduced to indicator lights or speed restrictions.. He swore down death on them and the flashes of stabbing reflected light that pierced his eyes. He prayed through gritted teeth for the world to end so he could embrace the sight of them all trying vainly to escape a fate they all richly deserved.

The feeling passed and with it it's transient pleasure, leaving him to nurse a more vindictive need that beggared the mind and soul. Let them endure it, this ritual of minutes, hours, days, weeks, let them, like that faggot mincing out of the Spar with all his energies self-invested in his sculpted body; whilst all the time his being was being corroded by the flesh-eating rust that had been regularly pumped into him by the oblong, purple-capped dispenser of his lingering death. All the clothes, moisturisers and faghags won't bring Humpty Bum Bumpty back together again. Ha! Let time mark out their lives, let them feel keenly every tedious assault upon their senses and prolong this living purgatory, where everything between the entering and the departing, meant nothing.

He walked on under the personal animosity of the heat passing the off-licence where some scholar had advised in blue paint not to buy Isreli goods and the need for spelling lessons, no doubt too! Across the traffic island with a road on either side sat Gerry's shop, where a recent big bang had produced a galaxy of orange and yellow stars advertising the beginning of the spring sale. He hurried past in case Gerry would see him which would involve a conversation he had no strength or time for.

He turned into Clifton street its sloping road leading to the city centre, past the derelict church for the derelict faith, past the bunker of the Orange Hall with that fascist cunt King Billy the ballbeg lording it over the road astride his horse, his sword still raised to centuries of ascendancy, prejudice, and hate; paid for by an embattled Pope to protect his authority. Poor old Ireland, once again, the victim of its geography, he supposed. He passed the new solid housing of the benefit classes designed to contain them within their estates, discreet social engineering, most of them were thankful for. They were great solid chunks of taxpayers money, in redbrick and double-glazing. All their windows beset by lace curtains that were unveiled to showcase the ceramic obscenities of over-sized Dickensian urchins, vases and various breeds of dog. He didn't dare to contemplate the what the inside of those houses held, the large blown-up photos of their holidays in Majorca, with their children named after the latest popular TV soap like Chantelle, Madison and Corey smiling big, benefit smiles. Jeezus, he could look no more, he lowered his eyes and concentrated on the road.

Fifteen more hate-filled minutes later he was at his desk busily arranging papers to create an impression of work having been done. He eyed bumpkin-head hiding her mouth behind the receiver, but her corpulent cheeks betrayed her smile at his feverish toil against impossible time.

The case for spontaneous human combustion would arrive soon, bearing down on him with that limited repertoire of complaints, chides and farrago of moans that had him wanting to set fire to her himself rather than waiting for his prayers to be answered.

There would be a breathless rush through the door, seeking out bumpkin-head for morsels of encouragement and succour before descending on him with a lecture on punctuality, lacing the boots of that particular moral obligation with the tedious expectations for and on those fortunate to have a job. All aboard the bi-polar express. Sweet holy fuck.

The office door groaned open and she who eats to conquer, she who stoops to confer entered. She had crossed the office floor to conspire with bumpkin-head on some insanely inane matter. Gradually, the sharp horizon of the file he had raised to prevent immediate eye contact in advance of her arrival lowered to reveal her new head. Nestled above her fat, freckled trunk of a neck, constructed in a carefully bouffanted mass, was a vision in purple rinse. Jeezus, you'd need the heart of lion to go near that. *Too bleedin' right me ole china.*

"Good morning." The first shot across his bough. The irregular shaped cruiser rotated within the material of her dress and undergarments and landed at his desk. He could only hazard a guess at the strength of the charge of static electricity she produced, perhaps enough to power a small town he imagined, somewhere where bumpkin would live. She saddled up close to his side, ignoring the pretence he made of the file he was holding. She began nudging him with a large, fat, baby pink elbow. "Here, pay attention you, you've a lot to catch up on. Oh drop dead, so I can, given the energy, dance around your considerable carcass; he smarted, as the elastic band on his over-stretched patience snapped under her persistence to issue breath. Her tiny, brittle voice prattled on about new procedures that had been issued from Head Office no less. Implementing these new procedures would involve creating new formats and transferring existing databases to the new system. She recited the memo verbatim et litteratim.

"Would that include the databases we, or should I say, that I created on the G drive?" He asked, struggling to maintain an air of innocence and interest. Her green eyes darted from the side of their sockets to the other scanning the memo for an answer to his enquiry. There she was, this modern day Luddite, in charge, officially, of a computerised section. She smelt of lemon, too much make-up and hairspray, no doubt required to keep that industrial nylon she had for hair in place. He rested his chin in the cup of his hand whilst she squawked away in her tiny shrill voice like some gargantuan parakeet. He whiled away the time loathing everything about her, this refugee from the real world. The Service, give me your inept, your incompetent, your lazy indolent masses and you can have roles devoid of purpose and meaning. Oh, this stupefying stasis, stifling and starched; stuffed full with the cellulite of self-satisfaction and self-gratification. They were shameless in their pursuit of social stratification; contributing earnestly to the great farce.

"I'll have to check up on that would be a more honest answer." She said sharply with the note of a sniff of condescension

"Alright, I can get that done." He broke in, grasping the opportunity during a rare pause to remove her from his desk and fuck off and explode into vapour.

"Well then," her body crackling within the strangulated wrapping as she straightened up, "I can go and get my coffee now." She added, checking her ridiculously small watch on her fat pink wrist. She set the memo down in front of him and he watched her walk to the door, watched as she and bumpkin-head dripped smiles to each other. He decided to withdraw into a transgressed sulk and offer only withering looks and curt replies to bumpkin-head for the rest of the morning.

He sat at his desk viewing the minutiae of the everyday office, of every office everyone; with the notice boards pasted with everywhere reports no-one read, holiday postcards from the Costa's people saved towards to sit blistered and bloated in everywhere theme pubs, photographs of leaving do's, jokey notices that never raised a smile, the menus of local sandwich outlets. He looked over to Bumpkin's desk, tracing the intestinal leads, linking it to the network printers and fax, along the skirting and behind the filing cabinets where they disappeared. Above the filing cabinets sitting at a slant, the white board that mapped out the attendance of the working week. The list still contained Kieran's name, the boy who had up until his recent and untimely and unlikely promotion had sat opposite him. Two foot seven inches multiplied by two he had sat opposite to be precise, the width to his working desk, five foot three inches in length, the dimensions to his working life.

"New boy arrives here today. Strange day to come to your new place," Bumpkin head mused, "on a friday. Apparently he's from another department and he's been allowed to come over today to familiarise himself with the travel and the parking, you know what it's like here." Bumpkin-head piped up in an attempt to end the protracted silence that had enveloped the office since the case for spontaneous human combustion had left. He did not answer, not least because he was indifferent to what she had to say, he was; but it was more to exacerbate the impression that he was punishing her. Instead of meeting her need for conversation, he examined the range of coloured paper clips he liked to keep about his desk.

"About time too, I say." Bumpkin-head broke out again. He turned his attention to the ancient crystal set taped down at the side of his trays. Balls, he had just missed the news. The weather forecast catalogued intermittent showers across our wee province with high winds making driving conditions particularly difficult out and around Ballybollocks somewhere.

The radio voice, inhumanely upbeat, struggled against crossfire of static. Perhaps the case for spontaneous human combustion was passing along the corridor, her fat mitts clasping her coffee and some iced dainties.

Kieran, half-man, half-flexi, again sprung to his mind, his erstwhile image sitting, staring vacantly out of the window singing tunelessly to whatever played on the radio. He thought of the many times it had invoked in him the urge to grab the sharpest pencil he could find and plunge it into that empty head of his. His insipid face, with it's thin angular features that Bumpkin thought was handsome in a certain light. That same face would, no doubt, be staring out a different window, in possession of an executive position. This was all before his untimely and undeserved promotion, a guy who could turn the delivery of invoices to the fourth floor into a full days work, a guy who was advised if he stared out the window in the mornings he would have nothing to look forward to in the afternoon. He took all the admonishments with grace and humour, laughing at the annoyance his absence caused. This had Brendan thinking there was more to the boy than met the eye; perhaps he too saw the great farce, the absurdity of the grades, structures and hierarchical nature of a system that stifled the self. How could he have failed where Kieran succeeded, all his work, the innovations, the development of the databases, his system of monitoring the work, all these things met their fuckin' set criterion, yet within those twenty to twenty five minutes he had failed to persuade them he was good enough. He hated himself for wanting it so badly, because as they all knew it was a fuckin' joke, the whole system was.

Only the memory of the flexi blitz lifted his mood. It was the case for spontaneous human combustions' petty retribution for Kieran's unlikely and unjustified promotion. To be seen to being fair, everyone's sheet was taken that Thursday morning the penultimate before Kieran left. He knew her changes would reflect the level of antipathy she held for each individual, bearing that in mind when the sheets were returned he made a quick mental calculation on viewing Kieran's sheet that she hated him three and a half times more than she did him. Oh, she added, she would be checking that the sheet she had amended would be the one he presented to his new line manager. So there! The irony of the whole episode lay in the fact that it was her reports, written in hope to make Kieran more marketable and therefore facilitate his transfer request, had given him his move out of the office on promotion. At the time he could have laughed. Unfortunately, for him this same procedure of selection had deemed him unsuitable, unworthy, found wanting or lacking in qualities that Kieran apparently had. He rationalised it as the natural selection of the feeble-minded, pliable, malleable and open to manipulation to the higher levels of absurdity. Anyway, fuck it, he thought, he had more within him that could not be assessed and quantified in a series of questions set against appointed criteria.

He winced, remembering the leaving party, a turgid little event attended by low-level civil servants. He had already made Kieran an honoury member of the Flat Earth Society, due to his habitual residence in West Belfast that appeared to make most of the inhabitants fearful of travelling beyond Castle Street lest they should fall off the planet. When he arrived in the office over two years ago, he did not know where the Albert Clock was, nor the law courts, which was highly unusual from an inhabitant of that community he called him a Morlock. All this made The Case For... laughed heartily at the attack he had made upon Kieran, fuelled by drink and resentment and in no small part her amusement, he continued until Bumpkin made him go to the bar with her. She scolded him about his behaviour, his meanness, how petty, how he looked like 'a performing dog' for The Case For...The Unionists in the company were gorging on the internecine conflict, pandering as it did to their pre-conceptions of a large swathe of the

Nationalist community. Shame, shame on you Brendan. He could still hear her voice choking with disappointment at his tirade. He felt sick to his stomach, as again he realised he had no loyalties, no community, nothing to defend but the people he liked and considered friends. He sensed an urge to cry at the sight of Bumpkin genuinely upset and disappointed in him. He quickly apologised to her and went to toilet leaving her with the round of drink she had just bought. It was at this time he and Frances were beginning to unravel, his humour no longer assuaged her disappointment, his plans, in the face of any concrete developments, preparation or movement, appeared shallow and meaningless. He now consciously avoided the issue of a future. Later that evening, he had made amends with Bumpkin and allowed Kieran to score some points of his North Belfast constituency. He realised then that she would defend him even more stoutly if he were ever to be unfairly maligned. He was in an amenable, not yet forgiving, frame of mind when Bumpkin-head tried again to open lines of communication.

"Tea Brendan? Would you like some tea?" Her ballybollocks accent radiated a false, bright tempo, the mouthing of a hypocrite, not the penitent he desired.

"What?"

"Tea? Do you want a cup?"

"Yeah, why not, little milk, no sugar." He told her as he handed over his cup. "Here, where's Psychosomatic?"

"Margaret? She hasn't come in yet. Remember, she was talking about the problems

18

with the extension yesterday. She's been dealt a rotten hand with that house."

"And face. And personality." Brendan added. "What's wrong with it now?"

"They suspect subsidence in the kitchen extension. I told her to look at the deeds as they didn't build it, get in contact with the owners or their solicitors. I'll get Jerome to go through it if she wants. Now I'll get the tea." She said brighter than ever.

That gave the green light for her to generate a chorus of noise, drawers slammed, chairs rolled, her puffy cheeks blowing out a enquiry as to whether he would like a slice of home-made apple pie she had brought in or a blueberry muffin she had bought on her way to work. He grunted over to her that he would take a slice of apple pie. He watched her turn on her heels and depart the office to walk three doors down to the office kitchen.

He was keenly aware of her departure, the unconscious creaking of her shoes, the tenacious knitwear drawn down like sheet metal to the knee, smelling of soap and too much Sundays, her embryonic figure gestating rapidly towards middle age. Yet another plump doe-eyed cretin sleep-walking into life's next wonderful cycle. Eh John, wot you fink? Eh John did not respond, leaving him to deal entirely by himself, with his unkind thought.

He could feel his life mortally wounded, drained by daylight vampires who plagued his existence, hell-bent on some Mephistophelean plan to have him embrace the hordes of the living dead. Alone now, he found himself speculating on the kind of marriage she would have. Her engagement was now in its eighth month. Her fiancé, Jerome, worked in town planning, he liked squash, motorbikes and fishing for Godsake. Perhaps he should have assumed such an identity for the promotion board. And back to their marriage. Her simplicity so endearing at first, would collapse under intimacy and lift the smokescreen to reveal the true extent and depth of poverty to her character and his. But she would try to change, to adapt, but the capitulation would leave her despised and despising and you wouldn't even have the luxury in seeking solace in yourself. And a marriage in a small town, with small people would continue. But he delighted in the perceived rivalry Psychosomatic had developed. She had been married less that a year to John, a poor bastard of a self-employed heating engineer, who had become unwittingly embroiled in her demands to match Bumpkin's house and marriage plans. Her telephone calls to him got more frequent and her demands more vigorous, the patio had now become a conservatory, there was talk of upgrading the car and a holiday to Lake Garda to coincide with Bumpkin's planned honeymoon in Rome.

Gordon Bennett yer in a cheerful mood aintcha'?,All that palava says more about you, me ole china.

I know, he conceded.

After tea and a slice of Bumpkin-head's home made apple pie he settled down to the routine of his own work, Kieran's and now Psychosomatics as she had rang in sick, again. "What is it this time? Yellow parrot fever? Berri berri? Bitten by a fruit bat?" Bumpkin-head motioned with a wave of her hand for him to be quiet. She broke free of the receiver and placed one hand over the earpiece.

"She's got the flu." She hissed over to him. "She sounds terrible."

"So? She always does. The flu." He sneered back. "It's all in her head, no, in that big bugle of hers, make sure she's got a bed sheet handy in case she takes a sneezing fit." He said, getting up to go to the absentee's desk to check on what work needed to be done.

"Shush you!" Bumpkin-head laughed out and grimaced at the phone for her outburst.

"I don't think I've ever seen her without a hanky stuck to that bugle of hers, for the first two weeks I thought she was Michael Jackson." He snorted out a laugh. " Here, he added, " ask her did she walk up the aisle with a Kleenex for a veil." He took the work left in her top tray marked pending, more in hope than anything else and took it back to his desk.

"Sorry about that Margaret, I was talking to Brendan, he sends his regards." Bumpkin-head said returning to the call.

"Don't be keeping her on the phone too long, she'll be needing her rest." He called over and never looked up from the paperwork to see Bumpkin-heads reaction. He checked the post-it notes dotted along the bottom of his monitor to see if he had all the screens written down to complete their work. Bumpkin head kept up her pretence of concern and interest in psychosomatics symptoms and well-being. After the call which must have lasted a full ten minutes, Bumpkin placed the phone down. "You're right Brendan, she can be a lazy so and so."

Brendan shook his head in mock exasperation and accepted Bumpkin's offer to help out with the invoices "But before I begin, I need a smoke." He said, getting his cigarettes from his jacket.

"You said you were quitting." Bumpkin said, with genuine disappointment in her voice.

"I know, I say a lot of things." He replied, with the same genuine disappointment.

The smoke room was the former stationery room for The Personnel Branch, which had been moved to another building closer to the city centre and further away from the majority of disgruntled staff. Like all smoke rooms everywhere, it was the nerve centre of the building, it was said that if you wanted to know anything that was going on within the organisation, you would find it out in the smoking room. It was true. Due to the number of people, from a variety of Branches and ranks, the smoke room proved a treasure chest of information. Smoking proved to be salacious, a common bond that set them apart from the non-smokers, whom they resented. The room was silent as he approached the door still labelled stationery, not surprising he thought as he looked at his watch. The morning break ended fifteen minutes ago. He opened the door and saw that one smoker remained, sat in the corner under an open window.

"Jonny, my dear chap. Having a late break?"

Jonny looked up from a pile of papers he had before him on the coffee table. "Brendy, how's it going? Naw, was at the photocopier and sneaked in for a quickie. How's life's treating you?"

"Shite, but thanks for asking." Brendan answered, taking a seat opposite.

"Same here mate. You know that girl Marie in our office. Big tits, boils on her neck and missing an arse." Jonny added helpfully, blowing smoke out the open window.

"No, has she any distinguishing features?"

Jonny laughed. "Yeah, she's now bloody pregnant. Christ knows how." He added, sitting up in his seat. His small face, baby teeth and blue yes made him look like an overgrown schoolboy. "She's going off on maternity leave after next week and they're looking me to take on her work. All her filing, photocopying, making up the specs for the engineers. I'm not here that long and hardly know my own job. They're saying she might be off for six months. Would that be right?"

"No mate. They usually take a year." Brendan laughed.

"Fuck off." Jonny responded incredulously.

"Serious mate," Brendan told him, "first six months on full pay, then they take three to six months off on the sick."

"Fuck me, I wish I had a womb." Jonny said in a forlorn and deadpan voice that made Brendan cough out a smoky laugh.

"Here, I hope you didn't have a hand in her present situation Jonny."

"Well Brendy, it wouldn't have been a hand now."

"Well, it certainly wouldn't have been a foot." They both laughed and simultaneously put their cigarettes out. Jonny gathered up his papers form the table. "Gotta get back or the search party'll be out." He said, raising his long, thin frame up from the chair.

"Look Jonny, talk to Aine, she's your line manager, tell her you might not be able to cope with the extra workload. She has a duty of care for her staff. It's her job to make sure your not stressed out with too much work. I mean you have a job description, outlining your duties. I know that includes any other duties, but Marie's a grade above, so ask Aine if you are to receive acting up."

"I will Brendy, thanks for the advice, I'm a bit pissed off with the way no-one's come to me yet, but they're all saying I'll be doing it. Look," he said, standing by the door, his hand on the door handle, "I never got the chance during the week, as I was off, but, I'm sorry you didn't get the promotion. You should have, everyone in our office thinks so and no-one can believe that wanker Kieran got his. And he's already away. I haven't been in the Service long but the system stinks."

"Thanks Jonny. Appreciated mate."

"No problem, see ya later."

"Yeah, see ya." Brendan got up lighting another cigarette and stood by the window over-looking the car park. He listened for the door to open and close before he sat back down again in the chair. He smiled as he recalled one of the stories Jonny recounted in his time when he worked at a call centre conducting market research for various businesses. He had dropped out of A levels and his mother would not support his decision to take what he called his gap year. He left the call centre after a long and documented fractious relationship with his line manger. One day the line manager, 'a poisonous streak of shit' came in with a black eye and when a colleague leaned over to ask what had happened, he answered loud enough for him to hear, maybe he didn't get enough surveys done yesterday. This led to a stand-up argument and his attempt to blacken his other eye. He enjoyed that story as it just went to show that everyone can fuck up or get messed about and absorb it and make it part of you, part of your canon of material that made you up. It's how you deal with it and what you make of the stuff that life throws up is the measure of who you are. That's what he believed for what it was worth. It was Jonny who had disclosed Bumpkins indiscretion on the fourth floor with her friend Janice, who overheard Bumpkin's nickname for him. The wizard of Oz, all bluster, smoke and mirrors but at heart a pussycat.. After his initial shock and resentment, he mused on the connotations and rationalised that it was neither malicious or spiteful. He felt it best to remain quiet about the matter, to rise above it and remain magnanimous and the natural order of things was restored. He put the cigarette out having just lit it and got up to leave. He did not want to be alone, it just wasn't the promotion or lack of it, nor was it her who would not be named, there was something else lurking; something much deeper and much more threatening.

"And this, Brian, is the finance section. All payments generated by the Branch are processed in this office."

You had to hand it to her. She gave great pitch, well rehearsed, the duty of care tone perfect and the timing, exquisite. Her assertion that she was the senior manager, 'with overall' responsibility, as she manoeuvred her charge to the centre of the room, was pure theatre. An abundance of energy, fuelled by coffee and cake swept the room, first stop, Bumpkin-head and her reassuring gush of pleasantness. He made every effort to abstain from the charade, knocking out a rhythm on the impromptu drum kit built up around his desk. Yet he groaned inwardly at his brief sighting of Brian, before Brian slipped back, minnow-like, behind the case for spontaneous human combustion's vast frame.

He dropped both pens and picked up the invoice from TMT Ltd., complete public sector accounting personnel and administration specialists. For £7040.45 plus vat a month they'd need to be. He examined the breakdown of the costs on the invoices for two consultants to conduct an overview of the implementation and maintenance of the Krystal accounting system. Two consultants for four days, two of those days spent asking him and to a lesser extent, Bumpkin on the system and its processes, then disappeared into an office made available for them to do what he presumed was their consulting.. Taxpayers money well spent. Now he had to go through the outstanding queries, the payment transactions, discount dates, payments due, payments made; his only discretion was to decide who received discount based upon their payment history.

"This is Brendan, though he needs little introduction." She fixed him a smile he was obliged to reciprocate. "He'll be training you Brian." She added, chaperoning her charge into the seat opposite. Her driven personality was shamefully at odds with propriety. His theory was P.M.T., though that did not explain the duration or erratic shift in mood. Like the rest of her species she endured her cycle regularly, unlike the rest of her species, hers was

one women endured with several days off in the month. Mother nature, it seemed, had hers arse about face.

"Can I leave Brian in your capable hands?" The case for spontaneous human combustion asked sweetly, that almost had a sexual overtone to it that it made Brendan imagine her naked.

"Oh God." He confessed out loud his heartfelt revulsion at the image. He quickly composed himself straightening up in his chair. "Of course, are you going to show him the payment reconciliation's or shall I?" Brendan asked, maintaining an air of helpfulness.

"That as you know, will be part of your job in training Brian." She fussed, moving swiftly to the challenging intricacies of the electronic calculator, the stapler, tippex bottle and an array of pens set out on the desk for his arrival. She pointed out the PC and told him, "You'll get your passwords today, and you'll have three in total. System admin will email them when they are ready, Brendan, I've asked that they email them to you so that you can get Brian up and running."

"Fine." He said without looking up, having absconded into the outstanding accounts.

"Is that the monthly stats your working on?" She asked, picking up the cover sheet.

"It is."

"Can you have them on my desk by lunchtime?"

"I can." He answered, in his dutiful tone.

"Good, they were due yesterday after all." She said with a sniff.

"Yesterday was not possible, as you may, or may not, be aware the system was down yesterday afternoon, due to maintenance." He told her. "And I, sorry we," he nodded towards his colleague, ballbollocks, "now have additional work as we are down to just two to-day."

"Yes,yes, I know, she answered irritably, " that's why I insisted that Brian be brought over as soon as possible. Otherwise we'll fall even further back."

The case for human combustion had fulfilled her duty of care and entrusted Brian to him. She left the office passing Bumpkin-head issuing a breathless message regarding a meeting with Department heads.

His cheap woollen tie hung like a sickly red tongue from a white shirt that gripped a throat raped by a razor hours before and clashed vigorously with the brown check of his jacket. His parents, or whoever looked after him, had probably found it all a bit too risqué for a first day. His small brown eyes darted along the rims inducting the world he was surrounded by. "So, Brian, how's it hanging?" His greeting drew the of faintest of smiles on the surface of his thin, pale face.

"Ignore him Brian, he's just showing off." Bumpkin-head interjected, crossing the floor to intervene and act as mediator in the fraught first few moments. "You can read through this today Brian, it's a complete guide on the section, what we do and how it is carried out on the system. It's all there, step by step. He," she said, looking at Brendan, "wrote this out for me, she said then with much more emphasis, "it was the first and last nice thing he did for me."

"Well, I had to simplify everything for her, or she would still be struggling to get the door open." He did not wait for the smile Brian ought to have made and returned to the outstanding invoices. He watched Bumpkin with head lowered and felt a sliver of sadness at the prospect of her leaving one day. Now she was getting married, she wanted to be closer to home and had submitted a location transfer. He recalled how shocked he was at the depth of feeling it had aroused in him. He really was going to miss her when she left, she was refreshingly unencumbered by that female narcissism that always got in the way of real friendship . As they say, what you see is what you get. She, a simple, honest soul, wholly good-natured and kind. He smiled remembering the Head of Departments' last email detailing the recommendations from the internal audit. The Head, Seymour Clibberd, seriously they would do anything to avoid using a Saints name. All the same he was a nice man, serious, officious, meticulous, but a man of true mansuetude. The e-mail's wording was typically aphoristic which had Bumpkin perplexed, she kept asking him for the explanation of the words The Head had employed, what's negate mean? And onerous? When Brendan had explained, an exasperated Bumpkin asked, quite legitimately, why he didn't just say that in plain English. He replied that he was just being pleonastic. Bumpkin's look of deep puzzlement had him laughing. He's just intoxicated by the propensity of his own verbosity I suppose, Brendan shrugged. That's ok then she said simply and they both laughed. In truth he really was going to miss her, as it was a case of when, not if.

"So you need to read through this, it's concise and comprehensive and it's kept on the G drive. Sorry Brian, what's your surname, I was told, but I've forgotten."

"Mor...Mor...Morton." Brian stuttered, the colour drained from his throat to disperse around his face.

"Is that with three m's or four?" Brendan asked, without looking up, concealing the laugh all to himself. Bumpkin-head pressed ahead with her ringing line of enquiries. He left them to it occupying himself with the work psychosomatic had left pending.

He had the monthly report on the stats printed off, walking along the corridor towards the CFSHC's office, running a quick check over the columns, outstanding in red, those pending in orange, the nearest colour he could get to amber, those paid in green. At the base of each column, monies accrued, monies outstanding, invoice numbers, dates issued, received and a top ten of outstanding debtors. It could not have been made more simple and user-friendly, yet she still found fault. He had spent an entire afternoon explaining the new format, the colour scheme was based on traffic lights, red, amber and green. She looked over the spreadsheet and stated in an agitated tone that forbade another explanation, that she could not understand it and in the same tone said she would seek advice elsewhere, the emphasis on elsewhere inferred that the someone, somewhere would be infinitely more knowledgeable than him. Now the spreadsheet was standard practice (take note - promotion panel!) having been approved by that someone somewhere, she was begrudging in her acceptance and could not resist pointing out the scribbled improvements that she wanted.

She wasn't in her office when he knocked, so he went in and placed the report on her desk and sat down in her executive reclining manager armchair, black leather with tilt action £159.99 plus vat. Paid. Green column. Beneath his feet at the side of her desk sat her Masters leather flap over briefcase, split hide leather with central compartments and a three-sided zipped front flap containing organiser workstation gilt locks and trim £49.99 plus vat. Paid. Green column again. On the desk by the switched off, never switched on presumably, PC, her Kensington stalemate, stainless steel, complimented by matching chrome trim. £32.99 plus vat, she had written: doctors 2:45 TUES. And he had ordered two of those pens. One set aside as a birthday present. He got up and went over to her glass-fronted cabinet sat the management reports, the Branches procedures, Corporate and Business Plans and the flow chart on the new Rapide system. This was the new on-line system for all the invoicing and purchasing that he had trained on for a week in Head office and took great pleasure in reporting back to her to witness her discomfort at the introduction of another system she would not be able to master. He fingered the plants that sat as bookends for the reports, checking the labels on each, Peacelily and Diffenbachia. Between the two plants was a silver-framed photograph of two young children, her niece and nephew, in their school uniforms, their podgy, privileged smiling faces detonated a thought that the office was the closest thing he had to a family. He rapidly left her office, as an uncomfortable affinity with her solitude begin to envelope him.

"Sweet holy fuck." His cue to explode was lent to him by the forgery of a lunch he peered at in the plastic box. "Look at that." He held up the banana for anyone to inspect. "As black as Ali's cock." He lamented loudly and theatrically dropped it into the waste paper bin with a thick, plump thud. The sandwiches fared no better. Limp pieces of white bread frowned back at him, moist, the tuna not fully drained, and cut horizontally, not diagonally, the way he liked it. Granny brown wouldn't have been aware of the injustice, the imbalance, the world of difference between what he wanted and what he got. "To hell with this I'm outta here." He stated, dropping the contents of his lunchbox into the bin by his chair. He stood up and put his jacket on, willing Br…Br…Br…Brian to look up from his step by step guide, to splutter, stutter something so he could legitimately end his fledgling career. "I'm off out, back in a couple of pints." He smiled grimly.

Admittedly, his imbibed joviality was disingenuous and it was to poor Br.Br.Brian he targeted. "So Brian," he began, conscious not to stutter, " whadya' think of the place?"

Br…Br…Brian, the model of sobriety and rectitude, looked up from the notes he was immersed in, a crust of ginger eyelash protecting his eyes from making contact. "It's ni…nice."

Ni..nice? Brendan lit up a cigarette in deliberate defiance of the designated and well-defined non-smoking policy. What did that mean ni..nice, nothing. Innocuous drivel. Empowered by three pints of Carlsberg and a rushed vodka and a dash of orange, Bumpkin-head's absence, he decided to probe to discover the recesses of Br…Br…Brian's character. Hobbies? Likes? Dislikes, love, religion, politics. After several minutes of monosyllabic replies, shrugs, vacant looks and vacant smiles drove him into a coveted silence from which he would not emerge. He'd break the hearts of the peelers in Castlereagh, eh John? Wot you fink? He made a mental note to avoid Br…Br…Brian during inactive periods in case the vegetation was catching or at least until he returned to a normal colour. He laughed out loud at that one causing Br...Br...Brian to give up a startled look and quickly return to his guidance notes.

Bumpkin-head arrived in at three minutes to two, her face flushed with good company and a substantial lunch. She removed her coat put it over the back of her chair sat down, picked up the phone and gave him a look to put out his cigarette which he did in his cup.

At four twenty five he was completely and utterly desperate, anxious, hurting to alleviate the prospect of his day after he left the office. Murray hadn't called, B..B..Brian had left a scribbled note that Mrs O'Connell had called when he was out for lunch. He picked up the phone and quickly dialled. "Alright ballick breath, oh sorry Missus McCann, is Gerry there?" He joked for the benefit of Bri...Bri...Brian who had grown tired of the office guide and was finding his attention drawn to the information board on the wall plastered with various pieces of information on the union, the weekly lottery draw, discrimination at work, the usual 'oul shite that was of no interest and little use. His performance had Gerry on the other end of the line perplexed.

"Are you on something? What the fuck..." Gerry enquired.

"Never mind, wha'dya doing tonight?"

"Dunno, suppose I could get out, after all, I am injured at the mo."

"Right, so are you going out or what?" Brendan cut in impatiently.

"I'm a bit skint." Gerry's prevarication elicited another curt response.

"So dip into the emergency fund."

"Aye, alright then, call into the shop on your home from work."

"What for? Sure I'll see you in the pub." Brendan answered, detecting a noticeable dip in Gerry's voice that was a prelude to something of a more serious nature; and that usually meant one thing, or more precisely one person. "Alright," he relented, "but you'd better bloody well cheer up, and don't be depressing any customers."

"No can do, its shop policy." Gerry laughed back.

"Right then, I'll see you later." Brendan set the phone down, guillotining the potential for further degenerative sounds from that particular quarter. He sat back in his chair yawning loudly to chase the drone of Gerry's voice from his mind. Gerry was not the type of person to see the glass half-full, or half-empty for that matter, his philosophy was what's it matter, we're all going to die anyway.

Just before five the office fell under a spell of quiet contemplation as they turned their attention to their flexi-sheet. It was explained to Bri...Bri...Brian that they use the twenty-four hour clock and its seven-twenty five day, except for Wednesday, which was seven-twenty and with that said Bumpkin-head returned to her desk with Brendan's assertion that her days were more five or six twenty a day to keep her company. Not that B..B..Brian required the advice as the office he was in used the same system. He inscribed a nine o'clock start, a thirty, no forty minute lunch and a five fifteen finish. He had made fifteen minutes. He read down the accounting period, beginning the seventeenth, and could not help but is impressed by the imagination, ingenuity and consistency in his endeavours. *You should fire that orf to a publisher me ole china, it's got more fiction than anyfink you've ever written.*

True, eh John, very true.

"Hell, I'd better get on, otherwise I'll be in danger of leaving at the time I've signed off for." He smiled to Br...Br...Brian who gave a brief smile in return.

"Does anyone need a lift?" Bri…Bri…Brian's innocent question evoked another eruption on Brendan's part.

"Shite, balls and other swear words."

"What's wrong with you? Brian was only asking." Bumpkin-head laughed placing her bag over her shoulder. He managed to subdue the urge to get up and strangle her with her own knitwear.

"I forgot about the car." He shouted over to her, he took out his pocket diary, unable to remember how he had indexed Murray, it wasn't under 'B' for bastard, or 'T for twat, he finally found him under 'G' for gangster, it never crossed his mind to put him under 'M' for mechanic. He quickly dialled Murray's number he had written down in his diary. The line was engaged. "Shite." Bastard was probably on the phone to his bookie to place a bet. He got up and put his coat on, echoed the goodnights both of them made as he rushed towards the office door.

The rotted corrugated doors to Murray's lock-up were closed and the large rusted chain fastened with what looked like a new lock. He stood outside toeing the film of oil that had spread like a form of car blood down the sloping entrance. He knew Murray had gone, the garage was in a state of abeyance and he had grown tired of staring through the rusted holes in the doors. A weak beam of light from the roof of the lock-up provided little that was discernable amongst the impenetrable chunks of darkness. The lock-up yielded up nothing up but a pungent metallic air, fused with petrol, and diesel that burned at his nostrils.

He stood back from the doors and rattled them with a kick that reverberated throughout the lock-up and spat the taste of the place onto the knotted rusted chain that married one door to the other.

Rush hour traffic had ground to a halt; motorists sat camped in the cars marshalled by noisy youngsters armed with the sixth edition of the 'tele' and were now reaping a bumper harvest, thanks to the bomb scares paralysing the city. It was becoming a typical Friday evening.

He crossed the road past the immobilised cars, grateful to an extent to Murray the bastard for locking up early, otherwise he would have found himself amongst the throng of anxious motorists snapping up the paper or tuning into the radio for news of when, or if, they would ever get to the toilet. He moved onto the pavement turned left at the now unnecessary traffic lights and into the side street where the confectionery shop, butchers, the cheap electrical shop, good for knock off batteries and Gerry's clothes shop sat in the at the corner of the huddled row occupying an envious eye onto the main road where shoppers would pass on their way to town in cars, buses, aeroplanes, hot air balloons, rather than stop to look in at the wares on offer. It was a peculiarly local shop, for peculiarly local people.

Gerry worked for the owner who was also a Director at the football club Gerry played for, a bald, grasping little man, whose niggardly credo extended beyond his pocket and into his personality. It was a mutually beneficial arrangement between the two, but what if Gerry were sold, or dropped? What then? Gerry gave a shrug of his shoulders and said he would go back to quantity surveying even though he walked out of his job in that field and took up painting and decorating for a year.

He stopped at the window of Gerry's shop, hiding his face behind a large yellow star that shone out to passer-bys that the sale was out of this world. Gerry, his back to him held up a sweatshirt for two women to cast a critical eye over. Ho ho. It looked now as if

they wanted Gerry to try the sweatshirt on. Go on love, just to give us an idea what it's

like on. He watched Gerry slip the sweatshirt over his shirt and pull it down, "Now this

won't look half as good on your man as it is on me." Gerry smiled.

"Ach, away on with ye. " The woman with the straight ginger hair, combed down

over her shoulders, laughed, stepping back to get a better perspective of the sweatshirt.

Her companion with the 'my friend went to Florida and all I got was this lousy tee shirt,'

stepped back to join her in telepathic contemplation. Gerry stood modelling the

sweatshirt wondering where the fuck Brendan was, it was almost five thirty and the

woman with the pudding tits and lousy tee-shirt had just asked for the umpteenth time.

"And you don't have it in the red?"

"Not in large, only blue and green in large." He answered for the umpteenth time.

Half a fucking hour almost spent on a nine ninety-nine sweatshirt with two hundred and

seventy two quid in the till including float, he felt compelled to persevere.

Brendan grew tired, hot, hungry and bored of the scene and left Gerry to his fate.

He eased the sense of guilt rationalising that he would see him later and tell he had

worked late and had to see about the car.

Florida top joined Gerry at the counter opening her purse. "And it'll be exchanged

or refunded if it doesn't do, love?"

"Not a problem. Just hold on to the receipt, tell him to come back in with it and

I'll fix him up." Gerry answered, ringing in the sale.

"What, even in three years, when's he due out?" Florida top laughed and looked

to her friend who was rummaging through a wire basket holding an assortment of end of line stock. Gerry busied himself folding and placing the shirt along with the receipt into the bag, taking her ten pound note and placing one pence change beside the bag.

"Right ladies, is that us?" He asked, holding the bag out for Florida top to take.

"Come on Angela. Let this fella get to his home." She turned to her friend who dropped a pack of white sports socks bag into the wire basket.

"Here Sheila, them socks are only a pound." Her friend Angela said, lifting a pack of sports socks, made by six year olds in a sweatshop.

"Sure they'll still be there tomorra, come on. I've that glipes dinner to put on."

"Sure we'll call into the chippie on the way down, that'll do us. Right love we'll get out of your hair."

Gerry opened the door with it's clanging bell ringing above his head. He saw them off with a "thanks" a "take care" and "hang on to that receipt now". He got back "Oh, I will love." before he could close the door and click the snib on the lock. He walked to the main window and looked out one more time before crouching down to press the green button to set the shutters in motion. The phone rang. "Ballicks." he swore, thinking it was the Bald eagle, his nickname for the proprietor, wanting to know how much the shop had taken and what time he'd be up at the house to leave in the takings. But it wasn't. "Hello." He answered coldly.

"Yes, Gerry it's me. Sorry to disturb you at the hotbed of retail activity."

"Orflaith, I don't need this."

"Gerry, please be quiet. I have something to say. Don't interrupt until I'm finished, then you can say what you want. I want to talk about the future, I know it's way down on your list of priorities, every time I mention it, you run a mile."

"That's not strictly…"

"Gerry, please shut up and listen. Yes you do, you left a good job, no, a career, because you found it boring. Jeesus, you think I like working for the Executive, dealing with whiny deadbeats, it's not Las Vegas. Don't laugh, I'm being deadly serious. The real reason you left that job was because it was too grown-up, it came with responsibilities and prospects. A job with a future. Now, you're hiding away in that thrift shop."

"Now, hold on. I've had enough of this, I've had long day and I need to lock up." Gerry hotly interjected, feeling his face heat up like it did when he was told off by his mother, when he was a child.

"No, you hold on, I have held on long enough for you. Where will you be tonight? Some pub, with your re-born best friend, Brendan. Now he's split up from miss middle-class, the two of you have been inseparable. Where was he when he was all loved-up? No-where, that's where. Now you both have your childhoods back."

Gerry went over to the door whilst listening to Orflaith, he checked it was closed and then, holding the receiver tightly between his chin and shoulder managed to press the button to draw down the shutters. He grunted in agreement that this was the last chance and that they should meet sometime the next day to discuss things. "Like your little holiday." He grunted down the phone. That was on the table too, she told him. Where? Queen's? That's for froots.

"The Garrick then. I'd hate for you compromise your masculinity."

They agreed to meet at seven the next evening. He hung up without saying goodbye. He opened the till and began to count the takings. She was right of course, he never thought of their future to-gether. He somehow couldn't project their relationship beyond their next meeting. He stood at the table that masqueraded as a counter, feeling he had just been verbally mugged, in a well-planned ambush.

The gate to Granny Brown's house swung open catching the wall with a resounding clank that resonated with a condensed petulance.

"Lunch was superb, you excelled yourself today, Delia." His sarcasm hung over her as she dozed in the armchair. "Where's the washing?" He asked, not waiting for an answer he walked into the kitchen. "Well?" He shouted from the sink pouring himself a glass of water.

"Hold on, hold on." She told him impatiently, entering the kitchen, rubbing the small of her back. She heard the concealed "fucksake" but ignored it. "The washing's under the kitchen table in the big bag. I've dinner on, she added, going over to the cooker and lifting the lid of the enormous pot that bubbled with boiling water.

"If it's anything like that lunch. Thanks, but no thanks."

"Oh God, she groaned bending down to open the oven, "must've fell asleep on me side." She straightened up and turned the heat down on the oven and the big pot.

"I'll just get the washing then." He said, having made a show of ignoring her offer of dinner. He lifted the bag up on to the kitchen table and saw the clothes, ironed and neatly folded. It would have been churlish of him to point out that jeans should go on the bottom and shirts to the top. He left the bag and opened the fridge door. "Don't you have any coke?" He groaned loudly. "I'm parched."

"I didn't get up to Tesco today, but there's Fanta there. Are you sure you don't want dinner, I've made plenty and it'll just go to waste, it'd be a sin."

"Well, what is it then?" He tried his voice of vague interest and went over to the sink and poured himself a glass of water.

"Cauliflower, peas, potatoes…I can roast them the way you like and those chicken breasts without the bones."

He said ok. He said he was going to the bathroom to freshen up. He went to the bathroom and flung off his shoes and socks, pulled off his underwear and stood in the shower to wash down his genitals and legs. He dried off and slipped on fresh underwear and a pair of jeans he had taken from the bag in the kitchen. The jeans washed and pressed, imbued in him a sense of place and of situation that he sought. This would have cost him making the dinner and doing the washing up, back in his former life. Theirs had been a very modern relationship.

After a hot, wholesome meal he sat back in the settee to enjoy a cigarette with his tea. Twenty five past six. Pub by seven. He'd watched the end of the news. The smiling state mannequins recited the news . All the bomb alerts had turned out to be hoaxes. A shooting in some bog town had resulted in two minor injuries. The phoney war continued. If the state and its policy had been in peril we'd all be fucking dead. He finished his cigarette and stubbed it to a smoky death in the ashtray. "Thanks for dinner and the washing, I'm gonna head on, alright." He said, getting up to stretch his body. He collected his plate and mug and placed them in the sink full of shipwrecked pots and plates. He went to get the bag full of

washing and began separating the clothes into jeans, shirts, tee-shirts, underwear and socks. There were no towels. He used the double creases on the arms of his shirts to renew his war on the inequities of life, its terrible toll of minutiae.

"Do you need anything for home?" She asked. "Your towels are still drying, do you have any?"

"Aye, stacks. Don't be worrying" He said kindly.

He returned to the living room to get a cigarette and left her to the washing up. He paced the floor across the minefield of small carpets placed strategically at the entrance of the kitchen and the door into the living room and foot of the settee and chair. The material and patterns on each in various states of distress; with light and close inspection a hairy crumb-infested skin would reveal itself. The landscape was littered with shells of ash the remnants of some ferocious battle in the carcinogenic wars . He'd look and look and want to weep. He wanted them both to stop smoking, eat well and be in good health and good cheer; so they could be better disposed to embracing a better life.

"Here, take these up with ye." She said, holding a plastic bag bulging with deformities. "There's Rice Crispies, milk, a brown loaf, eggs and bacon there. Oh," she said, setting the bag down on the seat of her chair, "you'll be needing butter." She turned and moved hastily into the kitchen, returning moments later. "Its ordinary butter, not the low fat stuff you use, but it'll do ye until ye get to the shops."

"You shouldn't have gone to all this trouble, honestly Gran" He replied quietly, the depth of his appreciation and gratitude over-whelmed him momentarily, his voice glued to the roof of his mouth, his affection dulled, nullified, by years of loathing. "Give me those messages, you'll do yourself an injury." He said taking the bag. "I'll put all of this in the travel bag, I'll get the washing and be off."

"Okay son." She said, suddenly much older and smaller than he had ever seen or remembered her. Her body shrunk into her tee-shirt and cardigan, her long blue skirt hung down to her ankles and her old carpet slippers, Of course there was a cigarette burn hole on the hem of the skirt. He was angry at that and was determined that he would take her into town or to the shopping centres outside Belfast and get her some new clothes.

"And another thing," he said coming back into the living room with the washing, "when I get the car back, I'll take you shopping, anytime you need to do any major shopping. Like the old days. Ok? Now, whadya' I owe for the messages?" He said smoothing the bag of washing over the top of the messages.

"Ach, don't be daft. You hang onto yer money, you'll be needing it for that flat."

"Especially now, eh?" He laughed emptily. "Tell you what, we'll head up to Abbey centre some Saturday and I'll get you slippers and a new pair drawers." He laughed.

"Seriously, we'll get up and get some paint for your room. Now, don't be coming to the door, you have a cup of tea and sure Coronation street'll be on soon. Ok?"

"Ach, get on with ye." She smiled and waved him towards the living room door. "You'll ring me later, won't ye now?" She asked of him " Let me know how you're getting on up there. Will ye?" Her earnest request was met with a gentle squeeze of her forearm, and a long drawn out :"Yes maw." I will, I promise." He said out-manoeuvring the potential of an over- emotional farewell. "Now go on, get in and have a cup of tea and watch your soaps."

She saw off his gentle persuasion with an affectionate hand on his shoulder and left him to the door and watched him walk up the street, waved as he waved back and wished him a quiet place, a place which she would keep for him in her forever home. A place in her heart where the pains and hurt of this life were a distant memory and her family were to be reunited and reconciled, the way God would want it.

AMANEUNSIS

His Guinness was growing older before his eyes, its head changing from a healthy inviting cream to warehouse brown, the sign of rigor mortis. It appeared like a metaphor for something he could not care to think of. He took a large bite at the head; its tangy cut of its taste excited the senses and conjured the spectre of a world with infinite possibilities. Another bite and he was trying to attract the attention of the barman.

"Here, mate another pi...pi...pint of G..Guinness." The youthful barman kept his smile to himself as he returned from the end of the bar where he had been restocking the cooler with bottles of beer. Brendan smiled back at the result of his pretence. He lit up another of Granny Brown's cheap, revolting cigarettes from a pack pilfered from her ill-concealed store.

Minutes later he exchanged his empty glass for a fresh pint. "Che...che...cheers." The barman scooped the loose change Brendan had left on the bar and rang in the sale; he turned to the sound system inserted below the cash register. A collage of intermittent talk and music, one sweeping cacophonous pastiche penetrated the womb of the quiet bar until the barman's twiddling quest ended.

It stopped to allow the opening strains of a song he thought to be by James Taylor, creep stealthily into his consciousness, it's mournful cheat of a tune complimenting and enriching his melancholic mood. It presented itself like a parting gesture, a final indulgence to a part of his life that he could not say goodbye to. Farewells did not exist, only in physicality, but the mind, the heart, the soul, would not relinquish.

He sucked at his drink, the barman passed by placing coasters along the bar urging people to drink low alcohol lager. The couple did not look like drinkers, slim, clear-skinned, bright-eyed with stick-on smiles. The clothes and hairstyles suggested a much earlier era, so they would be a lot older, perhaps dead. So much for the healthy lifestyle! So fuck ye. Ha.

He returned to his pint and the music seeping out from the speakers hidden to him behind the bar. The drink and his mood invited more, more than the young barman could carry. Yet, there would never be enough to swamp the feelings cutting up his waking moments. He looked to the clock embedded into a mirror advertising a whiskey he had never heard of. Five past seven. What a stupid time. Five past seven, like ten forty, the time? Oh yes, its three seventeen, the exact time he entered that microwave of a room to face the flabby face of a failed mechanical engineer, member of a third rate golf club and protestant denomination. He sat, emasculated, between two shiny-faced careerists with a ball gripped in each hand. He kept metronome to his syllable, his thumb clicking the top his pen. If only you would wear sensible shoes, click in, white Primark shirts, click out, creased pants of a conservative nature and colour, click in, play the game, click out, be courteous, pleasant, professional, subservient, click in. Play golf, get married, endorse motorcycle racing and fishing. Click out. The case for spontaneous human combustion's perfunctory report had him fitted for purpose, but the ply board platform on which he had to build his case, creaked under the weight of thirty some minutes in that room. Unfortunately, it did not meet the criteria, nor his hopes and expectations.

No-where days, no-where months, time carved up; and measured by divisions that gave structure; yet no meaning to the passing of time. He imagined the barman didn't give it a thought; his concern lay only in closing time, when he could fuck everyone out.

He leaned forward on the bar allowing the spotlights puncturing the ceiling, drilling light down on his face, bathing him in an unforgiving brightness. He had to look away focusing on the orange lanterns pimpling the walls; the colour soothed him, inducing in him a need to put down on paper his thoughts, his feelings, to excogitate his mind. He wanted to purge the life he had lived so far and presumably live for a long time unless he did something. If he died now, his obituary would have grannies throughout our wee province tut-tutting and lamenting with 'a God love him', then pass on in search of something more interesting, more worthwhile.

He wanted big ideas, big themes, big issues, big contemplations; but the door to the bar opened allowing cold rush of outside noise to disturb his train of thought.

"Where'd you get to, I thought you were calling into the shop? And whadya' doin' here? Luckily, bumped into your Gran coming out of Vincey's shop, she told me you'd come in here."

"Take it you'd like a pint." He asked, as Gerry sat down at the bar beside him. So she had followed him again, for the third time this week when he had made feeble declarations that he was going to go back to the flat, only to end up in the bar and then back to her house. This bar was much better suited to his desire for relative peace and quiet. All the other bars would be packing up with guys off the sites, offices, the football crowd would be there to discuss the forthcoming weekend and their bets on it. Tonight he didn't want to drink within a democracy, with all those voices clamouring to be heard. Some voices, of course, heard more often than others like Cheeks, a brutish man of hard opinion, who conducted his sit-down, stand-up routine that made for nervous, ingratiating laughter. His large face and neck, bulging with urges and impulses; built-up over several days and requiring urgent release. And they used the cover of football to surreptitiously insult and denigrate each other ostensibly through their support of a particular team; but the malice often went way beyond that. The company was more akin to a mediaeval court where the rigid structure, based on birthright, who had significantly grown up together through the troubles. A tangible bond existed, like the Brits of who had endured the war years and longed for that Dunkirk spirit. Arriving in Belfast at thirteen, his accent, nature of his country locale, ensured his academic and social apartheid. The riots proved a great leveller, thank God for them. Don't let anyone try to tell you that Belfast is a city, in size and scope certainly, but in reality, it's a series of villages, with an accompanying mentality. He knew that his continued inclusion was dependent upon his remaining an asset to the company, providing a consistent level of conviviality and humour, as ostracism was a constant threat to a blow-in. Not tonight and not at his table. No fucking thank you. Not tonight, definitely not tonight, he confirmed with himself.

"Fuck, yes." Gerry spat out across the bar.

"Give us another Guinness and a pint of green, cheers." Brendan ordered of the barman who had hovered close to them as soon as Gerry entered, dispensing with the speech impediment he had employed to keep them both amused.

"A week." Gerry said bitterly. He stood up to take his jacket off and place it over the chair. A week? Brendan asked himself. A week what? Jeezus, he was deliberately being obtuse in an effort to engender the conversation he wanted. There was a catalogue of injustices to choose from and he lived under the dread knowledge that Gerry's charade would be played out until he asked. So he asked, "A week what?"

Gerry waited until his pint arrived and Brendan had paid for the round. " A week in Spain, that's what."

"Oh." Brendan replied simply and turned to finish his pint before the other arrived.

"It'd be mad to miss it." Gerry said, ridiculing her reasoning and caricaturing her voice.. "Her and that fuckpot Suzanne from work. Oh right oh, I'm off to shag some dago." Gerry managed to squeeze out in falsetto in between voracious gulps at his pint.

"You've been working on that." Brendan laughed and Gerry's foam ringed smile said that he had. "Let her go and with your best wishes." Brendan advised.

Gerry's smile vanished. "She doesn't even like Suzanne. Fuck that, I'm not giving in to her and her bloody whims."

"Knock it on the head then, if she's messing you about." He offered up to Gerry's dismal look. The elongated teeth that Gerry's bulbous red lips tried despairingly to accommodate disappeared into the last of his beer. "What?" He laughed back at the incredulity and suspicion pasted on Gerry's face.

"Oh aye and it's that simple." Gerry answered, stroking back his unfashionably long hair, leaving the unresolved, a fear that it evoked and would not confess, hanging in the uneasy silence between them. Gerry's girlfriend, Orflaith, was an attractive girl, tall, slender with long black hair. She worked as a housing officer, had a degree in social policy and seemed ambitious in one respect, to settle down with Gerry. He felt a burst of envy at that. She loved him, and she didn't care that it showed. She was funny when she was drunk, vociferous in her defence of Gerry, and embarrassingly affectionate. Brendan liked her, she appeared to take, what he accepted as a genuine interest, in his stories and his ramblings about University. He felt his Human CV severely lacking and its limitations more keenly as Gerry had his HND in quantity surveying. Gerry shouted to the barman for the same again, stealing the time he needed to allow the unspoken to go unsaid.

They both drank in silent, agitated haste, both in earnest and urgent need to be in that state they both craved, drunk, and inexcusably so.

Their destination: a place where everything held an exaggerated significance; a place where they themselves, held an exaggerated importance. The delicious idea of it hung expectantly in the taste buds of his mind, where it was savoured and feted. "I'm off to the bogs, keep an eye on my bag." He told Gerry, aware of his friend's penchant for networking a bar, even though the lounge was empty; the public bar would have its regulars.

When he returned from the toilet Gerry was standing over the table nearest the door talking to some pairing that had just come in. She with a blue cardigan entrusted to her plump, round-shouldered body and a smile sellotaped to her over-made up face. Him, bored to whatever tedious little drama Gerry had scripted. His dark brown eyes never left Gerry, wary of conversation.

As for Gerry, the social dissident; he kept up the talking, animating it with expansive hand movements. Jeezus, you had to love him sometimes. At last, Gerry's powers of telepathy were restored to him, the dark brown eyes had conveyed they had listened long enough and he bid the couple a bright 'cheers' and returned to the bar. His face longer than before, his words couched in solemnity, his conversation invested in the closure of some place, somewhere.

"The whole place is coming to a standstill, look at the shop for fucksake. If they're not on the rock and roll, they're coming from or going to prison, and a lot of it's on the slate.

And that miserly fuck charges a fortune in interest. It's dog eat dog, alright." A shadow descended on Gerry's face as he reached for his pint.

"Yeah, and for those who don't have the appetite, it's starve." He looked away to let the remark register and have it's inevitable impact.

"Profound stuff, sir." Gerry said, raising his pint glass in a toast to him.

Christ it was farcical. " Here, whadya' call that barman, he's new isn't he?"

"He must be, if you don't know him." Gerry laughed back.

Ingrate bastard he thought and signalled to the barman who was busying himself cleaning glasses. He ordered another round on Gerry's behalf.. It was eight thirteen, another stupid time, when he looked at his watch, timing Gerry's explanation, now in it's fourth going into it's fifth minute, on how and why his football bet had been beaten. The explanation had involved the weather, motorway travelling, managers who wore wigs, the moon entering Sagittarius all seemed to feature as he sat staring at his pint imagining his imminent death. His poor emaciated body discovered behind a barricaded door, eyes wide open, a serene peacefulness blanketing him. Coroner's verdict: death from fear. Police suspect foul play and are following a definite line of enquiry. They are desperately seeking a man answering to Gerry's description. He is not to be approached under any circumstances; considered a dangerous public menace.

"Here, Gerry interrupted himself, tugging at the cuff of Brendan's shirt, "have a jeff juke at who's just come in." Gerry smiled over to whoever had just entered the bar, moved closer to him, closing rank and in a hushed tone, told him. "Wee Concepta and her mates."

"Who?" Brendan asked heatedly, Gerry's descent into football and now girls had served to thicken his dull mood.

"Concepta and her mates." He reiterated. "You insulted them last Friday night up in Maginty's." Gerry revealed, unable to conceal his delight in recalling the moment Brendan had clearly forgotten. Gerry leaned into Brendan's shoulder, his breath brushing into the side of his face. "You said, Concepta! That's not a name, it's an inoculation against something." His fit of laughing emitted dots of spittle onto Brendan's cheek.

"Alright." Brendan retorted. "I didn't ask for a weather report." He said, making a demonstrable show of wiping the side of his face.

"And her fat mate." Gerry broke out again in a fit of laughter, he drew close again, reducing his voice to near whisper," you said her head looked like a helicopter landing pad, you told her to get to the bar and get the drinks in because her head would make an ideal tray. Man, you were in some form that night. Concepta and her mate took it as a bit of banter but the landing pad hates you. Jesus, that's right," Gerry slapped both thighs, his head falling back, his mouth wide open revealing all his back teeth and their fillings, "she had on a 'I love Rock n Roll' tee-shirt, and you said, clearly you love roll more than rock. I thought she was gonna deck you one." Gerry burst into another high pitched nasal fit of laughing.

"I don't remember any of that, sounds like a load of 'oul shite to me." But his derision lacked conviction in the face of Gerry's assured performance .

Gerry shushed him not to say another word. "Here, Concepta's coming to the bar."

Brendan did not care to look round when she presented herself at the bar beside Gerry, who presented himself as far too eager for her company. He stared straight ahead watching the ectoplasm of smoke leave his mouth, waft in swirling contortions in the freedom of the air before escaping invisibly through the wall. Christ if she could see you now, wallowing in a puddle of dissipation, Christ how fortunate she would count herself.

"And how are you?" Concepta had leaned over the bar to ask.

"Alright. Yourself?" He asked. She must have detected the reciprocated distance to his enquiry as she did not answer and preoccupied herself with the money she had taken from her purse. The bad impression he must have made was best left endured. He watched her in the large mirror at the bar. She was attractive, her oval-shaped face wreathed in the blackest, shiniest hair, layered like large sheaths that graced her shoulders. By now he could smell her perfume, he breathed in the general cleanliness peculiar to young women. So much fresher than granny brown's cough inducers he smoked to hasten his demise. In deference to an oasis of something clean and fresh in the bar he stubbed his cigarette out.

He glanced over at her when she reached out to collect the drinks she had ordered. The bright green top embraced her small, strong-looking body; and what looked like a sports bra flattened and spread her ample breasts. The top co-ordinated with the dark blue of her jeans, the make of which he could not identify from the side view he had. He noticed she wore one silver ring on her right hand and a matching small chain that hung slightly below the neck of her top.

"Would you like to join us?" She asked, the drinks gathered up in her two slender hands.

"Yeah, great, we'll be over." Gerry's bright advance into accepting her offer on behalf of them both, blistered on Brendan's mind, and one he tried to telegraph. But Gerry was not receiving under a near breathless "see youse in a minute, we'll get a drink in first."

Brendan watched her walk casually back to the table where her friends were entrenched and he guessed why he would have insulted her. He despised her kind of natural attractiveness that attracted the level of attention mere mortals struggled for and the throwaway nature that instinctively came with it.

"You coming?" Gerry asked, turning to him and motioning to the waitress that had just come on duty, for the same again.

"Do I have a bloody choice now?" Brendan snapped sourly.

"No. Not unless you want to be a lonely pint. Come on." Gerry laughed, compounding Brendan's feeling of desertion and betrayal. He toyed with the idea of telling him to fuck off, of getting up after he finished his pint and walking out. But he could not, no matter how much it appealed to leave Gerry alone with them. People were beginning to trickle in, the music and warmth had grown, a late bar: and the outside held nothing.

"Ok then, you lead." He said, getting off his chair. "So lead on McDuff."

"We're heading over to that snug." Gerry told the waitress, who has just began her shift and asked where they would like their drinks brought, and foraged ahead, approaching the table with a loud 'hello ladies' He joined moments later placing his travel bag by the side of the chair he took on the periphery of the enforced closeness of the cubicle. Here, in the oh-so-cosy niche they had carved for themselves he felt isolated and alienated, regretting not having acted upon his impulse to leave. He told himself he would be content with remaining outside of company whose incompatibility to his own, made ostracism a necessity, a blessing, if those existed. He lit up again and sat back to enjoy the sight and sound of Gerry ploughing on with a dearth of vocabulary and deed that was indicative of alcohol and genetics.

Concepta's two companions fell away into a he said, she said and I said goalless end-to-end mouthing that abandoned their friend to field Gerry's questions. Brendan began to feel sorry for her, he knew her friends' game, one fat, one skinny, both unattractive; both jealous of their friend, as their only access to men lay through her, and they hated her for it.

"It's true, honestly." Burst in upon the table. The affirmation rang with feigned shock designed specifically for attention.

"What's that Maureen?" Concepta asked, seizing the opportunity to relieve Gerry's siege. The fat one cast her a peremptory look that said they were prepared to allow her back in from the cold.

"What? What is it?" Gerry plundered, his outburst borne out of his annoyance of having Concepta taken from him.

Maureen glared back at Gerry refusing to be intimidated into not spoiling her show. "We were just talking about that wee girl Karen, the one who works in the bakery, you know, ginger girl. Big teeth." And everyone, with the exception of Brendan, went uh huh. "She lost her baby, she says miscarriage, but everyone knows she was off across the water just before." Maureen divulged with theatrical hand movements that intimated how secret this was and how foresworn everyone was now she had spoken of it.

Brendan hated her, not just in the now or the most recent past, but in the primordial swamp of the gene pool, he believed antithesis existed. There she sat, a resplendent fat turd, in an old woman's top covered in flora and faunae, you would have bought in Gerry's shop; with heavy balloons of flesh ensuring a bumper harvest. The small brown hairy mole on her lower lip operated once more. "It's for the best, if you ask me. She's a child herself." She followed up, sensing the isolation in her stated belief.

"I think it's wrong, I mean if she did that." Her thin friend, with both face cheeks slapped red that made her look like she was teething, found the courage to commit. Her painfully small voice played out in a reed-like body a tune so low that she had to repeat her charge.

"That's ok for you Tina, you'd be happy to let men make the decisions for you. A woman's body is her own, if you ask me."

"Aye, and you're welcome to it." Brendan heard himself say, purely in the interests of democracy. A ripple of apologetic sniggering broke out labelling her outcast and set the seal on her defiance.

"Who asked for your opinion?" She countered thunderously, rifling glares at her friends.

The gloves were off as the foetus-killer prepared to stand her ground. He relished the prospect of her attempt to regain the stature she imagined she had and was momentarily lost through his intervention.

"Abortions are morally wrong they are as repugnant, as they are avoidable." He found himself quoting from a piece in the Sunday Tribune on the abortion debate raging in the Republic. He cared nothing for the issue, though looking at his fat adversary; he found a strong case for the abortionist lobby. Eh John, wot you fink? *Too bleedin' right me ole son, best part of that old sort ran down 'er mum's legs.*

"Morally wrong?" She sneered back, "To who? Men, who make the rules on morality you mean."

"Balls." Was his equally sneering coup de gras. "You rant and rave on about your rights .Doesn't the child have the same rights?"

"It's not a child at that stage then, is it?" She countered looking at her friends for support, her face a fusion of anger and consternation.

"What is it then? A bloody melon?" His response dragged out the laughter that was begging in the company. Foetus, termination, words employed to dehumanise, desensitise to lose sight of the human who becomes collateral damage in the war of the sexes.

"Oh aye, murder is murder is murder." Maureen intoned in a deep Slovak-sounding accent. It was a good counter jab, but his remark, plus his higher work rate had caught the judges eyes. Na, na, na, na, na.

"Do you hate men or something?" This time Gerry entered the fray.

"It'd be better a place without them." She confirmed her catechism.

"In that case, you'd better go out and get a load of batteries." Brendan shot back. Gerry leaned forward laughing, Maureen gave a begrudging smile, leaving Concepta to explain the implications his remark alluded to, to her thin companion.

"That's disgusting." She said to a chorus of laughter.

Concepta stood up palming down the front of her top and made a signal known throughout the female world for her friends to join her in the ladies.

"Well, whadya' think? Gerry leaned across the table to ask as soon as the girls had made their excuses and left for the ladies. "She's alright, isn't she?"

"Who?" He asked lamely.

"Concepta! Who'd ya think? Laurel or Hardy there?" He replied nodding back to the seats the girls were occupying.

"I suppose." Brendan spelt his reply out in smoke. He wondered if he could send for help if he blew it high enough.

"I'm not waiting for her to come back from her holiday all tanned up and shagged out. Fuck that." Gerry spat out, lifting his pint.

"A pre-emptive strike." Brendan concluded, in a 'for fucksake get me out of here' puff of smoke.

"Yeah. Gerry smiled, straightening up, "I hear she's boyfriend trouble, so if she's in need of a shoulder…"

"Or cock."

"Precisely." Gerry laughed.

So this is what you're missing, Brendan thought, damning the barmaid to ten levels of Hell for her sloth. He caught her attention and signalled with a wave of his hand. As she approached, he informed Gerry that it was his round. This is what she has submitted herself back to, men like Gerry, men like him for Godsake. She was no wanton libertine, she worried about dry skin and gum disease. He felt like weeping again.

Concepta, foetus-killer and the Belsen non-survivor returned from the toilets in a conversation that maintained its momentum and integrity as they took their seats. They submerged themselves in a I said, she said, so I said verbal joust. Brendan excused himself and got up to go to the toilet, leaving Gerry substituted to a spectator by a strategy the girls had obviously formulated in the ladies.

Too many toilet blocks in the urinal hissed out a stinging rebuke of freshness that attacked the eyes and nose. Inches from his face a Neanderthal had dug up from the pit of his lungs a green, yellow chunk of heavy matter and left it for future generations to ponder on what kind of fucker would do that. Christ, he missed her so much, it was almost a physical ache, his emotional need cut across his shoulders and burned at his chest. He needed her to believe in colour, in grace, in fragrance again. Without her, the world was a construct of condensed atoms, without the intangible, invisible reason for life.

"Alright man." The over-friendly slap on his back had him urinating beyond the bowl and onto the wall. "You lot having a good time or what?" His unwelcome guest asked joining at the adjacent urinal, oblivious to it being clogged with fag ends and drowning in a frothy yellow brown coloured pool.

"Aye, not bad." He replied to his over-fragrant, cheaply dressed visitor. His beige, baggy trousers looked tired, washed out and over-ironed. He stood tiptoe and began pissing too loudly into the bowl. Brendan's peripheral vision caught sight of his collarless denim shirt, an ear pierced with a large gold ring, with a mountain range of volcanic acne afflicting his jaw line.

"Saw your girl the other night." He said, staring at the wall. "Wednesday, yeah Wednesday it was." He continued, staring down at the dribble he was now making into the bowl that was now in grave danger of over-flowing.

My girl? Brendan thought. What is that ferret-faced fuck talking about? My girl?

He felt a hot chill of recognition warm the calves of his legs and rise to fuel the accelerated engine room of his chest.

"She was in that new bar, the ones the boys blew up ages ago. Opened up a couple of weeks ago, you know, near the multiplex." He elucidated, filling in gaps to the unasked questions. "Looked like a family do." He added , straing down at his penis and then zipping up his fly. " The ma, da and another girl about her age."

"Her sister." Brendan found himself answering. "It was her da's birthday. I had to work late, so I didn't bother." He hated the inexplicable need he felt to explain his absence to this rodent.

"Not a bad place that, plenty of 'oul rare ones knocking about, you could get lucky there, if they're after a bit of rough." Ferret face laughed, shaking his penis rather too vigorously for Brendan's comfort.

Brendan went to the sink to wash his hands and let the jet of water hit the sink to drown out his 'Is that right.' Who the hell is this cunt? Why was he even talking to him? The ugly, ferret-faced fucker. Nice alliteration though. With his close-cropped blonde hair gelled to his head and with white eyebrows that reminded him of a suffering rabbit.

"She not in tonight, then?" Ferret-face asked standing at the hand drier, not having washed his hands.

"No, she's studying. She's got exams coming up." The whirring noise from the hand drier covered his walk over to the toilet cubicle to unroll some toilet tissue to dry his hands.

"Better get back in. See ya later." Ferret face shouted over to him.

"Aye." Brendan returned at him, wiping his hands dry, plunging the rolled up ball of tissue into the toilet standing over it watching it sink. He felt weak, emptied from the inside, like he had been vacuumed internally. It was much too much, much too soon, to hear of her from something like that. To know she still existed outside of him, where ferret-face and his ilk could look upon her and worse, could even talk to her. These vacuous predators, what if one were cunning enough. Oh God, he felt sick to his stomach. *Existed?. She's 'aving the time of 'er life, me ole china.*

Fuck off, this is neither the time nor place, eh John. He was in no mood to barter or bargain with Eh John.

He found his way out of the toilet and into the evening crowd that had materialised; he sidestepped his way through the walled human turmoil to the end of the bar where the payphone waited.

He took a moment to pause, to collect and synthesise his thoughts, he dug a hand into a pocket and lifted the receiver, placing a twenty pence piece at the slot, he dialled. Breep, breep, breep. Hello dead man calling. He turned his back to shield his call from the noise of the bar, holding the receiver tight to his ear he prayed for an answer. God, or whatever went for it these days listened.

"Hello?" The stone-cutting tone of her mother made him crumble.

He pushed the coin into the slot. "Hello." His voice unintentionally louder than he had planned. "May I speak to Frances?"

"One moment, who shall I say is calling?"

"Brendan, Brendan McConnell" He answered, steadying his voice and standing straight, yet he trembled in an age of silence that followed. Why did he say his full name? Had he needed to, had they all forgotten him already? Was he so penitent as not to be so presumptuous that they would still know him on a first name basis? Hurry up, stop standing there up to your neck in the deep pile, disgusted by the pub sounds, unable to believe people were actually up and out at this time of the night.

."Just a moment." Her crisp tone remained unchanged, and broke away from the phone. She would race off to raise the alarm. He took the opportunity to slot in a pound coin preparing for a long engagement. Shall I tell him your out. Good idea mumee. Better still, get dadee tell him I'm dead. Oh, you're too precious darling. I'll tell him you're out shagging your new beau, shall I? Ooh, yes mumee, that's much better. He listened to the mechanical pool of noise in the earpiece pleading for it to be broken.

"Hello?"

Thank God and all his Angels and Saints. "Frances, it's me."

"Yes, I gathered as much." She answered with all warmth of a headstone.

"What do you mean? Because it's from the pub?" His attempt at humour seemed ill fated with her voice remaining in neutral as she 'yes'. Nonetheless, it was soul soaring to hear her voice amongst the swamp of strangers. She had, in recent history, slipped from what he had known to what he thought he knew. Now that parcel of imagined thought had been tore open, bringing her to life. "How are you?" He asked.

"Fine."

"Good, good, I'm glad."

It was answered with the phone's silence.

"I'm sorry, I didn't mean to disturb you. Just thought I'd call to see how you are?" He followed up trying to subvert the entrenched silence.

"What fir?"

"What?"

"What fir?"

"I just wanted to see if you're okay, that's all."

"Why?"

"Because I was concerned, is that a crime?" He answered her, his mouth dry and his lips heavy and numb.

"There's no need, I'm fine."

"Good. I'm just wondering why I bothered now." He laughed a little laugh to rupture the stillborn atmosphere that had developed in the mouth and earpiece of the phone.

"I just wanted to see how you were, that's all."

"What fir?"

"Would you please stop that what fir stuff? It's hateful."

"You hate a lot."

"Sorry?" He asked, pushing the telephone tight to his ear.

"Nothing." She sniffed into the phone.

"Could you explain what you mean by that?" He asked, trying to maintain a jovial tone to his voice. "Is it that 'big book of things I hate' book I showed you? You know remember? After you pestered me for you to see it. It's was just observations, that was all. Okay there were quiet a lot." He snorted a laugh down the phone. He was aware he was babbling, but he did not realise how much he missed her voice, the life-force restored to his being.

"I don't have to explain a thing to you." Her voice was now strong, strident with an element of steel behind it.

"I know, I know you don't," he surrendered, "just a minute, sorry." He said, turning to see what had caused the uproarious noise in the bar. To loud cheers and whistles a kiss-O-gram had entered the bar. His friends jostled through a young man to the centre of the bar. A chair was placed for him to sit on and a laughing girl took a photograph. Brendan returned to the call smiling. "I think it's someone's birthday, it's hard to hear yourself think with all this racket."

"I have to go."

"What? Why? Wait, please. Hold on a moment. I still have some credit left." He laughed out his desperate plea.

"Ring someone else then." She instructed harshly.

"I was hoping to speak to you." He had to shout to be heard over the noise of the chanting crowd.

"What fir?" She let a laugh escape at the resumption of her tone and pronunciation. It was her way of maintaining her distance, of intimating her implacable will to keep him dead to her. It was a cold, calculated demonstration of her complete break and her embrace of new life; a life without him.

"About anything. Everything." He grasped, shouting again to be heard above the din caused by the strip-O-gram removing her clients' shirt.

"I've nothing to talk about, I have to go, mummy wants to use the phone."

"What fir?" He laughed back.

"I'm going." She snapped.

"Hold on. I'm sorry, listen, let me ring you again sometime." The plea was met by a deadpool of unwished for mechanised noise.

"No, it's not a good idea."

"Why not?" He sprang. "Just to keep in touch, just a call." A rush of hot energy saw him complete the last few words.

"Maybe, perhaps, I don't know…I have to go, really."

"I'll let you go on then, now I've a definite maybe." He laughed again. She may have said okay or bugger off, but the crowd erupted as the kiss-O-gram left the bar. "Bye." He squeezed in before the breep, breep, breep. He listened to the death throes of the call for a moment or two longer before replacing the receiver. How could he live on an unsustainable diet of maybes, perhaps, ifs and buts? He turned sensing someone to his right where a girl waited, fingering her purse. She smiled as he caught her eye and pointed to the phone.

"Are you finished?" She asked.

"I believe I am." He answered, squeezing past as he allowed her access to the phone. He stood and took from his breast pocket a ten pack, he lit up a cigarette. Christ of Almighty the smoke preached out above the heads of the rabble. How could she treat him like that? Talk to him in that distant, detached, depersonalised manner. She had condemned him to the past. He had wanted to tell her about his disappointment at not getting promotion. He was thankful now he had never been given the chance. She, most likely, would have portrayed it as indicative of the failure he was destined to have become. *Leave it aht me ole china, you know why she aint talking, eh, remember? Heh, heh, heh.* Go to hell.

She had done it by the book, the way they discussed when Jamielee, her small, blonde friend from class with a spiteful effervescence and athletic snobbishness borne of her Shankill Road mother and Fermanagh father who had made a fortune from scrap metal; rang one evening. Jamie-lee had incurred her wrath, when in a drunken strop had told her she was losing her identity to the relationship she and Brendan had formed. Approach the call as if you were taking an ordinary call, preferably upbeat, drop the tone and language, just be neutral, yet decisive. The caller would be made penitent and therefore vulnerable and more likely made contrite; waiting to be administered a lesson in the art of chastisement. It was a matter of timing and tone. He smiled fondly at her laughter, when he said Courtney, who was studying, nay, reading as she referred to it, social anthropology; had her assignment waiting at home for her.

He stood close to the bar ringed by people, separated from the drink he craved, shaking with frustration and foolishness. Once again, he had proved to be the architect of his own diminution. He pushed his way to the front of the crowd, past those who had been served and were standing in his path just to be a fucking nuisance. He got to the bar and shouted to the barman, who approached him with a smile he had smiled ever since he arrived in the bar. The barman acknowledged his order and turned to the optics to serve him the double vodka and dash of orange. He paid for his drink and took the glass turning to face the noise, smoke and clothing of the crowd.

There they were, the guys, casually dressed, loud, animated with attempted cleverness, acting impulsively; self-contained units, revolving in orbits of their making. Their dolls circulating, antennae raised, receptive to what their guys had to say for themselves. Positioned reflections, fulfilling self-ordained public roles, listening attentively for what they had to say, smiling strategically and on more daring forays venture an opinion, rarely their own, but some contrived response dovetailing with their men's that you couldn't see the join. There would be willy language to upset them into fits of giggles, everyone would snatch, there's one!, at double-entendres, sanctioned by their titters, ooh er, there's another.

Look at them he thought savagely conspiring with his smoke, circling in adolescent perpetuity, damned to act out some form of life of some sorts. God, did you stand so long, long enough to plot and plan your escape? He gulped down the drink in his glass.

He felt an uneasy euphoria, a recklessness of mind, an area that forgave him his soul and his life's unfulfilled promise. He breathed in deeply, his nostrils drawing in the indiscernible, losing meaning and perspective, he was becoming subsumed, his senses pummelled by the now, the before and a hereafter. He raised his glass to the assimilation. God, he could write another entire volume of 'My big book of things I hate'. First line, I hate Frances.

If he were to find her in the street lying in a pool of blood, he would kick her in the mouth so she couldn't call for help. There. It was a great concept, but never-ending he discovered which is why he thought a clever way to complete the book was to leave it unfinished and have half the book contain blank pages so the dear reader could take over authorship with their own particular hates. He stayed at the bar and ordered another double which he gulped down.

He returned to the table in a vicious mood, taking his seat and the pint that had performed hopscotch around the table, its movement marked in rings of a homemade asphalt of beer and ash.

"Where'd you get to? I'm sitting here like a spare one. Here, guess who yer man is?" Gerry asked, now sitting almost shoulder to shoulder with him. "Concepta's boyfriend ." Gerry hissed the answer to his rhetorical question into Brendan's face. "Yeah, I think he goes to the gym, I know his bake." Gerry mused.

"So what!" Brendan snapped back, looking over to the young man ensconced between foetus-killer and Concepta, his hands clasped between his legs assuming the pose of attentive listener, his bright blue eyes moving intelligently between his two companions.

"Fucking fruit or what?" Gerry's condemnation attempted to involve him in his conspiracy against the boyfriend and by implication, Concepta herself. He knew what lay beneath Gerry's overtures, his patter had fallen on fallow ground and the ole mutton dagger wouldn't be stabbing anyone tonight. Eh John? Poor Gerry, how he remembered his child-like displays of petulance when his wooing felt flat. The years they spent in the Donegal

Street nightclubs, bonded by their youthful lust, their love of The fall, Bauhaus, Joy Division, Psychedelic furs, The Cramps, Smiths, Spear of Destiny, bands that no-one in their immediate circle liked or even had heard of. They were in the dark years of ugly violence, but the clubs gave them an escape into a world of make-believe. The music, the fashion, their leather trousers, their heads shaved around the sides, the hair teased up with a half jar of hair gel; was two fingers up to the environment they were cast in. Great times, he remembered, with the clubs open until the early hours, the parties that would run into Sunday afternoons and they could imagine themselves to be anywhere and anyone they wanted to be. Fuck, it was so long ago. Then the club scene, Madchester, it was indiscernible at first, dance music came and went, then industrial rave and with it the irruption of Thatcher's generation and the fruition of her creed. It was aggressive, selfish, mean and with a voracious, vulgar appetite. The love of music was replaced by the love of money. The scene remained local fuelled by the drugs of the gangsters and criminals with the acquiescence of the paramilitaries. Now to-days youth were lost to an orchestrated and designed scene conducted in barbarous acts of corporate manipulation with profit aforethought. Capitalism posing as anarchy packaged and presented for mass consumption. Sickening. Jeezus, he sounded like a hippie. He sounded old.

"Are you going to get a liquor in?" He asked, as Gerry's fear of the woodwork at the bar was bordering on the pathological.

"I've no money left." Gerry's laconic reply was followed up by a theatrical show of rubbing both his pockets with the palms of his hands..

"So you'll not be getting a fucking drink in then." He responded murderously to the news. Gerry shrank back in his seat; his only source of succour in a world of diminishing returns, had gone. Brendan drained the last of his stout from the glass, bent down, picked up his bag from beneath the table and put on his jacket. He stood up and bidding no-one in particular a 'good-night' he left the table.

Frances set the receiver down and looked up the hall towards the living room door which was ajar. She could see her mother's shadow fixed against the living room wall where it had remained throughout her phone call. She did not mind that her mother was eavesdropping, perhaps now, after that performance her mother would stop worrying and fussing over her. It seemed her mother had her cue to move, the shadow stood up from sitting on the armrest of the sofa, straightened her cardigan and spoke. "Are you finished dear? With the phone I mean?"

"Yes, mum."

"Oh good," she said, her head appearing at the living room door, "I was hoping to hear from Agnes. It's bridge on Thursday. Hot chocolate?" She enquired, remaining steadfast in her vigil at the door.

"Yes, thanks. I'll be with you in a moment, mum."

"Ok, sweetheart."

"Mum, there's no need to worry. There's no going back." She told her mother, who had left the hall, but remained standing at the living room side of the door.

"I know. We don't want or need anything from, well, you know. Thank God your father and your brother…well. I'll get that chocolate, need one myself." The shadow glided over the wall and through the living room door into the kitchen where the door was closed behind her. Frances got up and returned to the living room and raised the volume of the television to audible. She knew she had made the right decision to return home, it was the best and most secure place to be. This is where could lick her wounds and put the plans she had in mind into action. She just did not need her mothers encroachment into the an area that was personal and could only be resolved by her, with her family's assistant not interference. She immediately and bitterly regretted her decision in telling her mother the real reason for the break-up and was given cause on daily basis to regret it further. Her mother's implicit warning that her father and brother never find out felt more like manipulation than maternal concern.

He felt weak, almost unable to carry the weight of his travel bag. He used the shield of bodies to conduct his path to the door until someone stepped out of line and knocked against him, the weight of the back pulled him back and he almost lost his footing. "Sorry there mate." A voice apologised from the main body of those gathered around him. "Are you stupid, as well as badly dressed?" He shouted over at his assailant and forged ahead through the static bodies using his bag as an icebreaker. Outside he embraced the chill of the night time air. Inside the babble of life would continue until the barman got his wish and fucked them all out. *Poor Gerry eh?, 'aving to face the golden boy of Concepta's wet ones, eh?* Serve the fucker right, he thought, putting the travel bag over his shoulder and digging both hands into his pockets in search of warmth, he walked.

Women and their bloody causes, because they got it stuck to 'em, their sanctity intruded upon, everyone has to pay. "Jeeezus." Brendan let out a gasp of frozen air, held rigid by the promiscuous line of thought that now shook his senses. *Oi, she'll be getting' the big skin 'ead with the one eye soon enuff, pukin' aht all that accumulated want and need.* "Shut fucking up!" He ordered, walking on purposefully to dispel the images eh John conjured up in his mind and escape the cold biting at his nose and ears. They could abort the whole of the next generation for all was concerned, returning to foetus killer and her fat issue. Serve us all bloody right; give the world a break from their ever-demanding children and their adoring progenitors who'd descend into baby sanitary talk about number ones and number twoseys. To hell with that, no way he would endure all that abstinence and self-denial in what was a pitifully short life.

The way he felt about kids walking along the road, he could murder one, but he'd have to settle for a chinkers. He made a laugh at the joke he'd prepared and stumbled up to the door of the heavily lit takeaway.

It was empty of the late night crowd, they were still encased in the bars and clubs, he couldn't have endured all that loudness, loose change and slabbering. The European girl sat behind the counter, bored and dulled into a zombie-like stupor which chaperoned her movement to the order pad. He walked over to the giant yellow menu, taking a few moments to scan it before ordering his usual dish.

"What's your order?"

"A number seven with lashings of your deeelicious curry."

The greasy haired girl stood up, reached for her pen and jotted down his order. He watched her scribble it down, curious to see her handwriting and spelling. But she proved too circumspect and proficient, peeling off the page with a small riiip sound, turning in one movement. Turning in one movement, she rapped the small hatch in the centre of the tiled wall and returned to her seat. The hatch opened immediately and a small jaundiced hand retrieved the order and disappeared as quickly behind the sliding hatch.

Behind the serving hatch he could hear a flurry of activity and noise as the chinkers worked like blacks to a symphony of woks and sizzle, jabbering away in that high-pitched nasal nonsense they spoke. Probably laughing at stupid bastards like you paying outlandish prices for the stomach-burners they served up. He walked over to the large window the fronted the take-away, set his back down and looked out onto the road, his eyes drawn to the moving lights of the traffic; red going down, white coming up. Their constant movement captivated his attention, soon his look had fallen into a stare, lulled by the lights hypnotic effect on his tired, aching sight of it all.

"Here's your order." The plain girl had his order placed in plastic bag and set on the counter as he fished in his pockets for the money. One rolled up fiver and an assortment of loose change. He counted out three pound coins, a fifty pence piece and two tens. The exact amount. He placed the money down on the counter. "Suppose a fork's out of the question?"

He said, shoving the fiver back into his pocket. The dull girl did not look up as she took the money across, her mouth moving as she counted.

"Forks another five pence." She said sullenly, his remark failing to engage her small grey eyes as they watched him roll the five pence across to the counter towards her. She collected the coin, and dipped her arm under the counter and handed over a plastic fork; as if he was going to flee the country with it, for forksake.

He wrestled the weight of the travel bag back onto his shoulder that had now assumed the density and weight of a malevolent dwarf on his back, took his order and placed the fork in his coat pocket wished the dull girl a 'goodnight'. He left the dull, plain, greasy girl to gazing into the black and white portable her employers had kindly provided for her entertainment.

"Long live fish and chips." He smuggled out onto the street laughing at his own joke. The green man, green person, let's be politically correct in this enlightened age, alerted him to put his best foot forward. He did his utmost to follow the illuminated example, arms stiffened, one behind his back, one in front, he marched across the road in elongated strides. He laughed at the sight he must have made to the taxi drivers and police land rovers parked at the solid white line. The province's two growth industries, all touting for business they would surely get. *Wot a bleedin' country, eh. A bleedin' bog.* Aye well , you lot played a big part in making it that way Brendan rounded on the cockney sound full of scathing derision.

He had negotiated the road just as his green friend disappeared, he could feel his breath hot and heavy from his exertions, here he was a chip of the oul sod's block. Eh? You belligerent, bellicose, boorish bollocks. She's probably praying for you. Reconcile him, O Lord, to his fate as one of life's great arseholes.

"Christ the night." He sucked out of the night air, stumbling into the church railings marking the beginning to his street. He stopped to rest staring at the debris left by early evening revellers, beer cans and plastic bags of various sizes and colours. He forced himself from the support of the railings drawing in the freshness of the damp earthiness of the church grounds. The trees, this small facet of ignored beauty, lying hitherto concealed, revealed a fractured moment and reminded him:

The bullet threaded a note hole through flesh. A shout. A plea. Again. Faces without mercy danced around the beast in the playground of the devil, playing his tune, paying his price. No-one saw the humanity witnessed only to an inhuman audience.

Leave it aht me ole chum, you'll never be a writer and she ain't wurf it, no bird is. Only a matter of the ole sweet and sublime before she's stuck on the end of some guy's pole.

"Fuck off! Please." He begged, falling back against the unforgiving surface of the wall of the church. Was this to be his Kunstlerroman? Christ, she had a word for everything. He could never understand how writers gave their characters complete understanding of their environment and provide them with the language to fully describe their world. People weren't omnipotent. Those tress he had passed so often. Did he know what type they were? Were they coniferous? Deciduous? What type of tree were they? All he could tell you was that there were big and graceful looking and shed their leaves in autumn The Church, what type of religious architecture was it? What did it convey in its historical context, all this was hidden to him. A real writer would know, he would find out and employ it to his craft. . Some bollocks of a writer would have their character tell you their name both in English and Latin and that's bollocks.

His feet were clay, his thighs butter on hot toast almost unable to support him. The door, unchanged in its structure and composition from the day he slammed it behind him in a rush of noise and purposelessness. A wake of silence shadowed his hand as he inserted the key. The lock moved with the familiar clunking mechanism, and the door opened without pressure. A vacuum of uninviting stillness beckoned

A bewildering tennis ball of trepidation and expectation rose to lodge in his throat. He waited in absurd hope that the silence ridiculed.

He crossed the threshold into the darkened womb of the hall dispelling the stillborn atmosphere by slamming the door firmly shut behind him. The living room door was ajar, it never closed properly, it was a running complaint of hers, particularly during the winter months. He had gone and bought 'willy' the snake, the 'adorable' draught excluder that he dutifully placed at the foot of the door each evening. (Now gone).

He pushed the door open with his fingertips, his eyes growing accustomed to the dark, a dark accentuated by the curtains drawn over a still-life setting hewn in recognisable and familiar shapes.

Come on mate, he thought, encouraging himself to move, you're chinkers'll get cold, aware of the past thickening in and around him. He moved swiftly, dropping the travel bag to the floor and setting the takeaway on the seat of the armchair. He stooped down to reach for the four-gang plug socket. He found the holes after several sliding attempts and gave life to the green, red and blue lights of the hi-fi. He reached over to the table lamp that rolled out light over the room like a sheet of muslin and suddenly he felt stranded. Again, he had to move swiftly picking up the takeaway he took it into the kitchen switching the light on he placed the food beside the sink and went to the fridge. He opened the door to the fridge praying the beer he had left over from one of the International matches he wanted to watch, but cancelled due to bad weather. A solid inedible block of cheese, two frosted tomatoes, a carton of juice and milk, well past its drink by date, a tub of butter and six cans of Budweiser. Praise be! He snatched one from the group breaking its plastic attachment and caressed its tinny chill, its body responding to the pressure of his hand. He plucked the metal ring, a beery gasp escaped and he drank until his mouth could hold no more. There knew you'd drink it, he could hear a sneering voice say.

He swallowed hard and repeated the exercise until the tin had been drained; he dropped the empty tin onto the floor in defiance of her obsession with keeping the kitchen clean. He opened the fridge door again and took another tin, opened it and sipped slowly looking at the takeaway he knew he would not eat. He lifted the bag and placed it in the fridge knowing he would not eat it in the morning either.

Then it was there, or more accurately, there it wasn't. The pine wall clock (his), gone, stripped of the wall. At least the spice rack was still in place; perhaps she couldn't find a screwdriver. The fuckpot. He lifted his tin and went into the living room ready to play 'I spy with my little eye things she took 'cos she ain't coming back'. He had looked about the floor of the hall when he stepped in, hoping for a note or letter and he felt absurd that, even now, he was looking about the room for one.

He went over to the pine shelves he had put up to house books, cd's and cassettes. The top shelf he announced pompously would be devoted to literature, the lower to music. He looked along the row of books (his) all corralled into a taut formation Marquez, Greene, Fowles, Joyce, Eco, O'Brien, O'Connor, poetry anthologies, Steinbeck and an error of judgement he had made twice with Brian Moore.

Musically, he suffered from the same sporadic inconsistency, nothing to suggest a person with a strong taste or opinion, but one formed by an opinion he wanted of himself in others. REM, U2, Fleetwood Mac, Motown, big groups, mainstream and universally appealing, (all his) his cd's and cassettes sat in a reduced stack, which suggested a methodical, if not, clinical removal (hers). Fuck it, give me, MC5, Prefab Sprout, Steely Dan anyday. There's sunshine in every chord. Fuck she had Rumours by Fleetwood Mac, who didn't, but couldn't tell you who Peter Green was. He swiped the shelf with his arm sending cds and cassettes clattering to the floor to disrupt the neat little end she had made of him.

He turned to face the room, the Van Gogh print of sunflowers (his) remained crucified to the wall, the tv/video unit (his), the leather settee (also his), the armchair, non-matching (his) all kept faith with him, reflecting the investment he, not her, had made. Proof, if it were needed, of his, not hers, level of commitment. There wasn't anything she could not lift up, pick off and take away.

He breathed into the half empty can remembering the savings book he discovered in her bottom drawer whilst searching for a clean tee shirt for her after her nightly bath. Studded, regular little deposits of faithlessness, like a prayer book of a non-believer. Apostate!

He sat down on the settee, lit up a cigarette (all his), wondering if she intended for him to find it. He pulled the ashtray stolen from a bar closer (no outright owner) and flicked the ash beyond the ashtray onto the table. He stood up and walked to the window and drew the curtains open (his, after a months of the landlord's hideous purple drapes).

Outside nothing stirred, autumn had usurped the pretence of summer; it too deserted him. He drew the curtain close and faced the echoes of a previous incarnation. She admired me brayed the Van Gogh, she loved to lounge on me yawned the settee, remember how she'd brush her shiny dark hair with me the mirror hit out. "So what!" He let out a throbbing shiver of anger. "Holy fuck, I'm arguing with the furniture." And he laughed a laugh at the absurdity of his reduction and the need to parody himself. He drained the last of the tin and went to the bathroom. Small, pink (her idea) making a mental note to paint it out; blue, red, green, black, purple with yellow spots.

The toilet seat was up (her idea) and he pissed directly into the bowl, not around the sides, so no-one (her) could hear. He zipped up and in deliberate defiance slapped the toilet seat down, washed his hands and went to the airing cupboard to get a towel. Pink, cream, yellow and orange (hers) gone, his blue, red, green (his) neatly folded, remained. The toilet tissue, from pack of four, gone; except for one dangling, necktie on the holder, in case he needed a shite. Ta. He dried his hands on a green towel and placed it over the radiator.

He looked over to the bath at the head of which sat a depleted group of shampoos and bath salts (his) between the taps. It was time. Time for the biggy. He switched off the bathroom light with a sharp tug on the handle and made a long step from the bathroom door to the bedroom door. He pushed down on the handle and pushed open the door. He was shocked to discover he could still smell her; conjuring up the idea of her waiting, hair and body washed, moisturised and perfumed. He flicked on the light and an outstretched quilt (his), flat, oblong coated in coloured geometric lines rolled out to poke fun.

On the shelves, the family of fluffy pets (hers) gone. Glass jars, candles, joysticks and Betty Boo alarm clock (all hers) gone. It was a fraud of a place, the white immaculate ness of the walls impeached as barren indictments of him. He turned and slapped the switch off and went hurriedly back to the living room, buoyed slightly by the contrast of mood it offered.

He went into the kitchen zipped open his travel bag and carefully removing the clothes, placed them on the one barstool, he retrieved the food granny brown had given him and placed them in the fridge, left the clothes remaining on the chair and took another tin of beer and retired to the settee. "Look at it this way." He said, getting up from the settee and going over to the video unit, switched the television on, grabbed the remote took out the writing pad and pen from the drawer (both his) and sat back on the settee. He pressed down on the mute button on the remote control for the television and went over to the wicker hamper beneath the window (his, no, not the window, the hamper, he sniggered) and found the shoe box where he kept his writing. He took the box out, closed the hamper and sat down on the settee. He opened the box and the first item he saw was his scribbled poem 'Orang-utan' At the top of the page was her hand-written note. 'Well done. Excellent work. Keep writing. Keep focused.' And she had drawn a large star, with another note beside it 'Imagine it as gold'

I saw an Orang-utan in town yesterday

I said hello and asked what he was doing

I am working for a man

He beats me black and blue

I've always said, you humans,

You belong in a zoo

He rubbed his eyes and focused. He would prove to her. No, not her, himself, that he wasn't just 'a smart mouth in a bar.' He lifted out his short story 'Bygones'

The bullet threaded a neat hole through flesh, a shout. A plea. Again. Faces without mercy danced around the beast in the playground of the Devil, playing his tune, paying his price. No-one saw the humanity witnessed only to an inhuman audience. Fingers broken, unbowed, clawing needlessly through blood and dirt. Clothes made ridiculous trappings; shoes wrought from sweat-stained feet. The only reality lay in contact. Euphoria. An intoxicating pot pourri of fear and excitement.

Brendan got up and got himself another beer and returned to the settee. Hit her. Hard. Harder. Him holding the female. Rare control. Dominate. Humiliate. To kill. The ultimate expression. No-one watched. The others working to-gether. The Chapel spire, phallic like, impotent symbol of a creed that failed to take root. To the ground it fell. Fucksake watch the trousers. Laughter. The woman shuddering inside a cheap plastic raincoat. Do her. Norman likes her. Laughter again. Too old and too ugly. Too late.

Movement. Frantic. Compelling. Footsteps thudding past a rusted gate. Sniggers amongst the beer guts. Backseat dark. The smell and sound of new leather. Engine on. Music. Action everyone.

Mummy. Mummy. For a moment he thought he heard himself cry out. Afraid of self-righteous indignation. He was awake. His voice transported in time and in place. He was alive. The punishment block of a small room. Rain rattled the window. The draught pinching his nose and ears; his eyes on the tea-stained cup and ashtray of dead fag ends. Back amidst the nightmare of life. Inescapable. Incurable, carried with the malignancy bereft of hope or remission. His body cocooned in sackcloth waiting for the ashes.

Mummy. The voice shriller than before, puncturing the stillness of his tomb. The front door slammed shut. A plastic raincoat he wished. Rushing out, rushing off. Demanding, forever demanding. The product of his frenzy. He refused the flaccid lure of masturbation. He took a cigarette. Smoke filled his mouth, nose, throat and lungs. The hollow chamber of his stomach echoed.

The kitchen cold to his naked feet. Warm smells escaping. He drained the last of the milk in the carton left at the sink, allowing it to trickle down his chin, just to have the feel of something.

Money. The curse of the drinking classes. Possessed. Upstairs trouser, jacket, shirt yielded the price of two pints. An hour if you sipped.

"You know, this isn't too bad." Brendan said in a toast to himself. "Wot you fink eh John?" Eh John did not reply, preferring to wait until the drink and the distraction had ended.

Into the bitches lair. The big room, warm and comfortable. Perfume ignited the air. He lingered over the underwear. An earlier life. Bygones. The crying child impressed on his mind. He slammed the drawer shut. The other room. A tidy, comfortable version of his mothers. A girl's room he scorned. He struck gold in a rich seam inside a pencil case. Two ten pound notes and several

pound coins. Sneaky shite. His face sombre. Accusing. Eyes of his mother, blue

and cold.

Outside a concrete sky burnished the angled grey slabs of his world duller. He

walked towards a pack of cigarettes, a paper and hot breakfast. Around his

ankles, stiffened denim. Muddy shackles.

"That's good stuff, even if I say so myself." Brendan said, getting up to get

another tin. He returned to the settee and lit up a cigarette and settled back to read.

Moments later he left the unruly warmth of the shop shielding the

precious company of a cigarette from the constant rain. He was back home. Laid

before him the back pages. He sat down, concentrated and ate.

Friends, rain and mud synchronised on screen. The smoke masking the

sharpness of the pristine presentation. Painted face, good clothes incongruous to

the death of a policeman. Bitterness and grievance knitted.

He did not recognise the scene. The ugly rock of a chapel, the skeletal trees, the

mud. A woman's voice, quiet, choking on incomprehension. Jimmy was sixty-

four, a loving family man with five children. A silhouette engulfed in loss.

Everyone's a Saint. He smacked the arm of the chair. The muted thickness of his

response descended on him. He plunged in the deafening pool of profanity. The

woman knew no better. A fenian whore who lies down with her priests. You, son

of Cain are no better than they.

He escaped out onto the street clutching the paper immersed in the selections

and race meetings. His bet placed he was at the bar barking out an order to

Parkinson, a bag of old bones, his name reflecting the disease that seemed to afflict him. He shunned the company of an elderly patron, his eyes ran along the rows of distilled amnesiacs. Two glasses, one small, one large, both shaking. Dark liquid rinsed the wretchedness from inside his mouth. He watched in the mirror as the alcohol bit. His face the colour and texture of kneaded dough. Bar room pallor. The wages of sin.

He ordered again. Unemployed. Unemployable. Approaching the big four O. Best wishes. Not love. Never that. Her unlove fatal. His child lost to the truth. The pain returned to the base of his spine causing him to swear aloud. Fuck where are they. He hated to be alone. His life without abstract meaning or apology.

A voice hailed. Blessed relief as the three appeared before him. Benny, his tight-lipped grin, Dougie stroking his stubbled chin. Sammy, looming head and shoulders above the pair. Drinks were ordered, Norman scrambled over to the table to join them. An air unforgivable air of seriousness. Dougie state of urgency barely contained by the beer mats. Active, comical eyes about to burst their sockets.

Sammy demanded calm. Dougie championed his cause, sitting close to him, his much smaller frame eclipsed by the sun he revolved around. Sammy dominated,
sheer size guaranteed attention. His great shaven head lowered, the tightly grouped band grew tighter. Norman moved in tasting the comradeship forming on the numbness of his mouth. There would be talk, the execution had been sanctioned, there would be no debate. Sammy's pedigree was impeccable. Fifteen

years for the murder of an IRA intelligence unit posing as a courting couple on the wrong side of the Crumlin Road. The claim denounced by the RUC and IRA, as both organisations acting together to rubbish the action. No-one was to break with routine. Dougie raised his glass to that. Laughter. Norman became absorbed by the hard, lean faces, stubble, smoke and beer. A secret life hidden from empty eyes. He basked in a sense of protectiveness.

The bet. At the bar two races, two winners, glory. One required for a good return. The race began. One mile. The purple shirt of the jockey, the white noseband of the horse edging home with three lengths to go. Run, run you brute. Docket in the grip of a sweating hand. A cry leapt out, deep, rich and throaty against a lifetime, against the insults and banter from the resurrected table. Seventy-eight pounds or thereabouts, twenty for the injured party. The means. A certain end.

Home is the leper. The clatter of plate and cold blue eyes, body trembling with anger. Blindly rushing, clutching at the system, to remove the poison. He gripped, shouting, screaming, pain streaming, queuing in his mouth. The raincoat, the rain, the mud. Suddenly the force was spent. He fell from the heights of his pain laying side by side with her convulsed form. He was lost, his hands unable to reach out and touch what he longed for.
It was much too late, her body rigid. He was alone.

A burst of thunderous knocking on the door rose his shell, serious looking faces, fresh, clean, scrubbed with disdain. He nodded in dumb compliance he did not glance back.

He travelled inside the bumping, clanking metal of the chugging grey beast. 'Sammy had been arrested, squealed like a pig' A young unsmiling face sat facing him. He did not stir. The thought of prison did not alarm him. He had served time in the worst of them.

Ends.

"Eh John? Wot you fink? Not too shabby, eh?" Brendan sat back on the settee, feeling the need to be congratulated. Eh John was not to be engaged in backslapping. *It's waffle, lacks substance, like the author. Wot yer goin' to do wiv that, nuthin' She were dead raight about you. And she's still not 'ere, probably wiv sum geezer raight now.*

"Oh yeah, let's see about that. Eh shall we?" He flicked the writing pad to a blank page. "Right then," he said, pen in hand, "chance's of meeting mister right." He headlined the page. "Let's look at the probability. But first, let's have another tin. Eh?" He returned from the kitchen with another beer from the fridge. "Ok" He said pulling the coffee table closer. "First, place: Belfast. Naw let's be generous, give her the whole of our wee province.

Population? Say one and half million, half of them women." He scribbled down his figure saying to himself. " Leaving us with seven hundred and fifty thousand."

Yeah, 'cos we know she ain't no dickie dodger, he, he.

"Shut up! Let's not be crude about this." Brendan retorted. "Right. Age.Again, being generous here. Between twenty and forty. Take away another four hundred thousand, leaving three hundred and fifty thousand."

That's a lot of cock, he,he.

"You're becoming a bore, eh John!" Brendan snapped. "So, if we feed in physical appearance, height, weight, personality, character, then…" He sat chewing his pen for a moment as these elements reduced the number. "Say about a hundred thousand. Don't say it, I've more data to factor in." He advised eh John. He took a gulp of beer. "Now some fine tuning. They'd need to interesting, thoughtful, considerate, intelligent…"

Wot was she doin' wiv you then?, he,he. Don't forget ambition and drive.

"Not listening." Brendan continued and wrote down the figure of ten thousand. "And into this figure we will enter, good taste, generosity, ambition, love of animals, especially cats. And" he added the last factor in silence, writing drive and ambition, acknowledging eh John was right, "and we're down to a thousand. And this figure can be whittled down further with someone who will run baths, errands, make breakfast in bed, clean, massage aches and pains, listen to her grumbling, show concern for her worries and alleviate her foul moods by buying her something. What's that leave us with?" He did not write down a figure, but the set pen on the writing pad. "You know wot, eh John, a good man really is hard to find." He took a sip from the beer can. "Any way you took it well old chum, no doubt about that."

He remembered the night she arrived home later than usual from her psychology class setting her bag down in the hall and breezing into the kitchen without a word. He heard the kettle boil and her call out if he would like a cup tea. Before he could answer she came out to stand at the kitchen door munching on a handful of fruit and fibre.

You not staying? He thought he would ask given that she had not removed her coat. No. Not after tonight. Would you like a biscuit with your tea? She asked. Oh yes, I think this calls for a digestive. No a Kitkat, seeing this is a break. Some bright bastard somewhere, probably in Germany, would have a syndrome to describe his behavioural response as she stood at the kitchen entrance denying him the smile that should have been on is lips.

It was the casual and quiet way of the way she poured the boiled water into the mugs that alarmed him. He stood by the kitchen door, his face betraying his need for an explanation. She returned at him in that high octane way that was always a prelude to a desertion. He pressed on, his voice at shouting level. There was a history of quiet. Then, at last, as she swallowed down the last of her cereal 'There's no, there's no...'

No what? he demanded. He could have struck her for the laugh that she made to the mugs of tea. 'Herzlickeit. There's no herzlickeit.' She gushed. What? What the hell is that? Is it like fellatio? he laughed, wiping the bubbles of mucus membrane propagating in both nostrils.

"It's not you, it's me. I'm no good at relationships, I've told you."

That old chestnut.

Fuck off, he said it three times to cover his escape back into the living room He sat down on the floor his back resting against the settee cocooned in a little place he had made between his legs; filling it with his breath. He followed the stitching in his jeans that tracked down the leg like a tiny ho chi min trail to the hem and wished he was part, if not, all thread. Inanimate, with a purpose, a design behind his existence.

He knew it was real when he heard the spoon in the kitchen chime out the Angelus. His felt the muscles in his face fail him as her small smile radiated the end and a residual pity for him. She returned from the kitchen and left a cup of tea on the carpet at his feet and she took her cup over to the window. " I saw something today that made me think about this," she said quietly, if she smoked, she would be puffing furiously on a cigarette, " there was a couple outside the boutique holding each other kissing and when they separated, she sort of skipped away, like she was on air, back to work presumably. I mean this wasn't a girl, she was a young woman, well dressed, not a teenager and I watched the guy watching her skip up the street, her back to him and he blew her a kiss." She stopped to take a sip of tea and wipe her coat of invisible dust.

"Maybe it was glue he was on." He offered without a trace of humour.

"Everything's just one big joke to you." She said, the fire returning to her soul. "It struck me then that we don't have that anymore, the excitement, the bliss, the euphoria..." Her voice trailed off and she returned to wiping her coat.

"All relationships start on an unnatural high, then they settle into something more realistic, something that can be maintained. Something that is sustainable. It can't all be Mills and Boon. I didn't think I was with Barbara Cartland." This time he laughed, but he knew it was misplaced, mistimed and another pathetic stand-up routine ignored the reality of the situation. How much of his real life was he to laugh away? No wonder she had tired of him..

"I don't love you, not the way I did. I care deeply about you. I do." She lowered her head and examined the contents of her cup. "When Una was here."

"What's she got to do with this?" He demanded, standing up to the challenge, suddenly in the grip of an anger that startled the both of them. He stood up to challenge her.

"Nothing. Nothing directly." She said quickly and the fear in her voice made him feel immediately ashamed of his outburst. "When she was here," She said at last, as he sat back down in the settee and lit up a cigarette ignoring her rule of no smoking in the flat. The fact that she did not admonish him for smoking told him that she did not care because she was not staying, "when she was here, I thought your behaviour towards her was more than rude, it was distant, the way you go at times. It was a side to you I knew existed, but not to that extent and it made me feel ashamed and embarrassed and in some way part responsible. I had to talk to her and make excuses, saying you were under pressure at work. But your behaviour was downright cruel and if I didn't know better, you seemed to be enjoying it. To be honest I was defending myself too, I didn't want her thinking I supported behaviour like that."

"Perish the thought." Brendan struck out quietly to himself.

"She said that you were sent to Belfast because you had so much promise and your family thought you'd get a much better education here and go onto university."

"The great white hick of hope." He laughed bitterly.

"Yes, that's what they all thought, but what have you done? You're stuck in that same job, in the same career. When you didn't get that Careers Officer post, you moped around the flat for days, even though you hate the job and the service. I know you've the intelligence to do so much better, but you don't do anything. It's like your happy to make sarcastic comments about your situation and place in the world and do nothing about it." She finished.

"It's a bit difficult to go Uni with a full-time job and a flat to pay for." He told her in his defence.

"Lots of mature students do it and a lot of them have children, you have that assistance programme in work and I know you've done everything regarding the flat, I know, but…"

He got up from the settee. "You condescending…" he left the final word for the kitchen. "Bitch." He spat out the word into the sink, suppressing it to a hot whisper that burned his lips. "Not all of us can have the luxury of a middle-class background, with disposable income."

He shouted back at her into the living room.

"I work too." She shouted back. "That's not fair."

"What? In that doss house once a week" He retorted. "You spend most of that time sleeping, you said so yourself."

"You asshole. That's my job and my career, hopefully, one day. You may be in need of somewhere like one day. I'm still working, supporting, was supporting, this flat and studying."

"Not anymore though, eh?" He snapped back, louder than before.

"Look I know", she said coming to the kitchen door, "I'm partly to blame, you could do so much more, maybe I'm holding you back as well."

"Oh Jesus, don't be a martyr on my account, please." He sneered back.

Much discussion followed between the meeting of Brendan O'Connell and Frances Preston. Miss Preston was quoted as using the words 'Indolent, sarcastic, mean' Mr O'Connell throughout the meeting was heard to use the words 'bourgeoise, predictable, superficial, laboured, mean (the last word was previously used by Miss P, but Mr O'C wanted it ascribed to him as it applied) and his final coup de gras, boring. Then he did one more unspeakable thing in their relationship, he begged. But it was over, a deep realisation had seeped into his consciousness. He knew as she stood by the kitchen door popping bran flakes into her mouth like she was ay the movies, that she had already left him. Her return to a bright and breezy tone and demeanour conveyed her neutrality within the situation. She was of it, but outside and beyond it. Her attitude ad movement did not invite discussion and certainly ruled out any hope of reconciliation. She had discovered, against all her warnings and precaution, that he had been the smartest mouth in the bar that night; Brendan concluded for her.

On our first meeting I did think you were gay, she admitted, and on the second she confessed, concealing her laugh with a hand freed from the cereal box. I never met a guy who was so obsessed with clothes. I caught you more than once looking in shop windows, not at what was behind them. What's wrong with taking pride in your appearance, you could take a leaf out of my book, he added unkindly. Sorry, for dragging you down, but I won't be cramping your style any further, she returned frostily. He apologised, but it was too late for apologies. She leaned against the door frame and delved into the cereal box again, resuming to her bright and breezy tone. Look at the number of shirts you have, and you treat them better than you did your sister. Fabric softener, ironed to perfection. I ironed yours too, cos your too lazy. Well, I'll be doing my own from now on. No, you won't, mumee will, giving you more time to shave your legs. He was set free now by her signposting her departure. What I've come to realise, she snapped, gripping the cereal box until it crumpled, outside of a smart turn of phrase, she stopped, smiling at some recollection, her mind invested in a different time and place, that all you were, are, she hastily added, is a wardrobe full of clothes. You bitch, he thought as she made her stage exit to change props. She returned to the living room with two cups of tea.

"It's like boxes? Boxes, you say. Yes, another one of life's great mysteries. Love. Where does it go, when it goes? It must still exist, the emotional rationale for its existence, it must remain, uprooted, but still, it must survive, like a virus. But why boxes? You buy an item, say a video. You take it out. And for whatever reason you want to return it. And you have to repack it and does it go back into its original packing? Does it fuck." He laughed, reaching for his lighter. "It's," he stopped to light a cigarette, "an unscrupulous marketing ploy, and that says more about mere commerce. No wot I mean Eh John, wot you fink? Innit? He sat back, exhausted, he had reached the end of his rationalisation and was left feeling the true burden of his situation.

Eh John did not care for the analogy or the conversation, preferring to retire to the bedroom and wait for the drink and its distraction to end. But to Brendan it proved that writers cannot allow their characters omnipotence, he knew what he meant by the analogy. So fuck *him*. How can you put into words life's momentous events. He knew eh John would say it's because you ain't no writer. He was probably right. But then again, he was pissed.

"Oh Christ." He screamed into his hands from the bottom of his anguish. No-one heard, nothing cared to. The creature comforts, restored to the natural status in the world could and would say nothing. Now it was only a matter of time that all of this would be filled with her absence and she with someone else. Her thoughts, her laughter, her smiles, her scent, a fine layer of perfume and creams, her long clean fingernails; her beautifully kept hair, shiny and clean, her colourful clothes machine-washed and pressed. Even the funny way she ate, chewing speedily like some small animal, her concerns, her loves, her dislikes; all, all of this and much more would be gathered up and invested in another.

How could she claim that he was insensitive? How dare she! It was him who always had to initiate rapturous declarations of undying love. Love wasn't in her emotional vocabulary. The cunt.

When would the sanctity of indifference and its faraway longing come; and relieve the insurmountable sense of loss and the terror of its permanence? A bubble of breath escaped from his lips and echoed around the half-empty tin. His whole being felt like a frozen mass of disjointed needs and wants, mid-thoughts and half-feeling that had no origin and no end. A being of maladjustments. Malformed: a jumbled mass of mental processes that were without foundation. He stared at the television screen, a silent pornography of images that catalogued the expulsion of the human spirit. The venom spread quickly in his blood, hastened by the alcohol fat and fixed in his veins. Around him lay the contamination inflicted by her loss. Self had no basis and he sat in the shade of its under-nourished meaning. Somewhere, somehow, the development had been lost, usurped. Weltschmerz. Yet again, she was right.

What's the real reason, all this Herzlickeit balls was a smokescreen, what's the truth, he dared to ask again; he willed her to answer. Tell me, I need to hear it. She suddenly became very quiet, lowering her head, as if she was about to plunge into the cup. "I just, I just don't want this anymore." She said, in a voice so flat, so deflated that the very air within her body had been removed. It made her sound almost kind, sympathetic even. She invented a speck on her jeans which she concentrated her attention. He sat back down on the sofa, consciously taking a breath, his hand trembled as he sucked in a smoke. She was gone, all that remained was to remove her physical presence. She gain her degree, get that career she longed for, she, of course, would meet someone, her sort always do. And rightly so, he quickly concluded, she deserved her happiness and at that moment he wish her all the love the world had to offer.

"God, I can't stand this." He got up and emptied the last of the beer into the sink. "There's no way I can bear self-analysis, not now." He opened the fridge door and removed the take-away and placed it in the bin, the idea of heating it up in the morning was the kind of drunken, disgusting act she would have him do now. "You won't do this to me." He told her.

Just then the phone rang, he ran to it sitting on the table in the hall. "Hello." He answered his breath heavy and laboured.

" Sorry to bother you son, it's only me. So you got home ok, that's good"

"Yes Gran, I'm fine and why aren't you in bed yet? It's really late." He said sitting down by the table deflated, but heartened by the soft and caring tone of her voice.

"Aye, I know, there was a film I wanted to watch…"

"But you fell asleep." He entered, laughing.

"How'd you guess?" She gave a throaty laugh, causing a fit of coughing, during which he told her she would have to stop smoking, "I know son, I will God spares me, this Lent. I'm going to bed now, and I just wanted to know you were ok."

"Thanks Gran, I'm ok, just takes time I suppose."

"You'll be alright, everything'll work itself it out, you'll see."

"God I hope so Gran."

"It will. You get back to your studying and writing, it'll be the making of ye. And get out and see your friends. You'll see if things are meant for ye they'll happen. And you let yer woman run on. No woman's worth it and I'm tellin' ye as one." She stopped, presumably to allow her words of wisdom to sink into her grandsons head. "Here, I wasn't going to say til' ye, until tamarra. Ye've enough on your plate right now, God knows. Una rang, not long after you left."

"Una? Really? What did she want?" He tried to sound surprised and interested.

"She said she'd been trying to get you at your flat all last week, she was asking if there was something wrong. I told her nothing, I wouldn't let her or anyone know your business."

"Thanks Gran, I suppose I'll have to ring her at some stage to see what she wants. She probably wants to come up to Belfast and wants somewhere to stay."

"Oh no doubt madam wants to do that. She's got big ideas about herself that one."

"Granny!" Brendan mildly admonished, laughing. He didn't know if he should have speculated about Una's reasons for calling, in case Gran felt offended. He knew that on her last visit she had not called to see her. He did not object, how could he, he hadn't called in five days and that was to borrow money for petrol.

"Well, you know what that one is like." His granny said, without a trace of malice.

"I do Gran, I do."

"Look, everything will work out with the help of God, and remember just ask Saint Anthony for help, he's never let me down."

"I will Gran. I promise" He answered sincerely. "Well goodnight Gran. I'll see you tomorrow at some stage. If you want I'll go out shopping with you."

"Don't worry about that, you get a good rest. Goodnight and God bless son."

"Goodnight Gran, God bless you too." He replaced the receiver, feeling an overwhelming urge to cry coming from his gut, initiated by the care and concern of another human being for him. Something he thought that was lost to him and even more relieved to feel the same concern and love for another human being other than himself. He feared if he they had spoken longer, he would have gone back to her house to stay and never faced what he knew he must.

He returned to the living room, tearing the plugs out of the sockets in a frenzy of movement that blanked and sealed the room behind him. He entered the bedroom and switched on the bedside lamp allowing his body to fall heavily onto the bed. The bed felt cold, enormous and dispossessed. He kicked off his boots and let them fall to the floor; he undid the buttons of his shirt. He undid his belt buckle, unbuttoned his jeans, sat up to take off his shirt and jeans, and flung them both to a corner of the room. He got in under the duvet and wrapped it around him. He lay there not knowing where sleep would come. Eh John?, who had been sleeping he guessed, slid up beside him whispering, *cud 'ave 'ad that wee sort, wot's 'er face, back at the pub. The ole mutton cud 'av seen sum action, if yud tried 'ard enuff instead of all this moping abawt, gawd almighty.*

"Go away!" Brendan shouted into the pillow, turning from the light.

Come on, me ole saucer and plate, they're all the bleeding same lying down, or 'angin' from the light bulb, he, he. There'll be sum 'ard 'un dryin' 'er eyes, bet a pony on it, there there dahlin' ave a suck on that, he, he.

Brendan turned and stared up at the ceiling lying flat and motionless, thinking back to the pub when Concepta approached him, smiling her cherry lips and white teeth, wanting to know why he hadn't rejoined their company at the table. And he would reply he thought she and Gerry were an item and she would laugh at the absurd notion saying he wasn't her type. He would ask who was and with hot breath and a wet tongue she'd whisper into his ear "you are!" She would be forced close him by someone stealing up to the bar and the bones of her hips would be pressed against his and a nervous expectancy would rise and bubble in both their stomachs. And they would hold, with her laughing a healthy, wholesome laugh that was both sensual and infectious. Oh, if only it wasn't a sexually inactive hour he'd say. Not for me, she'd say, not with you and she would ask him to drink up and meet her outside. Quickly they'd be back at the flat, her fleshy thighs apart waiting for him to finish caressing her breasts, her tee-shirt pulled up around her chest as his greedy mouth devoured, her hands frantically searching for his swollen penis. To do those forbidden things in a realm without limits, no human, no divine, a world of satisfaction, salaciousness, sated and without sin. Wet and open mouths clasping and grasping, shoulders and elbows burning, fingers in frenzied motion. A film of sweat oiled bodies, perfectly proportioned, bent over a rounded, shiny body, an ever-present smile, the grotesque acquiescence for the ugly ritual of clashing plastic.

His fevered endeavour was over, he rolled to one side, his toil ending in dry wretchedness. The table lamp illuminating an ancient shame that bit with renewed vigour. He slipped further into the duvet trying to embrace warmth and familiarity smelling the fabric that still held faint traces of her. He turned from the light, leaving it to burn, knowing the dark would only bring the world BF (Before Frances). He shut his eyes, her fading smell enough to evoke a maelstrom of memories. Her long smooth legs entangled with his, their feet cupped together, both sets entrenched against the outside world. The nights he lay watching her sleep, her small, delicate breaths, how beautiful she looked and then he would be gripped by a terror of this beauty revealed to the outside world. He turned and kissed where her head would have lay and recoiled immediately from the act, making a spit to remove the residue of his weakness.

He lay angry with himself for the scenarios he conjured up in his mind to keep sight of her. If someone asked where she was, "oh, she's at her parents, she's not well, she's at class" Yet every time he nailed those lies with a sneering line of probing questions. He adopted the habit of talking to her, with her, calling out for her, but she had been unable to hear him, or she was sleeping. Finally, in desperation, he had imagined that she was dead, but that was unsustainable; given the inherent danger of a chance encounter with her very much alive ghost.

High above him, spanning the width of the skylight, shivery line of cobweb twitched in a light draught, a sister shadowing it's every move. He stared, fascinated by the delicate balance of its fragile existence, and for a moment he was aware of the peace he was experiencing. How he would like to lie there and not feel; to just lie there and be.

For gawsake take a day orf. All you need is a good sort, get the ole parts moving, no wot I mean. Lissen, the Guinness clouds are suffocatin' yer brain.

Brendan fought the language and what it imparted, he fought harder the return of her image and in the no-man's land between the two fronts, carefully concealed memories squeezed into his consciousness, teasing anxiety-ridden, heat-filled mornings of a much older life to the now and ever-present. The school and the showers, the struggle and the startling feeling of expectant pleasure he had often sought, but only found alone. He struggled to break free, frightened of discovery. They lay side by side on the tiled floor. They may have lay there for hours in complete silence, if not for the caretaker barking in that he wanted to close up. They did not speak to one another; they avoided each other and joined other groups, where new alliances formed. Days later, a rumour spread throughout the school centring on their fall-out. The rumour proved deliciously wicked and worthy of circulation, it came to his attention only after it had been recycled, reworked and embellished. School politics demanded that confrontation was the only avenue in which to resolve the matter. Arrangements were quickly and professionally handled. The two faced each other in the handball court after school. He fought with the commitment of a coward and the conviction of a liar, his greater fear and desperation won the day. In ancient fashion he was held aloft, exonerated before his peers, the gods declared him vindicated and the vanquished made outcast. A week later the other boy was removed from school after a series of assaults. Years later he met a member of that assembled mob at a administrative development course; he was one of those who had bayed for blood. During the course of their short conversation in the afternoon break he was told that the old queer he had given a hiding to, had died in England. No other information was available.

'Ere 'member frowing all that religious shit out the winda, he, he, 'member that bible, the colouring pens, eh?

Brendan remembered. 'The 'commie kazi kid,' the boy who did not believe in God or his ma. Beware the child who could abandon and defy the two greatest forces known. He engendered both awe and derision in equal measure. Sure all the kids hated going to Mass, hated and cursed those who made them. They mocked, they laughed in groups at his stated belief that it was all a myth, the love of God and one's family, one power based on the fear of another, a fear that held it altogether. All keek, like the stories they all publicly scorned, but privately believed and subscribed to. He gave them a for instance, reading the Bible backwards would conjure up the Devil himself or if you repeated the F word enough times in a row, you would start sinking into Hell. KEEK. And to prove it to the assembly of half-believers, he put it to the effing test.

He began slowly, and began to make a tune to keep the momentum and their interest, stopping only to wet his mouth by nibbling on his tongue. He carried on despite their protests and shouts to 'wise up fucksake', 'he's an eejit, a show-off', the boys who had gathered began to feign interests far away from the ongoing recital, but their eyes never strayed too far from the ground under which the apostate stood, half-expecting, half-wishing. Yet nothing happened. It felt like an age before he would stop, his mouth had become dry and tingly. Someone with a watch said it was over five minutes. There. See. Keek. He believed he had freed those who had witnessed and now they were all on the road to full emancipation.

He began his own crusade at home, tentatively, surreptitiously, through stealth and endeavour over a period of weeks. The un-protective cross, stuck in the wall above his bed was taken down, put into a waste bag and left in the outside bin. Fat lot of use He was, stuck up there. Out too the Sacred Heart in the kitchen. Call that pain. Out too the so-called holy water his aunt Sheila had brought back from Knock to cure all. Of course it didn't. The severe rash on his face remained despite several applications. A trip to the doctors and a course of antibiotics worked that little miracle. Out too, those insufferable religious tracts to Saints sealed in plastic; prayers to this and this. Scapulars, that was what they were called. *Oh, get the catholic boy!* Fuck you English pagan dog. Saints for everything under the sun. If there is a Saint for deliverance from fire, as he was sure there was, he'll save youse.

Of course his family did not see what he was attempting to do, they were far too ignorant, far too institutionalised to comprehend. The big guns were called for, after it became clear that threats from his father, the wee talks from his mother and the kicking and threat of something much worse from the bastard were evidently not enough to halt his campaign. In fact, it seemed to propel the boy into further and more audacious acts of what they considered mindless acts of sacrilege. His iconoclasm grew in strength and audacity, the football boots the bastard had just bought was suddenly, inexplicably lost; clothing, money too.

He was taken to see Father Peter, the parish priest, he could not for the life of him remember the surname of this antiquated shell of a man, who tried to be all pally with him. The young boy glared and said nothing, his reticence compounded by his mother's tearful chattering and pathetic pandering to the old man; all the while smoking and not touching her tea. "He's sickening for something Father, we're all at a loss", on and on she went in that phoney voice she used for the man from the Pru, or anyone with a 'position' as she saw it; and all the while the old man with the shiny black trousers and bony knees was getting older and older whilst having to listen to her load of keek.

He had decided that the old priest was a kind, but stupid man and allowed the priest to usher him out of the warm, well-lit room into the hall so he could have a private word with his mother. He counted ten whole minutes on the big clock stuck on the wall, full minutes that tick-tocked his exploration of the claret coloured carpet, the wooden varnished walls, the large paintings of capped men, with chains; one was an archbishop of the diocese who was called Patrick Mullins, painted by a man called Walsh '52. He was a stern looking fucker. He sat on the large leather chair, the same colour as the carpet, hard and creaking, studded along the arms with brass buttons on which he spent two whole minutes trying to remove one.

Then, just twelve seconds before another full minute had elapsed, the door opened and quiet voices could be heard. The priest saw them to the front door blessing them both, he wished them a 'God bless' as he scratched several stray grey hairs blown back down over his forehead by the strong breeze that swirled around them outside.

They walked in silence. He in guilt, for the silence he gave to his mother, then in anger, for the silence she gave to him.

Brother Curren was a big, bastard bogger. He had been summoned to his office the following Monday to be confronted by a square head, chin and shoulders, thick glasses, behind which sat the smallest, darkest eyes. An air of calm normality pervaded the small office, imbuing the office with an unnerving stillness. The grey filing cabinets, the giant portrait of Edmund Rice, the rich red carpet, everything looked normal, if practical and solemn. So Mister McConnell he begins, with a quiet, understated authority voice that sent sweat racing slalom-like down the spine. You've been something of a nuisance, he says, causing the school and you're family some bother then. He always said then at the end of each sentence like a verbal punctuation mark, then. Har, har.

He set to one side the piece of paper he had made a poor show of interest in. He tried to look bored, but his eyes danced behind the thick glass. He raised both hands, big and padded in flesh, up to his face, then, big and padded in flesh, used his hands to remove his glasses; which he held at arms length his small eyes squinting through them like he was about to take aim at something. Without them on, he looked almost vulnerable. Then he locks them back on his head, behind tiny flat ears and stands up. Christ the night, he looks about ten feet tall, with a shock of angry, unforgiving black hair, shaved all around the sides. The floor creaks with the weight of him, he walks slowly, in equi-distant steps to the small window with its metal frame slicing up the condemning, dark clouds like the graphs he couldn't do and says to it: What to do, what to do then. He turns to face him, his eyes now swimming in dark pools, his padded cheeks flushed, the alarmingly small, cruel nose pointed straight at him. What to do, do you know McConnell, do you know then? He asks, but the boy knew not to answer.

No I fucking don't. Just let me out of here and I swear you'll never hear of me again. I'll leave town, turn protestant, anything. Well? He asks. Directly and louder than before.

No sir, he was startled into replying, it was all he managed from his dry mouth, his voice disappearing into his lap. No. Well nor do I then. He moved so quickly it seemed like he hadn't budged an inch, but he was upon him instantly, using techniques all the boys joked that he had picked up in concentration camps throughout his travels in the most cruel and wicked of countries. Catching the flesh on either cheek, between fingers and thumbs, twisting until the boy was virtually off the ground and then allowed to fall back into the chair. An enormous hand clapped out the sound of the world sending him and the chair onto the floor, where he was raised to his feet by the same hand only this time clamped to his lock. The boy fought very hard against the deliriously wild impulse to cry out for help. He vented it through his teeth, through the gaps in his lips, hot wind rushes of beating breath that forced saliva out of his mouth. He plunged into a black world of burning, pulling pain where the only sound he could hear was his and even then he did not recognise. Suddenly he was released and the bogger had returned to sit behind his desk.

The boy stood not knowing if he was meant to sit or stand on legs without strength, with all the muscles in flight, causing him to involuntarily shudder and with his heart battering a request to leave too. The room appeared brighter, whiter, merging in an un-walled vacuum of light and sound. He wondered if he had fainted or died, but bogger's voice emanated out of the brightness ordering him to lift up the chair and set it where it had been, that he was not to cause his presence to be required in his office again, then.

His life with the familial Bastard deteriorated rapidly. He was the big man now, playing for the local team with talk of county and for the family, role of most favoured son. But for him, the looks, the threats, the silences deepened. At school he had become persona non grata, ostracised by those who had formerly sought his company, now, it was too great a risk to associate with one earmarked for special attention by the bogger. This was the stratagem behind bogfear. His schoolwork had to be handed in at the end of each day and on Friday's he would have to wait at the office to receive extra curricula work for the weekend.

The day of some big game arrived and the bastard was up for honours. He had to remain at home while the rest of the family went to the game. Not that he or the family minded. Alone and upstairs in the bedroom he tried hard to grasp the formula for quadratic equations, failing, he envisaged bogger's reaction. The Bogfear took hold of him, a phenomenon, known throughout the school took hold, the fear converted to anger when he thought of how everyone in the world was enjoying their lives free from Bog-fear and bog-persecution.

The rage began in the bedroom, ripping up the schoolwork, reducing it to the absurdity it had become, he tore the textbook, he smashed the drawers, throwing the clothes over the room and kicking the drawers until they cracked and splintered. He grabbed a bundle of the Bastard's clothes and along with a box of matches he hid with his cigarettes under the base of the wardrobe took them out to the back garden. He took all his textbooks and jotters and built a pyre. While it burned he rushed upstairs he went to his parents room and taking a large pair of scissors he went back into his room and repeatedly stabbed the Bastards bed, ripping up the pillow and cutting up the bedclothes. He grabbed what he could from what he had cut up and returned to the fire and threw them on.

Judging from the Bastards reaction, you would have thought he had killed someone. The beating he got left him thinking he would be deaf for the rest of his life, unfortunately the ringing eased after a couple of hours, in time for him to listen to all the keek they had to say.

The da kept moaning through the drink to no-one in particular that there'd be no luck in the house if something wasn't done. Of course he didn't know what to do and if he did he wouldn't do it of course. Uncle Michael, on his ma's side of the family, was summoned in to ask the boy the reason behind his behaviour. The kind man with the pale blue eyes and a gentle voice knelt before him in the living room. The boy wished the greatest wish that he could answer the sad round face, but the reason was lost, obliterated by the hate and rage, that they had become reasons within themselves.

Maybe he just liked it, maybe he was just bad and should be carted off to the big home run by boggers like the da kept saying. In that big, grey mansion, miles from anything, boy- hating boggers would flay the flesh off your body for the salvation of your soul. Uncle Michael told him he wasn't a bad boy, just a good person doing bad things. The boy still could not answer, even though he was terrified of the big house and what they could do to his body, as for his soul, they could have that for nothing.

The boy sat in intransigent silence against his mother, Uncle Michael sat in front as they watched the estate pass by, then the town, then the road up past Moore's field and over the brow of Murray's hill, the furthest he had ever been; as a new road, new hills, new fences and walls filled his view. He occupied himself staring out to the faraway as the occasional helicopter or plane darted across the sky all the while keeping in touch with eh John? who he had brought along with him in case of trouble.

All this genuflecting to the past, where was it getting him? Fuck it. He had to end this inertia, otherwise he would live and die amidst a host of unrealised hopes and unfulfilled dreams; swept along like so many, bound to a finite number of minor triumphs and defeats constituting a nothing life. He was lost, estranged from himself, who he was, what he could yet be, the composite of traits, and components he took from others. And now they were unravelling, fragmenting before him and he was found to be without basis. He would remain at the mercy of others, he thought bitterly, continually deferring to their expectations and demands. Always at their behest, never to be himself

Goron bennet, what's all this palava? 'Av a day orf will ya?

What's this? Don't tell me the 'ard drinking, womanising diamond geezer, straight out of the school of 'ard knocks, is worried? The bloke who raced arand Landan town, bangin' up the 'ard cases and birds, no lip, no shit from nawan; don't tell me he 'as lost his bottol? Wouldn't you like to go back and give the Paddies the wot for. Wouldn't he like to go back and see where he was born? Ha! It's just occurred to me. You're Irish too!

Fack orf, being born in a barn don't make ya an 'orse

Touche, you cockney cunt. Brendan conceded.

Brendan sat up in the bed propping up the pillows to support his back. Una was his ticket back. Christ the times he regretted giving her his number. He would call her tomorrow; he had her number in his diary under 'T' for tries too hard. Yes, he would phone.

The thought pressed heavily on his mind, he felt eased in that peculiar, particular way that plans yet to come into fruition have on the mind. He'd go back, tell them, show them. Yes that was the only way forward, he thought wearily. Heavy cumulus clouds of lead weighed on his eyes and they closed.

When he awoke, he felt differently, he did not feel the customary gloom and it's strident companions of anger, frustration and hopelessness. Perhaps they were with eh John? He did not feel alone or isolated, but he was uneasy with the sense of elation and hope, usually daylight and it's accompanying sobriety robbed him of it's strength and conviction. Not to-day though, he told himself. He swept aside the duvet and rolled out of the bed standing unsteadily as he rubbed his face. He stripped off his tee-shirt and socks and took them into the bathroom where he binned them in the wicker basket (his). He stepped into the bath and ran a shower peeing down into the bath watching it mix with the hot soapy water. He got out of the bath and towelled himself down, shaved and brushed his teeth. He returned to the bedroom, opened the top right hand drawer (his), and took out a clean pair of underpants and socks.

He sat on the bed putting the socks on wondering what to wear. He stood up and opened the wardrobe (also his). What to wear, he thought again, after all this was business. Something casual, yet smart, something that said I mean business, but in an understated way; something that strongly suggested emotional and financial independence.

God, it was so much easier when she was here, she would pick out a shirt and trousers or jeans that always seem to match perfectly the occasion. He had a role then, boyfriend, partner, pain in the arse. Stop it. No more of her, no more time to be wasted on the past. Jeans, it would have to be. Navy, the new ones, just washed and ironed. He went into the living room, grabbed the pile of clothes from the chair in both arms, returned with them to the bedroom, and laid them out on to the bed. He put the jeans on with a fresh white tee-shirt. Now shoes or boots, footwear was crucial, it announced the man, they would be a great support, they would need to be strong, sturdy, well-polished and expensive looking. He decided on the Doc Martens half boot, they satisfied all the criteria he had set. He sat on the bed, dug both feet into the boots, and fastened the laces as tightly as he could.

As the bacon sizzled under a low grill, the eggs bobbed in too much water he got out the vacuum cleaner from the hall cupboard and began to clean the flat. Talc smudges, crumbs and hair, her dust, all traces of her would be removed, eviscerated. He took a cloth and wiped off the his and her toothpaste spots in the bathroom mirror. He gathered up the tissues, the cotton buds, hairclips anything of her and placed them in a plastic bag which he would take out to the bin in the entry. After breakfast, he would go to the shop, get cigarettes, his last packet he assured himself, a newspaper, chewing gum, then ring Una and call to Murray's to collect the car. The idea of planning excited and assured him that he was doing the right thing, he was on the right course, no other voice, but his own, could be heard. He would call to his Granny's but would not tell her of his plan. She would make a fuss, she'd want him to bring down 'some wee things', perhaps she would ask to go with him for the 'wee drive and some company'. It also held the danger of her contacting the old goosestepper and forewarning her. God help her, how she had missed the landmarks in that family, Terence's twenty first, Una's first job, the parents' thirtieth anniversary, but she never mentioned it, she never complained or made a fuss, she seemed happy enough with the occasional phone call. He knew she sent cards on birthdays and money too. Bless her. He'd make things up to her too, he'd take her shopping in the car, he'd move back to Grans, yes, that's what he would do; save up towards a house, they were actually good company for each other. Truth be told, he enjoyed the verbal jousting between them. He'd go back to evening class, go running and cycling again, he would take her over to the local once a week into the lounge on a week night when it was reasonably quiet. Yes, things would be much better; he could feel it.

After breakfast at the coffee table in the living room he sat back to enjoy a cigarette, the last one in the pack. As he sat smoking and drinking his tea he found the lapse into inactivity inclining him to doubt his chosen course of action. He began to ridicule the plan, the whole idea now seemed absurd, and depressingly, unnecessary. He quickly smoked the cigarette and finished his tea, and took his mug and plate into the kitchen. He set them in the sink, went to the bedroom to get his denim jacket and umbrella, took the plastic bag full of her and left the flat hastily buttoning his jacket on the descent to the front door.

He made his way to the shops, stopping at the entry to deposit the plastic bag in a bin left in the entry, mentally noting what he needed to do in the sequence of events that would fulfil his plan. He got cigarettes, the newspaper and chewing gum, then he would call Una. He had decided against calling her from the flat, at least in the telephone box he could control the length of the call. This was what he needed, this was the action that would propel him to a new life, this was the catharsis people read of, spoke of, but rarely knew themselves. Convinced of this, he walked briskly towards the telephone box at the junction of the road near the set of traffic lights that he hated to be held up at; because they were at the slip road that led onto the main road, the red light lasted an eternity. Eh John? would go to, he would return him to the place where they had found each other, in the glory hole beneath the stairs.

He stood sheltered from the light drizzle in the telephone box and lit up a cigarette, he dialled the number of Una's salon, he knew it by heart as it comprised of only two different digits. He stood with his back to the saturday shoppers making their pilgrimage to and from the supermarket. Outside everyone, everything looked painted in the colour of wet concrete. As he waited for the call to be answered he read off the graffiti scrawled above the phone UTH rules, whoever or whatever they were, CFC shite, Celtic and INLA, Grainne loved Connor and Connor loved cocks according to some scribe who had inserted his own observation between the two lovers in thick blue marker. He laughed aloud and was taken by surprise by the punctilious voice answering his call. He quickly inserted twenty pence; hesitating as the young female voice repeated, "Good morning, Quinnsential , can I help you?" He asked for Una and he was asked to hold. The girl's accent was as he remembered the town, except for her attempted polished and professional enunciation. He slipped in another twenty pence and waited, turning quickly behind him startled by the roar of a bus passing by in wet metal haste with its cargo of silent, staring passengers. The voice returned to the phone informing him that Una would be along in a minute if he didn't mind holding. He didn't and thanked her. He tapped out a count with the toe of his boot on the side of the telephone box, one boot, two boot, three boot, four fucking boot.

"Hello, this is Una, can I help you?"

"Yes, I'd like to make an appointment." He said, in a light, haughty tone.

"Certainly, let me get a pen and the diary. Could you speak up please, this must be a bad line"

"Oh, come on, don't you know who this is?" He asked, dropping the adopted tone in his voice.

"Is that you Micky?" She hissed, " I told you not to bother me at work or at home for that matter."

"Who on earth is Micky?"

"Who is this?"

"It's me" He smiled down the phone, enjoying her obvious annoyance.

"Who me?" She asked, impatiently.

"You torture me for ages to call you and when I do you can't remember your own brother. I'm hanging up."

"Brendan! She shrieked down the phone, "don't you dare hang up. The lines not so good I couldn't make out it was you."

"Easy on the old ears there, sis." He smiled down the phone.

"Oh shite, sorry, I think I've taken a few years off our Saturday blue rinse brigade. I can't believe it." She said, her voice returning to its normal level. "God, this is such a brilliant surprise." Her enthusiasm was heart warming and infectious. She repeated that she couldn't believe it, that it was brilliant to hear from him. When he told her he was thinking of coming down, she launched into an ecstatic, breathless preamble of what she was going to do, she had so much to tell him, she said it would be brilliant. He stopped her by telling her he had to put in another twenty pence.

"What time are you coming down?" She asked as soon as the money was accepted in the phone.

"Evening time about six-ish, I imagine." He replied.

"Right, well I have a friend's hair to do after work, which I can cancel, I can do that tomorrow. God, I can't wait to tell mum."

"No." He shouted, surprised at the sternness and hostility in his voice. "No, Una don't". He said more calmly, composing himself. "Please don't tell anyone, not Terence, no-one. I want this to be a surprise."

"Alright I won't. Don't bite me head off. I promise. It'll be a surprise alright. I can't remember the last time you were home."

"Well then, don't spoil it for them or for me, please. I'm sorry for over-reacting"

"I won't, I promise." Una said, this time her voice as solemn as her promise.

"Thanks, look I have to go. I'll see you at the house then. Don't forget to look out for me and answer the door. It'll be after six. Ok?"

"Ok, this is going to be brilliant." She said. "I've so much to tell you."

Yeah, he said and said his goodbye. He remained at the phone to ring Murray after reassuring Una once again that he would be down. He dialled Murray's number and waited impatiently for it to answer. Outside the rain had become heavier; the bands of clouds were locking to-gether to release their overnight store in a torrential downpour. All week they had remained fixed above with the absurd yellow dot darting in between gaps to make them sweat. The weather, like the people, was incomprehensible, fluctuating wildly from the darkest of deed to the sunniest of humour, to think they loved and killed over such a place.

Una sat by the phone, her initial delight subdued somewhat by Brendan's voice, its tone seemed to suggest something was wrong. The fact that he was coming home made her think it could be serious. God, she hoped not, she had her own agenda and did not want it to be sidelined by any other issue. His voice sounded subdued, and he was quite dismissive when she asked how Frances was. She's alright he said, but she knew something was wrong.

She knew those relationship conversations quite well now. She remembered her only visit to their flat and how uncomfortable, even unwelcoming he had been at first. She put it down to nerves, the fact they were strangers to one another and she was conscious of Frances watching them to-gether. Frances was lovely, tall and thin with a beautiful oval face and clear skin, with bright green eyes that seemed to moisten when she smiled. Una noticed immediately that Frances' haircut was expensive, it was beautifully trimmed and maintained. She noticed how Brendan barely took his eyes from her when she was in the room. He had changed of course, he was taller, broader in the chest, his body sturdy, it looked like he had been training. His hair shaved all around the sides and back leaving a crop of dirty fair hair that looked as if had not ever been brushed, combed or conditioned. She always hated the way men could get away with the minimum of grooming. His voice became gentler as they spoke and his green-blue eyes brightened as he spoke to Frances.

She was concerned that Frances would see how distant a brother and sister could appear. She wondered what Frances would think of them as a family and what Brendan had told her of his time at the family home. She never knew why he had left, she asked her mother repeatedly until she got bored of 'it's for the best', 'he'll do better at his studies in Belfast and go on to university. The differing answers always amounted to the same thing and haunted her; that when the time came, she would lose Terence too. All she knew at that age was that the house was quieter, lighter; there were the normal family rows but nothing like those when Brendan was there. She maintained a guilt all these years, blaming herself for telling her mother about the day she opened her bedroom door to find her brother playing on the floor with her dolls. But he wasn't playing, he wasn't laughing but speaking harsh and ugly words she had heard bad grown-ups say outside. All her dolls were unclothed and Brendan's action man, also unclothed was on top of Molly her favourite doll.

"Una. Una, for Godsake."

"Huh, what is it?" She turned, startled.

"You've left Mrs O'Neill under the dryer. I turned it off before the wee women's head melted."

"Oh Fiona, I'm sorry, I was miles away. I'll get to her now." Una left the reception and walked towards Mrs O'Neill with the sound of clashing plastic resonating in her head.

"Come on, answer." He demanded of the phone, spinning round from a couple waiting to cross the road and who had obviously heard his shout. At last, another young voice; this time coarser, with made in Belfast stamped on every syllable. It had saved a wasted journey. Murray wasn't there, he had buggered off to the races, Leopardstown or the Curragh, the boy didn't know exactly where, but somewhere down south. The car remained untouched and the garage left in the hands of someone who could barely change oil by the sound of him. The boy knew that Murray was waiting on a part for the car. He said he would tell Murray he called. Make sure you do Brendan told him slamming the phone down. There seemed little point in giving the boy a hard time.

Christ the night, he'd have to go by bus. He could ring Una back, tell her about the car, but then he'd have to live with Eh John's constant sniping, his mocking of his attempts At change and his abject failure to do so. No. He would go back, even by bus. He would see this as a challenge to his resolve and he would meet it head on. He left the telephone box and put up his umbrella. No, he wouldn't let Una down, he wouldn't let himself down. Was this how his new life would manifest itself? Concern for others? Love of one's nearest and dearest? Naw, that'd be going too far, he mocked, buttoning up his jacket, holding the umbrella against the rain.

He took the short cut over the sodden grass of the church grounds, enjoying the cool grassy freshness in his nostrils and discovering that his right boot had sprung a leak. The sole seeped, probably a slice worn across the sole through time and overuse; it didn't matter, he'd wear the new pair he had bought for the winter. Nothing would deny him his newly found purpose and emerging self. Spurred by this, he tramped across to the side gate sucking in deeply his first taste of new breath.

Back at the flat he dried off in the bathroom, taking off his boots and changed into a fresh pair of socks. He examined the sole of the right boot, he was right, a thin mouth of a slice grimaced across the width of the sole; he decided he would wear those boots only in dry weather.

After lunch he took his tea after toying with the idea of coffee, if he was honest with himself, he only drank coffee to co-join her love of it. Carrying the mug cautiously over to the window, he looked out over the dampened piece of park where the swings and slide sat abandoned. He watched the rain wondering if she was watching it too, maybe it did not rain where she was now, perhaps she was out shopping, or sleeping soundly in a room somewhere in her parent's house. It was galling to imagine that all they would ever share was the lousy weather.

It seemed appropriate, they had little else in common, not enough when they were together. He cheated; he feigned interests, her interests, affecting a conciliatory manner, deferential to all her needs and wants; professing a love of the arts and an interest in her chosen subjects, Psychology and German. His was a game in fatuous self-deceit; his real life was one of uncontrolled whimsy, senseless impossibilities, and lazy, directionless thinking, unattainable dreams.

She, on the other hand, never indulged in speculation or dreams; he said it was down to her lack of imagination. She replied he was full of it. He told her that she was guilty of far worse. And when she asked what that was, he told her she was boring. He tried to wrap it up as a joke, but the damage had been done. She remained tight-lipped and furious with him throughout the evening and only spoke to him to ask for a lift, as she just 'had' to go and see her sister.

For her, wishes and desires were tempered and moulded by specific, measurable, achievable, realistic, and time-bound objectives, (S.M.A.R.T.) an acronym he well remembered from an administrative development course he had attended On the drive to her sisters he pleaded for forgiveness as he had often suspected he had obtained and received more than he was entitled to. She kissed him on the cheek and told him she would get a lift back.

He withdrew from the window and went to the kitchen to wash out his mug; he stood at the sink allowing the water to run preparing himself to get ready to leave the flat. He would ring granny before leaving and tell he would call in tomorrow for dinner and she would be content to occupy herself with that. He knew he could not stay and do nothing; it was far too late for that.

In the bedroom he packed what little he would need, toothbrush and toothpaste, aftershave, deodorant, shaver, a towel a change of socks, underwear, tee-shirt and shirt the expensive white one that she thought he had paid far too much for. Christ, if only he had the car, the loss of such mobility and independence and the consequent dependence on public transport contrasted sharply with the image he had hoped to present. He zipped up the bag, took it into the living room, went to the curtains, and drew them within a foot of each other. He checked that all the plugs were removed from the sockets, closed every door and sat down to ring his granny. The phone rang, he counted ten rings before he put the phone down, thinking that she would be out shopping he put on his leather jacket and picked up his bag. He did not wait to look around the room, the next time he would see it, he would be different, changed. He went to the front door and made a final check of his pockets, wallet, cards, pen and keys. He left the flat and locked the door giving it a firm push to check it was securely closed and descended the flight of stairs.

He passed Gerry who was standing at the counter serving two young boys. He signalled with his hand his destination and purpose which Gerry responded to with his own hand signal making it his clear intention to join him.

In through the door of the lounge, the first customer; hardly surprising, he said to himself, checking his watch. Ten past twelve, you drunken bastard the face glared. No, not any more, no siree bob. He placed his bag by a stool at the bar and asked the barman if they were serving lunches.

"Certainly, I'll get you a menu." He returned with a menu. "Can I get you a drink?" He asked, wiping down the surface of the counter. He stood back with one hand on his hip and the other rubbing his beard painted in tiny stokes of grey.

"A pi..pi..pi..pint of Guinness, pl..pl..please." Brendan ordered.

"Certainly." The barman began pouring the pint, he turned out to be the charge hand

and had a young son who suffered from a similar speech impediment, so he understood what it was like and hoped Brendan did not mind him bringing the subject up.

"N… no, no, not at all." Brendan sym…sympathised with the man and for a moment both of them stared at the black liquid filling up the glass. The charge hand returned to him with the pint saying he thought it was down to his son's shyness.

"The wife gets him to read out things from his schoolbooks and she's mad keen on him to go to drama, she thinks it'll bring him out of himself."

"It cud..cud..help." Brendan replied, handing over the money for his drink. There'd be no more of it, he promised, just this last time he'd have to keep up the pretence or end up with a fat lip. He'd knock the fags on the head too; end the tyranny of tobacco, he swore. Stop the drinking, well not as much, he quickly qualified, two nights a week, that'd be enough. He would be more productive, useful, he would write and go to college and improve his career prospects, get the hell out of the service altogether maybe.

"You ready to order now sir?"

"Yes, I'll hav…have th..the cheeseburger no chi..chips, pl..please." He tha..tha…thanked the charge hand and returned the menu to him. He was at the threshold of a new beginning and to celebrate he took a large gulp of his Guinness. He set the pint back on the counter and thought of Una's voice, how vital it sounded, reverberating with youth and optimism. Qualities lost to him. Until now, he chastised himself. The last time he saw her it was through a mixture of pity and loathing. He and Frances had just moved into the flat when Una's persistence and France's persistent cajoling had brought her to their door one Saturday evening. He put it down to his euphoria at moving in with Frances that had allowed him be swayed, though as soon as he had agreed, he changed his mind. Frances would not hear of it, the sofa bed in the living room would be perfect and if he kept up his objections, he would

find it very comfortable. He obstinately maintained his position, accepting her visit under duress. After exhausting several avenues of enquiry trying to discover the reason behind his objection, Frances commented that it must be her he was ashamed of.

"Yes, it is." He laughed. He knew the game, trying to trap him into a storm of protest in her defence. Then bang, what is it? Are you ashamed of your own sister? Or, as he knew she was capable of, shrewdly draw the conclusion, that it was him he was unsure of. She stood directly in front of him, blocking the television he was pretending to watch, her long blue nightshirt capturing the silhouette of her slim, strong body within its transparent material.

"You're pathetic." She condemned, smiling and shaking her head, holding a look that hid her true opinion of him.

"Oh yeah." He replied, lunging towards her with both hands, she skipped past his greedy hands and ran to the bedroom shrieking with laughter. He pursued her into the room where they both stripped each other of their clothes and made love. After, with that heavenly exhaustion he felt after being with her he asked what drove her crazy in bed. "Biscuit crumbs." She giggled. And he laughed loudly and joyously at the line and her shy look over the duvet at him and they made love again.

On the Saturday morning he remained in the chair, flicking through the pages of a book by Caitlin Thomas on her life with her husband and poet Dylan. He was unwilling and unable to join in the welcome preparations that Frances had thrown herself into. It was enough that he had agreed to collect Una at the bus station. He watched her tidy up in a snatch and grab fashion to illustrate her annoyance with him. Eventually after continual demands that he do something and move his legs while she vacuumed he fled to the shop and spent a good half hour reading the paper in the park.

Una was marvellous. She rang from the bus station an hour before he was due to collect her insisting that she made her own way up to them; she wanted to get some shopping in town first. He gave her the telephone number of a reputable and reliable taxi firm and made her repeat the address of the flat so she would know where to go.

He waited in the living room while Frances dashed from the kitchen to the bathroom then back into the living room to stare out the window and ask for the umpteenth time if she knew their address. At twenty five past two Una arrived in a taxi, not one from the company he had advised her to get, but he did not mind as he raced down to help her with the shopping bags she was clutching in both hands.

Upstairs, in the living room she plunged both hands into one of the shopping bags and produced a flat warming present, a tasteful pot plant that she handed to Frances who proceeded to make an enormous fuss of. Frances left the room with it deciding it would be ideal for the bathroom. He asked Una for her jacket, which she took off and immediately he was struck by how well endowed she was, full, rounded breasts stretched the white material of her tee-shirt. He wondered how Frances would feel about her now as they reduced Frances' slender figure to almost a parody of womanhood.

Well, he said, conscious of the time he had spent taking in her curvaceous figure, I'll hang your jacket up. He returned to the living room to find her at the window with her back to him, he could see the hair had been cut into a tidy bob, the streaks and perms of her younger days cut away. He remembered the photographs she had sent to granny. He recalled how young and factitious she had looked in her ankle length blue dress; standing beside a young man with cropped black hair and a goatee beard. Now maturity had possessed her, in physicality and in the way she presented herself. I'll show you around shall I, he said, it shouldn't take long, he smiled. He escorted her room by room, leaving the kitchen out of the tour as Frances was preparing lunch. He knew Una's clatter of gum was the product of her nerves as she played her part to perfection, oohing and ahhing at the appropriate moments. He felt she had registered his concern and reticence about her visit and he felt shamed. He tried hard to keep her on the move, to keep her occupied and amused, but there was a only so much to see, even Una, who had become a martyr to her mouth, acknowledged as such, when she repeated the same compliment about the colour scheme of the living room. At that stage he decided to break France's retreat, she'd hidden long enough from his sister's great tits, he thought unkindly.

Frances, God love her, acted like she did not mind the intrusion of those breasts .If she felt self-conscious, she did not show it. He stayed for a moment and then slipped out of the kitchen to sit in the living room and watch a black and white movie about a girl who claimed to have seen a woman who claimed to be The Immaculate Conception, he recognised Vincent Price and the guy he thought was in the Exorcist. He listened to their mild laughter at his own culinary efforts. It delighted him to hear the edge of Una's harsh, uncultivated accent had softened. Her polite inquisitiveness, her nervous, bubbly laughter imbued with feminity made her his favourite in a field without competitors.

He returned to the kitchen and took a bottle of Sauvigon Blanc from the wine rack, opened the bottle poured out three glasses and rewarded them all with a glass. He asked that Una make a toast. She looked embarrassed and mumbled. "To you both, thank you for letting me into your home and I wish you both all the happiness in the world." He said he would drink to that. Frances said he would drink to anything and returned to her salad without touching her wine.

Guilt rested easily on you, shame, it had made a home. After lunch, he sat in on the feathers of light conversation that were kept in the air in an almost breathless exercise that wearied all concerned. As he listened a germ of hatred began to breed for Una's free and easy going manner. His demons begrudged her that which he had purchased. He went into the kitchen and poured himself another glass of wine ignoring Frances' look of warning.

That evening, they went to a restaurant, highly recommended by Carolyn, France's sister. It was central and expensive. But he was in an expansive, generous mood, much to do with the wine he had consumed. When asked by the waitress for his order, he asked for the duck, lightly drizzled, on a soft bed of interrogated lettuce and slightly slabbered at mangoes , with a red wine reduction. He burst out laughing, partly at the withering look from Frances, mostly because he was drunk. The meal went well after his episode, Frances looked at ease and at home in any setting, effortlessly conversing with Una. He marvelled that such a creature of grace was with him.

That night, after they had returned from the restaurant, Una slept on the sofa bed while he lay awake in the bed aware that Frances was studying him. "What's wrong with you? You hardly spoke tonight, well, not after your initial showing off. That's not like you at all, it was embarrassing. I really felt for Una. And she's really lovely." He did not answer, what was there to say, Una was a lovely young woman. "I don't understand you at all sometimes." Frances yawned, her breath infused with wine and late night Chinese. He leaned over to switch off the light wishing her sweet dreams as he did so. She bid him a goodnight and turned on her side, her back to him and settled quickly into a do not disturb.

Darkness comes in many forms; it is not just the absence of light. Even with Frances close to him, he felt alone. He watched through the skylight as the night fell upon the room. Above him, the dark stretched further reaching out to the stars, plucking them from view and removing all vestiges of light. He was back in the glory hole, clinging to his mother's coat, smelling in her smell, praying for her to come and get him, afraid to return to bed, afraid of the night, afraid of the morning. He sat wrapped up in her coat, shivering in cold damp, afraid of the wet patch on his bed being discovered before it dried in. The monstrous feet would be on the move soon, go, pass by, go to another bed, anyone's, crawl in to them with big hairy legs and big hairy arms. Oh merciful Jesus, for the briefest of the longest moments, he wanted to get up and walk to the sofa bed and disturb that blissful sleep with the nightmare she had been spared.

He gulped at his pint, biting into the glass, trying to dispel a cycle of memories, which should condemn him for an eternity. He drank mechanically, appealing for clemency, his sips acts of self-forgiveness. It should never have happened, not to you, not to anyone. There, he told himself, you see, you are getting better, before, you would have wished it on someone else.

He lunch arrived with a napkin and an array of sauces and condiments on a silver tray which was placed before him. He th..th..thanked the barman and ordered another pint. As he ate, the lunchtime crowd began to materialise, coming in for warmth and company, their comments centring on the weather. He was glad of the company and listened in on their idle conversations at the bar.

Just after one o'clock Gerry arrived at the bar with Marty, Gerry's Saturday assistant.

He stood beside Brandan and shouted out an order for drink, he turned to ask Marty what kind of lemonade he wanted. Marty turned from shaking his umbrella dry and told him to go fuck himself.

"Two Guinness and a green." Gerry ordered as the barman took Brendan's plate and removed the sauces. "Fucksake, get a sense a humour you." Gerry directed at Marty who stood on the other side of Brendan and smiled the smile that he too knew that Gerry was a wanker.

"Let's get over to a table. Here, Marty, order me a cheesburger, here, take the money for the pints." Gerry handed him a ten pound note .They had shut the shop for lunch Gerry explained as they took their seats. The rain, it seemed, had put off the expected rush for the end of summer sale. He turned and asked Marty to get some beer mats from the bar.

"Why? Are you crippled?" Marty asked, rubbing the fine blonde goatee that he had been growing for several weeks.

"Go on, bring some over, don't be such a pain in the arse" Gerry whined.

Marty remained at the bar shaking his large golf umbrella dry.

"He's a good kid, wee Riddler." Brendan observed.

"Yeah, he is." Brendan agreed, he was fond of Marty, fonder still of the non de guerre he had christened him with; borne of the scar that blighted his flat forehead, the result of a fall outside a pub. The resulting scar had knitted into an almost perfect question mark above tiny features squeezed into a busy face . Brendan derived an immense sense of satisfaction and pride from that, lending weight to his growing belief, to his claim of uniqueness, differentiating him from the herd. She could see that, couldn't she? Who else would have the wherewithal? There was another criterion impossible to meet. They had just finished eating their food. Brendan left his chips for anyone at the table to partake of.

"Here, Brendan, look who's just come in." Gerry said, nudging his leg. "It's Jimmy so it is. Here, Jimmy, come over when you get your pint."

"Be over in a minute, just getting a pint in, so I am." Jimmy shouted back.

"Fuck, this is too precious. Just what the doctor ordered." Gerry smiled, lifting up his pint in a toast.

Riddler and Jimmy returned to the table together. "No Harp on draught, so there isn't, the pumps off so it is." Jimmy complained, setting the large bottle of Harp down on the table. "Two quid a bottle it is." He added, staring at it as if he were his sworn enemy. "So it is." He directed at Gerry who had burst out laughing. " Do'ya think I'm lying, so I am."

"No, Gerry laughed. "I believe you, so I do."

"Some shite day out there now, so it is." Jimmy commented to Brendan.

"Aye, it is." Brendan answered, his lips crumbling into a wide smile.

"Me and Sheila's to go up to Glengormley, so we have, she wants a new bed for the kids so she does." Jimmy said, pouring his beer into the glass. "What's up with you?" Jimmy asked Brendan of Gerry as he turned to face the bar and laugh out loud.

"Could be anything, you know him Jimmy." Brendan answered

"Here Breny, you finished with them chips." Marty asked, as he drew the plate to him.

"Walt ahead Riddler." Brendan told him as he scoffed several chips into his month.

"Aye, I know, so I do.." Jimmy replied, his face tightening as he drew his glass up to his lips. The leather jacket his robust body was incarcerated in, stretched noisily. "You in here last night?" He asked Brendan, setting his glass down, his long tapered face, with it's peculiarly long nose and chin, stared at him, expecting an answer.. The long protruding front teeth gave him the appearance of a rather well-fed rodent and his eyes contained the alertness and cunning of the rodent.

"Yeah, we were in, surprised you and Sheila weren't in for the quiz upstairs."

"Quiz," Jimmy sneered, "lot of 'oul balls, lot of oul sad bastards so they are. Naw," he added, "I've been on the nightshift, so I have, trying to get the cabbage up for a holiday, so I am. Fucksake, I'm still paying for fucking Christmas, so I am."

"Aye, it's a bastard alright." Brendan replied, plunging into his pint so he could occupy his mouth and prevent it from betraying a laugh.

"Here Jimmy, Sheila's not been in yet to join the Christmas club?"

"The Christmas club? Fucksake, we've only just got out of jail with the summer club, so we have."

"Aye, but it's worth it. Some great bargains, when you join, you get twenty five per cent off purchases over fifty quid."

"Brilliant." Jimmy's deadpan response that lacked any interest or enthusiasm for Gerry's offer had Brendan and Riddler burst out laughing.

"Naw, I'm only joking, so I am." Jimmy said, placing a comforting pat on Gerry's withdrawn shoulders. "Sheila'll be in so she will. I want to get one of those coats, you're selling them cheap Sheila says, they're like crombies, but they're mohair so they are. They're some gear, so they are. Have any left?"

"No." Gerry replied with the same deadpan delivery Jimmy had employed to his Christmas club offer.

"Funny bastard so you are." Jimmy said playfully pushing him to one side.

"Put you down for two then." Gerry smiled back.

"My ballicks, two! I've to get the wee lad a new Man United strip, so I have." Jimmy announced, filling his glass from the large bottle. " Here, why aren't you playing

today?" Jimmy's nasal, sneering tone made every question he asked, however innocuous appear suffused with suspicion.

"Sure I got injured in the cup two weeks ago. Were you not at the game? That big bastard of a centre-half caught me on the ankle. Nothing too serious, just a knock, the physio said it's just bruising. So I'll be back training on Tuesday, then we'll see the boys shoot up the table."

"Yeah, right." Jimmy sneered." And I see your getting back to full fitness on the swally. You're gonna end up a pot-bellied, pub player talking shite about how you coulda been the next Best. Another bloody waster in a town full of them. Look at that lad, Toner, he's scored three, no four, if you count that goal that was ruled off-side when it wasn't, so it wasn't. He's like an x-ray with hair and he's filling yer boots."

"He's not that good, three in seven games. I got three in my last two." Gerry sat up, his voice deepened defensively." Anyway, that was against an amateur side."

"Here, Brendy, you're supposed to be his mate. If you were any kind of mate, you'd get him to get off that sauce, so you would." Jimmy levelled at Brendan.

Brendan turned to stare at Gerry. " Gerry, stop drinking and get back to training." He said, in a deadpan voice.

"Funny fuck." Jimmy muttered into his pint.

"Here Riddler, Did you order another round? Where is it?" Gerry turned to Marty, to conceal his widening smile. Marty, who had been quietly sipping his pint enjoying the covert

mocking of Jimmy, shot back. "Aye, I did. It's not my fault, I'm waiting on me pint too."
Marty fired back.

"So he did, I was at the bar when wee Marty ordered, so I was." Jimmy said, leaping
to Marty's defence and at that point Gerry and Brendan burst out laughing and
laughed louder as Marty had to spit out his mouthful of beer. The laughing continued
unabated due to Jimmy's consternation at their bewildering behaviour.

"What's up with youse two? Are youse on the wacky tabaccy?" Jimmy asked of the
group but received no answer as the laughing developed a momentum of its own.

" Fucksake, youse lot are fuckin' idiots. Youse must be on that 'oul laughing gear,
so youse must."

"Naw we're not." Gerry managed to answer.

"So we're not." Brendan followed up and the two fell into each other in a helpless fit
of laughing.

Jimmy looked at the both of them his eyes narrowing. "Know what they say, never
drink on an empty head so they do. Fuck, that's it so it is. I'd rather be in B and Q than listen
to this." Jimmy finished off the glass of beer and got up. "See you lads later, so I will." He
got up and left with the sounds of 'alright Jimmy' muffled by the continued laughter.

The barmaid arrived with the round of drinks with Marty, chiding her for not
bringing Gerry's drink as he had ordered. She smiled good-naturedly and said it would never
happen again. Marty left her the change from Gerry's tenner.

"Riddler, you can be a right dick sometimes." Gerry complained. "Here, that was so
funny with Jimmy, thought I was gonna throw my lunch up. Here, I'll give yez another
laugh." Gerry said, drawing his seat into the table." Two kids right. It's Christmas morning,

one kids out in a binliner, wielding this sword, two sticks taped together and this other kid drives up in a motorised Ferrari, best of gear, right?" Gerry paused, looking at his audience to assure himself they had the picture and were with him on the joke.

"Yeah, he didn't shop in Maplin's." Brendan said.

"But the other kid did." Marty entered and both of them fell into another fit of laughing.

"Yeah, yeah," Gerry hastily intervened fearing he was to be sidelined or Jimmied as he had cleverly put it, "So the kid in the sports car, he continued his voice raised louder than he had wished, asks the other kid what he's supposed to be. I'm a Ninja turtle, the other kid says. Whoosh he goes with his shitty little sword." Gerry says, making a wide sweep of his arm to coincide with another whoosh! "And the ninja kid asks the other what'd he get for Christmas. The other kid says, I got this car, all these new clothes and a computer and some other presents. Fuck me the kid in the Ninja outfit says, fuck, I wish I was a Mongol." Gerry's build up to the punchline resulted in a crescendo of laughter released in an outburst of short, sharp, nasal laughter.

Riddler sat impassively, while Brendan smiled only at Gerry's sneeze into his hands. "Fuck, I think that's a belter." Gerry managed to squeeze out between his fit of giggling.

"It's not funny, my niece's daughter has down's syndrome." Riddler said, his face and tone set in stone.

"Balls. What niece? I know them all. None of them have kids with that." Gerry felt his face involuntarily flush with the weight of his incredulity. "C'mon, fuck off." He smiled. But the smile withered under the gaze of Riddler's pale, unsmiling face. The moment dragged with Brendan searching the two faces in front of him. In Brendan's he sought solace and a helpline, to Riddler he searched for a break in the steel front he had put up.

Riddler lifted his pint. "Aye, I'm ballsing about, so I am." Riddler laughed. Brendan laughed out his relief, laughed louder at Gerry's undignified fall from grace. The laughter outlasted his protests that it wasn't funny to claim something like that. Gerry's downfall was complete and irrevocable by his own damning verdict on the incident.

"You wee cunt The only reason you near got me, is because you look like one."

Gerry tossed the shop keys over to Riddler. "Go on back and open up, it's near two and you've had your lunch. I'll be back shortly." It was petty retribution and from the sign Riddler aimed at the back of Gerry's head as Gerry turned to order another pint, Riddler knew it only too well.

As soon as Riddler had left to open the shop, Gerry spent the entire pint that had just arrived gleefully recounting how Orflaith's proposed holiday with her friend had fallen through. "She rang this morning, whinging about her mate and how she couldn't get the money in time. So being the considerate soul that I am, I offered to take her to the flicks the night, take her mind off the disappointment. I know it'll cheer me up no end." He ended laughing. He did not feel the need to explain to Brendan the true circumstances behind their meeting that night. The holiday was definitely off the agenda, otherwise he was walking, he was adamant about that.

"What'll you do about Concepta?" Brendan teased, feeling malicious because of his friend's good form and apparent fortune.

"She just have to live without me, poor cow." Gerry laughed again.

"Like so many." Brendan said quietly

"Like so many." Gerry concurred, raising his glass and smiling a toast, unable to distinguish the remark from a joke or an insult." You know, Jimmy has a point. I hate to say it, so I do." He said, smiling. "I've got physio next Monday, hopefully he'll let me do light training. Perhaps the swimmers, do you fancy it Brendan?"

"What?"

"Swimming. Monday nights?"

"No mate, this is as much liquid as I can stand." He said, tilting his pint at Gerry. He felt a twist of guilt burn at his face for not being more supportive in Gerry's rehabilitation. He knew he was a talented footballer. On a number of occasions he had turned up at the five-a-sides to play in goal. Outfield, he was too self-conscious, fearing the ball, fearing losing it, not able to control it or what to do with it in the frenetic pace and noise of the game. Gerry was a natural, the ball seemed to stay at his feet until he wanted to release it, usually in a neat one-two or more normally into the back of the net. He was carefree, cavalier, imperious to those around him as he dribbled, ran or tackled for the ball. He was graceful, purposeful and strong in possession of the ball, brave and organised throughout. Yes,he was really good and it gave rise to an ugly resentment Brendan held for him. He would pray for his swift recovery and return to the game Gerry loved, he would.

When Gerry took his leave from the table saying he would see him tomorrow, it was almost two thirty. "Better go, think I've ripped the arse out it with Riddler, I'll let him go early, fairs fair. See you tammara, all the boys should be out, about three? Alright Brendan?"

"Yeah, see ya then." He watched Gerry check his pockets and turn to wave at the door before leaving the pub. Brendan felt abandoned. Immediately he felt the social unacceptability to be sat occupying an entire table. The bar was the place designated for those who drank in solitude. Company, if sought or wanted, was never far away in the form of those patrons who lined the bar or those serving behind it. This is the way he would spend his life, he would drift unconsciously, over a period of time, until he found himself staring,

reflected in one of those men gathered at the bar. He had sought refuge here and in similar places over the past eleven days and he never saw himself as them, he always put his faith that because he recognised the pattern, he was saved, he could do something about it. Now it was time he did.

He took a seat along the bar furthest from the large television screen perched in the top left-hand corner above the ladies toilets and the horseracing that captivated those who sat at the bar, their heads at various angles, conversing or directed at the screen. He waited until the race was over which ended with an assortment of cries and comments that suggested no-one at the bar that had placed a bet won, before motioning to the barman for another pi..pi..pint. He hated himself for envying Gerry his good spirits, it made him feel even more diminished and far removed from the person he should be, could be, and would be. At least he did not wish for his baldy boss to have returned from his trip early having navigated a complex network of routes to evade the fashion police, to be waiting for him in the shop with his cards and a 'fuck ye'.

The barman had switched to the news and Brendan turned to look straight ahead, he had grown tired of the war-crimes in former Yugoslavia, the starvation in sub-Sahara Africa. He did look up to watch several of the elderly patrons who vied for the attention of the middle-aged barmaid collecting plates from one of the tables. She cheerfully spread her companionship amongst them in a spirited performance that was executed with such aplomb and adroitness that none of the men were neglected.

At one point, during an outburst of laughing, Brendan's opinion was sought on the relative condition of the men during a good-natured, but heated banter about the relative sex appeal of each of the men. He smiled up at them and apologised, but none of them were his type.

It was symptomatic of the kind of discussion that generously swamped an afternoon session. The laughter lasted too long, the jokes, anecdotes and one-liners repeated too often as they clung to the threads of a particular conversation because no-one was sure when and where the next one would come.

The sound of the tv was pumped up for the three fifteen at Doncaster. Christ, he'd little time, precious time to think before he had to act. The barman interrupted his thoughts as the pint he had had ordered minutes before was set before him. He paid his for his drink and went over to the payphone, the same payphone from the night before the one on which he spoke to Frances. The same phone, the same alcohol, the same. This is where he would stay, unable to move on, to move forward, although he did not quite know what these phrases actually meant, but he could see it in others who had done it. Like the guy he knew who had given up smoking and completed the Belfast marathon and had gone back to University and was now a community worker. Now that was moving in a direction, maybe it was not his direction. But he had nothing but admiration and an almost child like wonder of those who remained committed to themselves, they never strayed far from who they were and remained steadfast in their convictions. They ploughed on at their work, their own ambitions and remained who they were. They did not fall into themselves or others to be subsumed, afraid that if they were not around, they would be forgotten. He knew that his faith in himself, lay in the impact he made in others. Frances would never be like that, right now she would be eating well, sleeping well, studying, shopping, going out, making plans for her future life and sticking to them, not according to any schedule she had drawn up, but because that is who she was. The schedule to life lay within, not outside on a programme you have devised, to tick off those things listed to chart your progress. He dialled the number of the local taxi firm driven by his sense to progress, there was no tick for this, his dread was that he too was driven by a sense that there was very little to his self. No! He had no other way open to him, he told himself, as he struggled to answer the gruff voice asking him where he was going to. "City bus centre."

He returned to the bar to see a fourteen to one shot romp home to an impressive win by several lengths. Dockets produced, were examined like holy relics, then squeezed into tight yellow balls, and dreams of winning against a lifetime of losing were dropped to the floor or placed in ashtrays. He watched the paper baubles become flattened and kicked into the many hidden recesses of the bar floor and he knew he had to go.

An endless series of malignant red dots, a diatribe against police checkpoints from the obese taxi driver, coked in body odour and he was outside the bus depot handing over the fare he had kept in his hand throughout the journey. He thanked the driver and took his bag from the backseat and raced for cover from the rain which had just begun to fall, through the gates and over to the ticket booth to wait behind an elderly couple. His bus would be leaving in ten minutes, he paid for a return ticket and asked when the last bus would be leaving to return to Belfast. "Nine thirty." The man behind the strengthened glass told him through the tiny holes that radiated out in larger circles.

He took his ticket that grinded out from an unseen machine, scooped out his change from the steel basin, and patrolled up and down under cover of the bus shelter conscious not to join the other travellers, none of whom offered distraction. He walked back up to near the man in the glass booth and lit a cigarette, wondering if he would be smoking tomorrow, wondering how changed he would be, who he would become after his odyssey. He took a moment to examine his surroundings, to wonder if they too would be the same after. He watched the plastic sheets covering the scaffolding that battle-dressed the Grand Opera House flap wildly in the wind. The building had absorbed a great deal of the impact of a bomb attack directed at the The Ulster Unionist Party's headquarters several weeks ago. Its ornate façade was torn away in parts, like some beautiful face that was ravaged by a terrible act of personal savagery. He looked over to the Crown bar pockmarked with a rash of ugly wounds, blinded by the blast, it's windows replaced by wooden boarding, it's doors closed. The Philistines, he joked, flung the cigarette end out onto the depot bay, and made his way to the designated line printed on his ticket.

WELTSCHMERZ

Scenery from a countryside rolled past, he sat two rows up from the back of the bus, half-expecting end credits to flash up. He scanned the landscape staked by telephone poles, where lush green bushes grazed in herds corralled into neat little bundles by the imposition of man-made walls. The journey wore on and the land became poorer, more barren, its colour transmogrified from the strident green richness to a land washed of colour. Yet, the land became more familiar, intriguing and curiously reassuring to him. The comforting view was suddenly marred by a collection of flapping specks tracing a line between land and water. Perhaps they were Larks or fucking Curlews. Now, now he chastised, enough of that, you're on the mend now. Yeah, he thought wearily.

The lull of the engines rhythmic buoyancy forced tiredness on him. Above, the artificial lighting dulled and hurt his eyes, the condition becoming more pronounced with the evening dark stealing in upon the land. Belfast lay thirty odd miles behind him, at least that was when the last time he had bothered to glance out at the motorway signs posted along the route. He was sick of the endless boggy under-felt outside, sick of the view of his silent fellow travellers. Eight or nine of them sat quietly enduring the twists and turns of the undulating road they had embarked upon since leaving the motorway. His head ached and his mouth dry, he wished he had brought a can or bottle of coke, wished he had brought his walkman. He slumped further down in his seat and closed his eyes to it all.

He was jolted awake by the bus shuddering to a halt. He yawned loudly, stretching his legs under the empty seat in front. His fellow travellers had reduced to five in number and were already up and off their seats; anxious to escape their confinement. The bus door hissed open, allowing the uncomfortable build-up of travelled heat and smell to be released. He remained seated, finishing his yawn, attempting to shrug off the gauze of weariness draped over him as he slept. He watched the passengers shuffle down the aisle with their belongings, making their way towards the charmless block of glass and concrete of the terminus.

He waited until the last passenger stepped from the bus before raising himself from the unforgiving ledge of his seat, his legs ached with paralysis as he stood up to retrieve his travel bag from the overhead rack. He walked down the aisle following the path of his former travellers passing the bus driver still sat at his wheel. It appeared that the journey had taken its toll on the driver too. He was unshaven and rubbing his face, and then began scratching a large boiled egg of a stomach, a part of which was exposed through an unbuttoned part of his shirt. He could see his navy trousers creased in vexation at the crotch, angry lines forged in the cramped conditions of their internment. They parted company with an exchange of nods that suggested they had both survived some form of gruelling rites of passage that had made them for that moment the firmest of comrades.

Brendan stepped from the bus taking in a deep breath of cold wet air, deciding to avoid the well-trodden path through the illuminated tract of the terminus.

Several large, Georgian-style houses constituted Mace Drive, remnants of a more sedate age when the town was no more than a village. Here they rested, stored away memento's of an era before the estate was thrust upon them. He walked the drive past the large front gardens. The street lights only served to highlight their former grandeur. They sat in their own grounds, shunned and shunning, extravagant, elegant anachronisms that he felt an instant affinity with. He stopped at number seven, Mr O'Neill's, the scrap merchant, he remembered the estate gossip, the undercurrent of relish and excitement at the first Catholic to own a house on the drive. It was seen as part of the general social and political upheaval that was taking place throughout the province. As children they saw it as the only house they would climb the walls to scavenge for conkers and crab apples. It was an oasis all too brief as he passed the last house and was in Trench road that led to the estate and the house.

Welcome. Welcome to Moneyduff safari park. God, nothing could have prepared him for the sameness, if sameness could adequately describe they grey uniformity of the life- size pieces of lego like playthings fashioned by a thoughtless, malicious child.

He pulled the collar of his jacket up and walked shadowed by an evening shower. How he wished she was her with him, it was a journey he would have wanted to make with her, to make her understand and empathise with his failings, where they emanated from and see that they could be changed and that he could be changed and made worthy of her. He thought about her face, how he would scrutinise it as she slept, hoping to deconstruct hat whole from the composite parts and from it's individual parts he hoped to lessen the hold the sum possessed of his heart and soul. But the exercise never worked in the way he wished; in fact he found it all the more wondrous that someone with such beauty could be with him. And it made her love all the more miraculous and his hold on it, however brief, appear all the more tenuous. Fuck her, he thought savagely, he had to forget her as she would no doubt forget about him, otherwise he would never progress.

He trudged deliberately, the soles of his boots scraping the wet uncompromising surface of the main artery of Meadow Road. He glanced to either side of the road, his attention drawn to certain inhabitants lurking on the frayed edges of the street lighting. He felt his presence being watched with eyes full of curiosity and suspicion. He could hear them swearing down drink from over-sized plastic bottles, many of them lay strewn on the road emptied and discarded; he could hear them spitting out insults in an indiscriminate, indeterminate barrage that marked their territory.

Christ, it was barely six O'clock he thought. It wasn't hypocrisy, the circumstances for his drinking were a one-off. He hoped. He felt his legs stiffen in opposition as they took him closer to that place he once knew as home. From behind him, somewhere amongst the darkened recesses a voice screamed out a girl's name dragging out a rubble of laughter. He passed by two children around nine or ten who exchanged passes with what looked like a lump of dog excrement and he felt the disheartening malaise as thick and as dark as the encroaching night air sapping his will, smothering him with a feeling of ignorance and neglect that was almost tangible.

He stepped off the pavement and onto the road to avoid the corruption of children throwing cans for their skinny dogs to chase. The tenuous hold he had on his resolve loosened further and for a real moment he wanted to go back, but he thought of her derisiveness at his lack of strength of character and he cursed her. He walked on knowing he had left himself no choice but to follow.

A bruised sky heralded more rain. The clouds descended, closing in over the serrated spine of the mountain that imperiously encircled the estate and there they remained grid-locked over the estate.

'It's going to bucket.'

'You worried you're going to melt.'

'What's up with you? You've been a pain in the hole since you came home.'

His sister did not answer and continued to apply her make-up.

'Make sure you cover all them spots.'

'Bugger off fatboy.' She rounded on her brother as he ran to the staircase.

'No wonder Micky left ye.' Her brother hissed over, before skipping up the stairs laughing.

'I left him," she seethed, "because he's waster like you. Bastard.' She breathed out to her reflection, returning to the mirror and leaning in close to examine her face. Just a bit more foundation, she thought, delving into her make-up bag. She applied the foundation in light brush strokes concentrating in an area below her bottom lip where a cluster of tiny spots stubbornly resisted. Satisfied with the application she straightened up, smiled at herself and then to herself, her mouth an inviting line of strong and fast opinion a less attractive girl would find impossible to live by. She placed the make-up in her handbag and stopped before going into the living room to finger out some of the long loose curls of dark auburn hair that cascaded down to both shoulders. She made a final inspection of her dress, using the palm of her hand to iron out the material that failed to hug her trim, strong body.

'The mirror's free now fatboy, God knows what you're looking for though."

"Cheers, hope you got your bake camouflaged. It's alright," he called down, "I'll not be needing it now. I'm fine as I am."

"Yeah, as a fat moron." She let escape in a rush of hot breath through her teeth. She knew he had no intention of making use of the mirror, this was his way of getting back at her because she had kept Brendan's visit secret, even through his whining protests about invading his room to air the sofa bed without telling the real reason why. She told him, a friend might be staying overnight. As long as it wasn't one of her frooty boy hairdressers, one of the girls, he'd be alright with it, he said. He'd stand a better chance with one of the boys, she said. She had managed to conceal Brendan's arrival up to the moment she spotted him from her look-out point on the landing, walking towards the house.

She took her bag and walked into the living intending to speak to her mother about Brendan's visit as she had been very quiet since she knew of his arrival. She felt guilty concealing his visit from her. She didn't know what to make of her mother's reaction. It wasn't normal. It was quiet and pleasant, accepting more than inviting. She put it down to the time he had spent away, it was bound to create a distance. But she could not shake off the feeling that she was complicit in upsetting her in some way.

"Ah Una love, put us on a wee cup of tea." An outstretched arm offered up the empty teacup. Una dropped her handbag to the side of the settee and without a word took the cup from her mother's hand, turned and made her way out of the room. "And bring us in a wee slice of that madiera as well love."

Una did not reply, she pulled the living room door closed and went into the kitchen and vented her anger and frustration on the fridge door. "Shite." she swore, staring fiercely at the scuff mark her kick had made on her shoe. "I know where I'd like to stick her madeira." She got a cloth and wet it under the cold water and rubbed at the mark. She threw the cloth into the sink and filled the kettle throttling the handle as she slammed the plug into the socket.

In the living room Una's mother settled back in her armchair with an invigorated sense of pleasure at the prospect of another cup of tea to look forward to. She sat within almost her leg's length of the tv set, the glare from the screen illuminating her face and when she smiled at the activity on the screen her exposed a row of teeth too perfect to be real. The smile broadened deepening the lines around the edges of her mouth and eyes concentrating a patterned weave knitted by life's unremitting art.

Deirdre O'Connell had lived and worked in the town and its surrounding area, most of her life. At fourteen she went to work on one of the large farms picking potatoes and eventually acting as a general domestic, nursemaid and friend to the widowed Mrs Alexander, who lived on a large farmhouse, her husband had inherited from his grandparents. Her husband had been a bank manager and had no family background in farming, so they rented off most of the land and kept two acres mostly for their chickens, dogs and a horse that was roundly condemned as 'neither good to man nor baste'. She was a gentle woman with a genteel manner and voice, always impeccably dressed and idolised by her young employee who would adopt those qualities and mannerisms she so admired outside of her working day.

The best part to her role as companion was that she would accompany Mrs Alexander on those few occasions she went up to Belfast to visit with her sister whose husband was a doctor. On those journeys, travelling second class by train, the young girls head would be awash with dreams of a better, larger life than the small town could hold. Her imagination fired by the size of the city and the people and its sound and pace of life; its great buildings, the carts, cars and trams, the city hall with its great grounds and statues. She would wait in the front sitting room with a cup of tea while Mrs Alexander spoke to her sister in the next room as they discussed family matters. She would sit and imagine that she too would have a house in the city, filled with beautiful brass and glass ornaments, velvet curtains and a husband with a profession. That afternoon she and the widowed Mrs Alexander went to shop in Royal Avenue and it was in the elegant Robinson and Cleaver building that she met James. Mrs Alexander went in search of special ribbons for her sister's birthday, at the long counter of the haberdashers stood a young man and woman she presumed to be his mother.

He was tall, thin, with a handsome, boyish face. Big, blue eyes accentuated his boyishness even further. He walked away from the woman talking to the assistant at the counter and over to the glass casing she was looking into. He said the gloves and scarves he assumed she was looking at, would really suit her. She smiled and asked was that his mother he was with. He did not answer her question, but remarked on how lovely her accent was. She smiled again. He was eighteen and she was three weeks from her sixteenth birthday.

An echoing voice interrupted her thoughts. Instantly, the voice and the appeal were recognised. "How much?" She asked, shifting in her chair to reach for her purse buried beneath her back.

"A tenner ma, please." Her son pleaded, his hands spread in earnest exhortation as she facially baulked at the request.

"That girl of yours is getting more expensive." She remarked, opening her purse. Her son sat perched on the arm of her chair and leaned towards her."Doesn't your brother pay you enough?"

"Yeah, he pays enough, but I had to chip in for that new washing machine, remember? Anyway, there's no girl. No girl, but you." He said, planting a kiss on the top of her head, his lips feeling the coarse, greying hair that filled him with a burning shame.

"Get on with ye, go on and fetch us in me tea." She said, nudging him from the arm of the chair.

"Okay mum." Her son complied, relieved to have been given the opportunity to leave and to do something for her.

"Ma's tea ready yet?"

"You been tapping her again? Christ." Una swore, pouring the bolied water into the teapot. "You've no morals at all." Una said, slapping the lid down on the teapot, her anger and frustration subdued by the force of her actions. "Well, fatboy, you can take her tea into her, do something for your money." She said, moving aside to allow him to take the tray laid out with the teapot, cups, several slices of madeira and an assortment of biscuits.

"Ya-vol mein Fuehrer, have a day off Eva, you don't have to be a bitch all the time, you know," he said lifting up the tray. "Mum's been asking about you know who again."

"She's not stupid you know, except when it comes to the men in this house." Una snapped, wiping her hands dry on a teacloth. "Anyway, she's entitled to know, she's paying for the dates." She said and pulled a smile.

"Just open the door." Terence returned at her with contained fury, his face reddening as he stood with the tray experiencing an entire moment of impotency.

"Well? Are you bringing it in?" Una asked, holding the kitchen door open for him.

"I was just thinking." Terence said.

"I was wondering why you looked in pain." Una said.

"Give it a rest you," Terence retorted, "I was just thinking," he resumed, "there's only three cups. What about Brendan?" He asked, looking down upon the tray.

""Brendan'll get whatever he wants, when he gets down, ok?" Una told him firmly and opened the door as wide as it could be opened. Terence's grip on the tray tightened and took a couple of deep breaths before turning with the tray and walking it intop the living room. Una followed and sat down at the end of the settee furthest from her mother and close to the door. Terence set the tray on the coffee table bringing a cup and the plate with the Madiera over to his mother.

"Thanks son."

"Such a lovely boy." Una ridiculed.

Terence returned to the table and shovelled several large teaspoons of sugar into his cup.

"Have you worms or something? That's disgusting the amount of sugar you take." Terence dug the spoon once more into the sugar bowl and defiantly plopped another teaspoon of sugar into his cup.

"Well, it's your body." Una observed.

"I'm cuddly is all." Terence said sitting down at the opposite end of settee.

"Somebody must think so." Una replied and poured out her tea. She smiled back at the look of pained disquiet on Terence's face. He quickly took up the paper lying underneath the coffee table and read the lead story on the front page about the breakdown and remarkable rehabilitation of some star in some soap from years ago.

"Here Una, give us a smoke, will ya?" Terence placed the newspaper back underneath the table as he watched his sister light up.

"Take one, only one. I've a only a few left." She told him.

"Cheers, do you have a light?" He asked, standing over her twiddling the cigarette between his fingers.

"For Godsake." Una sighed, handing him up her lighter. Terence quickly lit up the cigarette and returned to his chair.

"You should go to Area cabs, they're selling them for one fifty." Terence informed her.

"It's only that foreign rubbish they sell. They're like wrapped up dung in paper those things." She replied.

"Better not let your father catch youse two smoking, you know he doesn't like youse smoking." Their mother cautioned, biting into a slice of madiera.

"Pity he doesn't feel the same way about drink." Una replied, exchanging raised eyebrows with her brother.

"Una, show him a bit of respect, he's your father." Her mother admonished, having withdrawn from taking another slice of cake to rebuke her daughter.

Una was about to tell her mother not to remind her of that sad fact, but it remained another thought she could not translate to words. All she could say was "Respect?" She rolled the word around her mouth like a new flavour and finding she had no taste for it, she sat back in the settee and blew a mouthful of smoke pointedly into the air.

Upstairs she heard the toilet being flushed. Terence on hearing it too got up from the settee and moved towards the door.

"Don't be tapping him fat boy." Una warned as he skipped over the arm of the settee.

"I won't, nothing wrong with wanting to see you bro', is there?" Terence declared smiling, leaving the room and running up the stairs.

Una sat on watching her mother staring at the TV, expecting a response. But she kept staring at the tv. She had been quiet since Terence opened his fat mouth to tell her Brendan was upstairs saying only that they would talk in their own good time. Una was not surprised or disappointed by her mother's reaction. To her knowledge she had never heard her ask about him, to her knowledge they had not talked on the phone and she was sure that they had never written to each other. She had kept her visit to him secret, lying about a colouring course she had to attend in Derry. When Brendan had rang her a second time in the afternoon from the pub, she thought he was drunk and she was angry and upset at his rambling about the car and having to get the bus. But he assured he was not drunk and that he would get the bus.

And she was relieved and thought now that he sounded unsure, reluctant, scared even. She told him it'd be alright and that she would meet him at the bus station if he wanted, or if he got the express he could call to the salon and they could walk to the house together. He said no to all this, saying that this was something he would have to do on his own. She said ok, that she would watch out for him and let him into the house to keep his visit a surprise. He said that would be fine and that he would see her soon. Again she worried that his news could prove so profound as to eclipse her plans.

When she set the phone down she felt a stab of guilt at taking advantage of his eagerness to be home with his family, was only to realise a deep desire borne of her own reasons.

"You hungover?"

Brendan brushed aside strands of hair obscuring his vision and smiled a greeting at the grinning figure of his brother standing on the top stair. The naked light directly above him on the landing further hampered his view. He winced as he tried to focus.

"Lampshades broken." Terence explained.

"Right." Brendan replied simply and walked to the bedroom where Una had laid out the sofa bed, a duvet and a pillow for his visit.

"Feeling any better?" Terence asked, following him up onto the landing and into the bedroom. "Una's been fussing about ever since she got home from work. She said the room needed tidying and she left the windows open. You'd think the room was boggin' for Godsake." Terence made a sniff at the offence it did not cause him.

"The sofa bed's fine."

"Aye, she got it all out aired and dusted." Terence said sitting down on the side of his bed. " I wouldn't lift a finger until she told me who it was for. She came off with some shite about a friend from work might be staying over tonight. Then when she told me, she told me not to breathe a word and not to come up and see you until you were ready to come down. What's all the cloak and dagger stuff about I asked her. But you know women, great at keeping secrets," he said in solemn voice, "and mum's hardly said a word." Terence made his observation quietly, before sitting down and then rolling onto his back lying supine on his bed.

" What are you doing with yerself now? Working away?" Brendan felt compelled to ask.

"Aye, working in our Martin's place, doing the wheel balancing, replacing tyres, stuff like that. It's not rocket science, you know. It's alright, he works me like a dog 'cause I'm family, he can't be seen to be doing me any favours, so he says." Terence said, staring up at the ceiling. "Money's not bad and he's going to do me a good deal on a car."

Brendan remained with his back to his brother and took out his deodorant and lifted his tee-shirt to spray both armpits. He stared down at the dresser where the figure of the impaled Christ had been resurrected. At its base lay the crushed filter of a cigarette. He imagined the Roman guards offering Him a last cigarette. He laughed thinking how Christ would have shouted in disbelief *'Are you crazy? Have you any idea the damage those things do to you?'*

He used the mirror to watch Terence now sat up on his bed, his brother appeared uncomfortable and strangely incongruous to his own environment. Though he noticed that he was wearing Timberland boots and Armani Jeans and that shirt, it looked a Pierre Cardin. Noticeably expensive tastes, particularly in a small town. Must have a man to impress he joked to himself. He remembered the last time he saw him, he was with Da and Una, they had made their way to Belfast for granny's sixtieth birthday, they had brought her a pair of slippers, a cardigan, a large box of chocolates and Una had come especially to cut her hair. He had bought her a radio so she could listen to radio Ulster and was taking her across the road to the local for her two glasses of orange where she would chat to the women whose mothers she knew. He was thankful that he had been working overtime that Saturday and had arrived into the house just as they were making their farewells. He remembered Una's hug

and whispered promise to come up on her own one day and see him. He remembered
Terence's expressionless look and his dyed black hair. He remembered da's 'heelo son' that
was directed at the carpet. The whole incident lasted no more than one or two minutes as da
said they had better go if they were to catch the bus. He watched granny give them all a last
hug, saving her last and longest for her son, a hug that ruptured an anger in him as they clung
so tightly to each other that it was apparent to all in the room how much they loved each
other.

Brendan put his deodorant back in the bag and looked at Terence sitting on his bed,
he had put on weight, his hair was cut short all around the head and his locks remained long,
a good inch below the earlobes. The weight did not sit well with him as he had not
broadened out and his round-shoulders gave the impression of a caved in chest when he sat
down. His ears still stuck out slightly giving him air of amiability and openness, perhaps
indicative of his personality. Brendan searched his travel bag for his wallet and watch.

"Here."

"What's this? " Terence asked, turning from the ranks of the Liverpool
championship-winning team taped above his bed.

"It's only a fiver, but it'll get you a drink."

" Wise up. You sure?" Terence asked, getting up from the bed. He tried to sound
surprised, but his mimed pretence of walking over to accept the note made the transaction
seem tawdry and his offer look cheap. Terence's ' thanks, thanks a lot, bro' propelled

Brendan to return to his travel bag searching for a way out.

"Right, you can go now." He said smiling, trying to make a joke of his most ardent
wish.

"Brother." Terence exclaimed, placing a hand over his chest as if mortally wounded. "You don't think it's just the money. God forbid." He pined, affecting to be mortally wounded..

"Go on. I've to get ready otherwise Una'll skin me alive."

"Cheers, are youse going to O'Brien's then? Una probably wouldn't go anywhere else in town. She thinks everywhere else is a dump. It's new, all done up like a hotel. It's where the trendies go first before they hit the clubs. " Terence said, pausing at the bedroom door. "Maybe I'll see you in there later."

"Maybe." Brendan replied brightly.

"I'll get on. I'll let her know you're nearly ready."

"Cheers." Brendan answered, making a show of rummaging through his bag for something vitally important.

"No worries, maybe I'll spend some of that money on ye." Terence laughed a hollow laugh that fell short somewhere between the door and his brother's feet.

"No problem." Brendan replied, not quite in keeping with the light-hearted nature that lubricated their exchange. He did not turn round, but kept up his search for the Holy Grail.

Terence left the room, pulling the bedroom door behind him and stood on the top landing. He pulled out the fiver and the tenner his pocket and pushed the fiver from his brother in with his own money, and slipped his mum's tenner into the other pocket.

Somehow it did not feel right that they share the same pocket, as they had come from vastly different sources. He felt little guilt in taking his money. It would have made his brother feel better to have given the hick a handout, he reasoned.

A thought blistered on his mind, he was an amateur in exploiting people in comparison to him. He used granny, stayed with her practically rent free for years, he heard his da say one night when he and his mum argued about inviting him to Martin's wedding. The da and Martin didn't want him there, but mum insisted that he be invited. All that arguing was for nothing. He was sick and he wasn't well enough to take granny down, conjunctivitis he said he had. Terence had to ask what that was and said that sounded terrible. So they had to get a friend of Martin's to collect her and so she travelled down with a complete stranger and his wife.

It was two years ago he last saw him when they went up to see granny for her birthday and he couldn't even look at them: you'd have thought they'd come up to the big smoke with straw sticking out of their mouths and manure on their feet. He said as much to da on the way home on the bus, but da excused Brendan saying it was hard for him being away so long, he probably didn't know what to say. Da sat on the bus a seat up from him and Una and said nothing more. But he could see da was upset. How hard was it for him to say something to his own family? Nobody talked about it. Una hissed at him to be quiet as he knew nothing about it. Neither did you, he answered back, his voice raised loud enough for it to bubble up over the seat and past their father's head. Una told him to keep quiet and he did, they all did, all the way home on the bus. Nobody talked about nothing in the house. Nothing important that is. Not like a real family. It was all big events, like who died, who got married, sports, jobs, furniture. Not what was really going on in their lives, how they felt.

Guilty? He thought to himself, self-consciously rubbing his pocket. Like fuck he did, he should've asked, demanded payment from the perfumed prick with his trendy clothes for all the missed birthdays and the shite he had to take at school from some of the Brothers just for being his brother.

Terence skipped down the stairs in need of company to escape a sense of alarm he could never identify when it came to his brother; like an old t.v. programme that scared you as a kid, but you couldn't remember the name or the character in the programme. But you knew the moment you could remember it, the unsettling fear would come flooding back.

The room had changed little, then again rarely do, they remain in their shape, fixed by their atoms, their history masked by a new coat of paint, some imitation pine furniture, a new piece of carpet and bed. Not the one he knew, not the one that played witness to his cold sweated-out nights and heat-filled mornings, the constituents of the pressure cooker that contained the innate shame and unholy excitement that was laid before him to choke on.

He should pack that bag and fuck off back home and never come back. And go back to what he questioned, the same insecurity that stymied every plan, aspiration and hope he would dare to have. No he must stick to his plan. The plan that had already undergone several revisions since you arrived in a matter of hours. You are no Caesar. Instead of I came, I saw, I conquered, you came had a wee peek-a-boo and decided you didn't have the courage to attack it head on. No, you'd be smarter. Suaviter in mod, fortiter in re. Fuck, he would implode her empire. In fact just like a Caesar. He thanked bogger for one aspect of his school years, an inherent fear of failing that saw him through the rest of his schooling and the eight GCSE'S he achieved.

He decided he would tell the truth about the lost years and offer Una the spare room and she could stay as long as she needed to. He would take her away for good and the ma would be unable to get her back, how could she? What could she say in her defence, in defence of the adults in that family? And in telling Una, he was in reality telling Terence too. He would find out, the house could not absorb the magnitude of another secret. And Terence, he'd have to stay behind to poison and cripple what was left. It was genius.

He sat down on the dresser and rewarded his plan with a cigarette, he would leave Jesus the drags.

There was a knock on the door which was pushed open. "You near ready? Do you want something to eat before you go? A sandwich or something?" Una asked, then apologised for her interruption.

"No thanks, I'm fine. I ate earlier." He told her.

She paced to and fro between the door and the head of Terence's bed. "Hasn't changed much, some things never do, some people too." She said quietly. Brendan imagined she was alluding to Terence. He could see she was trying to find a suitable place to sit, somewhere not too far, yet not too close from him. He did not answer what he thought was a rhetorical question from his sister. He sat on the dresser and continued to smoke his cigarette, his thoughts held captive miles away, fifty odd as the bus travels. He saw her in another time, another place, dashing energetically, and frantically collecting what she felt belonged to her. He could not see her crying, just determined.

"Brendan."

The thought broke through dispelling the images.

"You're still with us then?" She smiled, her timid attempt at humour unable to mask a deep swell of annoyance.

"Sorry, day dreaming there." He replied.

"That's ok." She glanced towards the door and she took a step towards the door, giving the impression he was about to become party to some conspiracy. "You know I never thought you'd come down. Thought I'd have to ring you again." She let out a little laugh that failed to disguise her deep disappointment.

"I'm here aren't I?" He said, not intending for it to sound so forceful and irritated as he felt, but his impatience had resurfaced, stewing in the cauldron of the room. "I'm sorry." He quickly apologised seeing her head lower to her chest. "I came down here because of you, you know" He said encouragingly.

"Well, if you really want to know." She answered, her head still lowered, "I've had the offer a job in Belfast as a senior stylist." She looked up and smiled, warmed by the thought. "I could eventually become the manager if I go on the training courses." She blurted out like a child breaking a foresworn oath it was never going to keep. Una looked to the poster of the dopey smiling faces of the footballers and thought most of them could with her expertise. She still felt an uncomfortable build up of heat in her centrally charged body fuelled by her hurt and anger at her brother's seeming indifference to her news, her life, her future.

Brendan fixed his eyes to the ceiling grasping for an appropriate and proportionate response. But time and circumstance was against him, all he could manage was "When?"

Una let out a sigh of resignation. "At the end of next month, if I accept it." Her voice fell and her gaze dropped back into her chest. She stared at her skirt and felt cheapened by her brother's reaction. The idea once released outside the protective, cosseted world of the mind and laid bare and made to look ostentatious and ridiculous. She faced the ogre that threatened her dream and wrestled it into submission. "I thought you, Brendan, of all people, would understand." She said, bursting out of the cloud of doubt that had settled in and around her silence. "I thought I could talk to you tonight about the whole thing."

"And you will." Brendan piped up in a bright voice. "We'll talk the whole thing through and I'll help whatever way I can. I promise."

Una's face broke into a broad smile. "Thanks Brendan." She said, standing up. "We'll go out, we can go to O'Briens, it's a bit like that one you, me and Frances went to into Belfast, remember? After that nice restaurant we were in. The Wharf, wasn't it?"

He remembered. Seriously south Belfast, wall-to-wall Benetton, skin cancer and well fed, healthy faces and bodies that espoused and eschewed a world he knew nothing of and a world that knew nothing of him. He wore his oldest jeans and most comfortable and washed out shirt . He did not want Una to think he endorsed this world and it informed Frances he was there under duress. Frances wore a spring dress that flowed to her ankles and a matching Pashmina tied around her head, with her hair, which for that occasion was a thunder flash of red, in ringlets that dripped from her slender neck. She looked serene, regal. He watched these two women and marvelled at their effortless beauty. He was keenly aware of the men and their furtive and at times overt glances over as they passed their table. Frances, dovetailed seamlessly into this world and he guessed, given time, Una would too. He sat despising the intensity of the middle-class at their recreation. All that work hard, play hard bollocks. Una was hideously over-whelmed, her face awash with wonderment and excitement, pointing out features of the bar and sharing the occasional girlish giggle with Frances at the antics of some people at the bar. Fuck you'd have thought Una had never seen a waitress or an electric light bulb before. Fuck. He resumed the performance he had scripted at the restaurant, making sneering observations that Frances did not want to laugh at, but despite herself she did and Una unsure of where her ally lay and keen to make a good impression, laughed too. If he was honest, he was terrified by the attractiveness, the casual wealth on show. The men were taller than he was used to, better, healthier looking, well-groomed and with a lot of great haircuts that Una just had to observe. Broad-shouldered with tight hips, a lot of these men pressed every biologically programmed button for the progression of the species. Frances belonged to this world, even Una, on appearance, did not look out of place.

"So we'll talk later then, ok?" Una said, determined to spell out her plan, to revive and resuscitate, to add flesh to the bare bones of a dream that had been her ethereal companion for weeks. She would ring Oliver later from the bar and tell him her news. It was time she kick-started this idea into life, as Oliver was too fond of saying, life is not a dress rehearsal. They would be together but not as Oliver had in mind. She would go and be with him, but on her own terms. She would not share his apartment and become his de facto live-in mistress and then only on the occasions he could get away from the demands of his ex-wife and their child. He had got the two Salons to run the one in town, the one in Belfast, the one she had pinned her hopes to. His wife, Majella, an attractive, ambitious woman whom Una admired, had got the salon in Bangor, the house, the car and holiday home in Portugal.

"Yes, of course, but you make sure you have everything in writing for this job. Get a contract down." Brendan told her. "Some people will promise the earth. Where is the salon?"

"Belfast, plus the one in town, of course. It belongs to the Oliver, Oliver Quinn, Quinnsation, corny, isn't it? The one in town, he bought that one over from his aunt when she retired. He learnt the profession with her. Anyway, it's close to Royal Avenue. The owner said he would get me a flat too, if I needed one." She added hastily, the idea that her dream hinged exclusively upon her brother's acquiescence; made the whole scheme seem impossibly fragile.

Brendan yawned deeply and unnecessarily and lit up another cigarette. "There's no need to move into a flat. You can come and stay with me. There should be enough room." He said, smiling, he lit up his cigarette. "Frances has left."

For a moment he could not believe he had actually said it. The admission felt like the expulsion of a cancer, but the surgery had had a traumatic effect. He resumed his smile to mask the sense of helplessness he felt. He wanted to sit down as he felt his knees almost buckle.

For a millennium nothing was said, no discernable movement was made.

"Jesus Brendan, I'm sorry I had no idea. What happened?" She asked. "Sorry, it's none of my business." She quickly added. "I'm so sorry." She repeated.

"Too long a story for now. But we'll talk about that later too. Gonna be an interesting night all round." Brendan smiled again.

"Isn't it?" Una smiled back at him. "And don't worry she'll come back. You know what us women are like." She added, feeling suddenly protective of her brother.

"Actually I don't" He laughed a small laugh. "Anyway, you can come and stay with me, if you want to. I could do with the rent." His laugh, this time, was genuine and a reciprocation of his goodwill.

Una interpreted his invitation to mean she could forge ahead with an outline of her plans and talked openly of how the move to Belfast had come about. She mentioned the owner of the salon several times and the retirement of the aunt and his buying of the business. Hairdressing. In the genes? Who would have thought it? She had the opportunity to be not only the senior stylist, some sort of honour he guessed; but the de facto manager. He was happy for her, truly he was, but right there and then he could have done without her chattering.

Una was saved from being thrown out of the window by the bedroom door opening quietly and slowly. "Got another one of them?" Terence asked, grinning a big grin at him.

"Here take one of these." Una told him, throwing her cigarette box to him. She was in a forgiving and generous mood.

"Whoops." Terence laughed, making an exaggerated fumble with the box managing to drop it to the floor.

"Get some when you're out, some Regal Kingsize. I'd like a few back."

"No problem, I'll get some," he said, getting the box from the floor and taking one out, "here Brendan, where you anywhere near that bomb last weekend? Saw it on the news, the town looked wrecked." The convivial tone to the subject matter struck a discordant note with his sister.

"It'll take more than some poxy bomb by some arseholes from the dark ages to send us all back there. And throw those cigarettes over here. Aren't you supposed to be meeting someone?" She asked dryly.

"For Godsake, I was only asking. And I'm not going out for a while yet." He argued back, holding up his watch to check on the time. "Oops," he said, frowning at the watch, "bit later than I thought, anyway I just wanted to know if granny and Brendan were alright, ok?" He finished.

"Sure." Una returned at him in a sneer. "Sure, da rang granny the other day to find out how they were and everything was fine. So less of the Galahad act You should go and use the remaining time you have left to smarten yourself up. Trust me, women appreciate a bit of an effort." She smiled sweetly at him, but the advice had the tone of an instruction.

"I'm fine, this is me best shirt and jeans, I've had a shower, brushed me teeth, and cleaned my arse for chrissake." He looked himself up and down self-conciously. "I'll head downstairs and clip me nose hair." He said sarcastically. "Better get off then." He said, surrendering a small wave to his brother. He left the room and Una waited until his footsteps had become an echo on the staircase.

"He's such a moron at times." She said, feeling it incumbent upon her to apologise as the only family member who was not and would not be a small mind in a small town.

"You'll miss him." Brendan said in earnest.

"Probably." Una replied, lighting up a cigarette.

"You smoke too much." Brendan gently chastised, silently accepting her offer of another cigarette.

"We both do." Una smiled, as he lit up again, "have you tried the patches?" She asked.

"Yeah, but you can't get a good drag out of them." He joked, hoping to carry the lighter mood forward to the night ahead. Una laughed even though she had heard the remark or something very similar before. But she shared an almost telepathic sense of securing the brighter mood.

"Suppose they only work if you really want to give up." She said.

"Suppose." He said to that.

For a moment they both said nothing. They ignored the first call of their mother's voice rising up the stairs in levels of agitation. Una placed a hand over her face allowing a long, lingering sigh to escape through the bars of her fingers.

"You don't have to go down, you're not a slave." Brendan told her, raising his voice to drown out the voice coming from the stairs.

"I have to, mum's backs playing up again, so I'm chief dishwasher and cleaner-upper for the time being." She told him, getting up from the bed. "Seems to come and go when it suits." She remarked quietly.

"Well, not for much longer, eh?" Brendan said, smiling as she came over to stub out her cigarette in the ashtray on the dresser. "Look, I'll go and make myself more beautiful, if that's possible and we'll get out of here for the night after you do what she wants, ok?" He said, struggling to keep hold of her as she walked towards the bedroom door.

"God, yes, " she sighed heavily, "I'll go and see what mum wants, won't be long, probably another cup of tea." She said, raising her sculpted eyebrows.

Walking downstairs she could not remember when and the why whatever existed between her and Oliver, began. Not an affair, that was far too mature, too passionate, to describe what they had. A relationship, certainly not, that hinted at affection, even love. A fling? No, too transient and cheap. They had only been together four times and the first time, she was sure was to be their last as he sat at the wheel of his car crying. He, riddled with guilt at his attempted sexual intercourse, her, desperately trying to get dressed as quickly as possible and get home. He kept apologising, his head firmly attached to the wheel, he had no idea what came over him; the divorce was more difficult than he had ever imagined. The effect it was having on his son, Thomas, was hurting him so much he wished he could turn back time and not concentrated so much on business. He laughed bitterly at that, now most of that he had worked for was going to his ex-wife in the divorce. He begged her to meet him again after work, in public, The Country Inn it was a couple of miles outside town on the road to Dungannon. She agreed so she could finally get home and have a shower. It was at their next meeting he told her of the salon in Belfast, he talked excitedly about a new start, away from the town and the past. He asked her she would like to work there, a bright, ambitious woman like her was deserving of so much better. She didn't know, it was all a bit sudden, quick. She would need time to think about it. She was flattered, she really was. To seal the deal, he offered her the position of senior stylist, he wanted someone he could trust, Patricia was leaving, her husband was moving South with his new job, and Una would be involved in the selection of the new décor, the hiring and firing, all the decisions affecting the business.

The next time they met it was a Sunday afternoon at the same venue, he had brought Thomas, his four year old son, a bright, smiling boy with his father's beguiling brown eyes and fair hair. She knew instantly, as she smiled pleasantly for the boy, that it was the job she craved and its location.

A middle-aged man faced his front door with atrophied, uncertain legs, his eyes burning in reaction to the abuse they had received in the smoke-filled bar all that day. His mind cast helplessly adrift, frustrating and complicating his every move. The door key became quicksilver in his clumsy attempts to get in from the sobering shower. He concentrated, focusing on the keyhole managing at last to slot the key in and turn the lock and the door opened invitingly. He clung to its frame, using it to support his entry. He quietly and gently slid the door shut behind him. He left the security of its guidance and began to remove his sodden raincoat; struggling with its extra weight. The coat hung precariously from one shoulder and fell to the floor, no longer able to defy the laws of hall gravity. Bastard thing, he thought at the coat, kicking out, sending it sprawling into a corner of the hall. His action brought wisps of wet grey hair to lash the side of his temple; he swept the strands back to the side of his head and walked towards the living room door.

"Sweet Jesus." Una muttered under her breath. Her father lay in the armchair nearest the fire, his eyes closed, his head resting to one side as an involuntary deep breath escaped through his nostrils. His head lolled further back into the chair, his face smeared in a jam of exploded blood vessels, his mouth trailed downwards to the left of his face in search of his chin like some imbecilic grin left over from a dirty joke he had been told in the bar.

Una stepped back from the stench of the alcohol and damp filtering through his heated body and clothes. There was movement of one thin spindly leg foraging out towards the fire seeking its warmth.

"Jim, Jim." His wife called over to him, getting up from her chair to lean over him. "Jim, she said gently, tenderly shaking his shoulder, "God, he's soaked through." She commented to her daughter on feeling his jumper.

"For Godsake, is this why you called me down, to look at this? I've seen it before." Una directed her disgust at her mother.

"Una love, go and stick your father's tea on, it's in the oven, just ready to be heated up." She said. "I'll get his shoes and socks off, his feet must be drenched." She said, returning to her husband.

"I'm supposed to be going out, remember?" Una protested angrily, but managing to subdue her anger into a elongated puff of hot breath from her tightening lips.

"Sure it'll not take long to heat up love, anyway it's early yet." Her mother said, looking up at the clock above the fire..

"God." Una cried out loud enough for anyone who cared to listen and turned, storming from the room.

"Ah Jim, love." His wife sighed pulling off his shoes, then his socks, that she laid before the fire. Looking at him slumbering she was reminded of the young man she fell in love with. The man who had hitched lifts to the town on lorries, vans and cars when he had missed the bus just to be with her. She remembered the day she and her mother coming back from mass had seen him at the bus stop, dishevelled and soaked through. He explained he had missed the bus and could not get a lift home. Her mother overcame her suspicion of a boy from the city and insisted that he come back to the house with them to dry off.

He explained over a large breakfast that her mother had made that he had spent the night in an open shed of someone's garden. That was the day she decided she would marry this boy. They lived for the first three years of marriage in his mother's house. He found a job labouring and started bricklaying, working on scaffolding anything to support her and the arrival of their first child. She found work in the Royal Victoria Hospital as a cleaner and her mother-in-law looked after Martin. It was a happy time, with enough money to rent a house of their own.

Then the troubles broke out, it was rioting at first then the guns appeared and people started dying, people they knew. Jim's job became ever more dangerous by the day as the workforce was mainly catholic and the areas they had to work in were almost entirely protestant. After the murder of one of the workforce, shot dead at his own doorstep waiting for the van to collect him, That was enough for Jim, he had had enough, he was terrified that he'd be next and he would be leaving her and the child alone. Sitting in his suit after the funeral of his workmate and friend, he told her that an offer to work and live in Australia had come up, it was a great opportunity to have fresh start, the chance to have a new life; a life without fear. She was adamant, she would not go. She was angry beyond words that he had already discussed it with his mother who said it was a great idea. She wouldn't go, she knew, HE knew nothing about Australia, it would be too hot, it was the other side of the world, they would know no-one and Martin was about to start school. And what about her family? Her father? Her sister? Didn't they matter? They'd be happy for us, Jim said, his face set in determination.

How could she travel so far? Given that she was pregnant again. She had not wanted to tell him so soon into the pregnancy, after the miscarriage from the year before; but seeing the determined look on her husband's face, she knew she had to.

A compromise was brokered that evening, they would leave Belfast and return to her hometown where the troubles had barely registered, he would find work in the new meat factory that was looking for workers and she could find work in the shirt factory her sister worked in. Jim was careful to hide his disappointment behind his zest and enthusiasm for the new home, the job and the new arrival. But she knew all the time he wanted the new life in a new country; his mind filled with a greater life of great wages, great weather, schools, beaches and a freedom from the everyday fear.

Now as she looked at him, drunk, his skin bleached red and dry with alcohol, his clothing still wet and his socks drying out by the fire, she wished, not for the first time in their marriage, that for his sake he had been a single man when that chance had come. He was right about this place, a man is not allowed to dream, this was no longer a land of Saints and Scholars, but of begrudging praise, spite and pettiness. She recalled widow Alexander's funeral. She had gone as a mourner, she was a young mother then, with a husband and a job but on her arrival had been urgently recruited to help out in the kitchen by the widow's sister.

She took off her coat and placed on an apron less her best dress get ruined and she saw to the guest's refreshments in the front and back rooms. She saw one of the nieces proudly displaying a broach, the widow had promised her. She never got to say the goodbye she had planned. She helped clear away the plates and cutlery, got her coat and left by way of the kitchen.

Terence slid open the zip of his brother's travel bag as quietly and as quickly as his act of stealth would allow. He rummaged through the clothes, a white shirt, Ben Sherman, no less a pair of shoes, Hush Puppies, nice, three pairs of socks and two pair of underpants. Maybe he had the two bob bits, he thought smiling at the prospect. Terence was astounded that his brother had packed so much for one nights stay. He's more like a girl, he thought unkindly. He found what he was looking for a small bag which he zipped open still in the travel bag. He took out a small, surprisingly heavy bottle that looked expensive. It had a black label with French writing. He removed the top and sprayed out a small amount of wet, cold, liquid onto his palm. He set the bottle back into the bag, rubbed both palms together, and rubbed both palms around his neck and throat. The odour was strong and pungent, yet fresh and clean, for some unknown reason it reminded him of sunshine. He should use some behind his ears, but he'd waste the whole bottle he joked at his own expense. He zipped up the small bag that contained the bottle, a razor, toothbrush and paste, some cotton buds and a few plasters. Fuck he was prepared if nothing else. He was sure his brother would not mind him the small indulgence. If anything, it was due him, given the disruption his visit had caused, he rationalised, zipping up the bag.

He went to the window and pulled the curtain aside cursing the rain, aware of the scent hanging around like a guilty vapour. Outside the rain hammered the window in continuous sheets that threatened to wash away the street, the estate even. He thought how he would look when he met her, as if it mattered. He'd wear his hat, his 'brickie's hat' she dubbed it. He scanned the room trying to remember where he had left it. Under his bed he spotted the old brown suitcase he had borrowed from his da for the school trip to Galway. It was a trip he had been chosen from the art class, four pupils in total and the art teacher, to attend art tutorials with some renowned landscape artist. He had done well that weekend, three charcoal sketches, a watercolours and one oil, one of the church and its surrounding grounds and another of an artist painting the scene with him in it. Mister Walsh, the art Teacher and local portrait painter of some renown chose this particular oil painting for special attention and an additional reward, a box of oils. Not that the trip was a competition, no, no, no, but Mister Walsh thought he would award the most imaginative piece, a piece, Mr Walsh said, 'that embodied what Shklovsky, a writer I know, said. That it is the purpose of art is to impart the sensation of things as they are perceived and not as they are known.' He never forgot that speech, writing it down and reading it as a tenant of his credo as an artist. It was Mister Walsh who had chosen his painting as demonstrating what Shklovsky had meant. He did not know what Mister Walsh had meant, very few mortals did, and if he was honest he still didn't. But he remembered the excitement and pride he felt as he told his mum and she had give him a big hug and bought him a new shirt as a present. She had wanted to get it framed and put up in the living room but Mister Walsh wanted it for the art class to inspire his younger classes and his peers. He had the painting for one day at the house so his mother could admire his work. She was so impressed by his work even though he had to explain what his painting was and what he was trying to convey; he was ecstatic, barely able to hold back the tears of joy to see how proud she was of him. Several weeks later there was a break-in at the school and the art class and the lab were destroyed in a fire. He knew it was several boys in fifth year who did it, the whole school knew by the end of the week. They hated the science teacher Mister Cahill whose father had been in the RIC, and the art class and in particular Mister Walsh, who devoted all his enthusiasm and energy on those in the class who exhibited an interest and talent.

But he did not let that deter him, he felt nothing stronger than his desire to be an artist, he dreamed of a job as an illustrator with Marvel comics, slavishly copying his superheroes from the comics he spent his pocket money on. He loved The Silver Surfer, empathising with his loneliness and his search for meaning in his exile to our galaxy. His artwork increased in quantity and quality as he honed his artist's eye for detail, but he could not find the interest or heart for any other subject and this was borne out when his exam results came through an 'A' in art and design, 'D's' and 'E's' in the rest. Art school was out.

He tried to get a job where he could utilise and develop his skills, to work at something he loved, he remembered reading or hearing somewhere a saying 'man who works at something he loves, never works a day in his life', beautiful. He submitted a portfolio of religious drawings he had made from a art book borrowed from the library, to a company that made stain glass windows for churches. He got an interview and they offered him a position fitting the fucking things.

He went over to the bed and nudged the box full of Jesus and the superheroes to the top of the bed out of his sight.

"Big date tonight, then?"

Terence swung round from the bed startled at the sound of the voice. "Jesus, you scared the shite out of me there." He exclaimed.

"Sorry bro." Brendan laughed, walking over to the dresser, rubbing the back of his neck with a towel.

"Are youse going to O'Brien's then? Terence asked, returning to the window conscious of the aroma helmeting his head.

"What was it before it became O'Brien's?" Brendan asked hoisting his travel bag onto the dresser and zipping it open

" Used to be Cassies, she used to give us bottles of lemonade in the summer. Cassie split years back to go and live with her son in Canada. Great old lady" Terence informed him.

"I had my first pint in there, after me uncle Michael's funeral." Brendan said quietly, remembering again the gentle man with the sad, blue eyes. He took out his toiletries bag. "Don't be laughing, a boy has to moisturise." Brendan laughed over to his brother as he squeezed out cream onto his hands and applied it onto his face and throat. "Bad night to be meeting the wee woman. Where are youse off to?"

"There's no wee woman." Terence's denial, although loud, lacked conviction.

"Well, now you've me really worried." Brendan said placing the cap back on his moisturiser and delving into the toiletries bag again. "Because you've went to some trouble to impress your mates. I only wear this on special occasions."

Terence felt his face flush as his brother held out the bottle of aftershave with the black label and the French writing.

"Hey, don't sweat it. I just hope she's worth it." Brendan smiled and began applying the aftershave to his face. "Here, what's wrong with this girl, you have to keep her a secret? Is she too ugly to bring home?" Brendan laughed.

"Fuck off she's not." Terence angrily denounced his brother's question.

"So this girl, she's not a... one of us then?" Brendan asked, exploiting the ugly nature to his enquiry to provoke a reaction.

"What if she isn't? Do you want yer money back?" Terence shouted, making a demonstrable show of digging a hand into his jean pocket.

"Don't be daft." Brendan asserted, turning to face him full on in case his brother attempted to execute what appeared to be on his tiny mind. "Wise up. I'm only winding you up. Don't be tarring me with the same brush as the clampits around here. I don't care what she is as long as the two of ye are happy." His overture seemed to placate his brother, he had to smile as his brother shoved the fiver back in his pocket, his anger abated.

"Shitehawk" Una swore, wrestling one of the kitchen chairs back against the table, her rage not fully vented as she took out a cigarette and broke several matches form the cooker trying to light it. "Hell roast that bony-arsed bagpipe of a drunk." She cursed, taking her lighter out of her bag. Once lit, she settled back against the fridge, her mind thrashing with ways on how to balance an old score. She went over to the oven and checked on the dinner, using a dishcloth she removed the plate. It had crossed her mind to let it burn, but looking at the potatoes, carrots, peas and sliced silverside she entertained the idea of spitting on it, or using the ash from her cigarette. Too crude, even for him she thought. Anyway he might not even notice.

She put the plate back in the oven. Above the oven, her attention centred on the pine rack containing the herbs and spices. She ran her eye along the small glass containers, studying the contents labels, deliberating on the best mix to use. Cheyenne pepper, with a trace of mixed herbs whetted her appetite for revenge. She took the dinner plate from the oven and placed it on the gas ring. She removed both from the rack, uncapped them and sprinkled three parts Cheyenne to two parts mixed herb. She replaced the containers and took another, pri pri, and for good measure sprinkled a measure of that onto the potatoes. She used a fork to mash the potatoes and using several carrots and peas to conceal further her sabotage. She replaced the plate back into the oven and sat down at the kitchen table to reward herself with the remainder of her cigarette. "Bastard." She swore, brushing a hand through her hair which had begun to flatten and gel into lamentable clumps lying heavily around her shoulders. The soft, sweet fragrance of her hair had now welded to an array of kitchen smells.

Terence brushed one arm of his leather jacket, it had seen better days, the cuffs were ragged, edged in wear and the shoulders threatened to explode, releasing his incarcerated body. But it had been his most expensive purchase, two weeks wages, a genuine bikers jacket with the Harley Davison motif splayed across the back. "God, I've had this jacket longer than pubic hair." He moaned theatrically, picking at the lapels.

"What, about two years?" His brother laughed.

"Aye that'd be right." Terence smiled wryly. "I'd better get on." He said, opening the bedroom door.

"Right you are, have a good night."

"And," Terence said, popping his head around the door, " by the way, she is one of us, well not exactly, that's another story; but it's not one of those love across the barricades bollocks." He smiled, and closed the door behind him. He wished it was that simple. He felt sure the circumstances he faced were much more difficult to overcome.

Poor Terence, Brendan thought, still tied by the balls to his maw's apron strings, still suckling at her teat to survive, employed by the Bastard. But he felt an elation that his brother's little secret with this girl, hidden from the ma for whatever reason, was another little indication of her crumbling empire. He thought he would ask Una why Terence kept the relationship secret. The oul doll must be slipping eh John? Wot you fink? Eh John did not reply, he remained under the stairs where he had banished himself since their arrival.

"He'll not eat that, you know. He hardly touches his dinner on a Saturday." Terence said, eyeing up the meal Una had taken from the oven and placed on the kitchen table.

"He'd bloody better." Una snapped. "I thought you'd be gone by now."

Her brother took out a chair and sat by the table placing his hopes on the unattended packet of cigarettes.

"Idle prick.!" Una exclaimed, slamming the oven door shut. She spun round at the sound of her brother's violent coughing.

"See what you get for stealing." She told him, snatching the packet from the table. "Ask in future." She said, turning her back on the red-faced burglar who appeared to be losing his fight for air. He got up and went to the sink and filled a glass of water which he gulped down.

"God, that's better. " He gasped, and coughed again and then spat into the sink which he washed down.

"For Godsake." Una protested.

"I've washed it away, alright." Terence replied, taking a strip of kitchen roll to wipe his mouth.

"Tell you what," Una said, "bring that tray in and I'll give you a couple, alright?"

"No problem, right is that everything there?" He asked pointing to the tray.

"No, hold on. His tea." Una said, waiting on the kettle to boil. When it had she poured the water into the cup, took out the teabag with her fingers, and handed him the cup. "That's all." She said sitting down at the table. "What are you standing there for? Bring in the tea." She told her brother who stood at the table.

"My cigarettes?" He reminded her.

"Jesus, you'll never die wanting." She said, taking out two cigarettes from the packet and rolling them across the table to him.

"Ta." He said, taking them and the one from the ashtray that almost claimed his life. "Here Brendan, keep the old H-stone open there, maitre'd coming through." He said as he passed his brother who held the door open for him as he carried the tray through to the living room.

"Dickhead." Una affirmed of her brother. Brendan laughed at the brutality of her remark. "Him and that da of ours are bloody useless. Christ, the two of them wouldn't raise their arses to fart."

Brendan met the mental picture of the pair in a collective effort with a burst of laughter.

"Aye, it's a hoot when you don't have to live with it. They've me ma robbed blind." She said unsmilingly, her face darkening.

Brendan stood at the sink finding the strident defence of the mother less humourous, he found it disquieting to see a deep undercurrent of respect for her. Yet it was forgiveable, understandable even, given the male role models she had to look to. It would seem the 'ghost' hadn't changed, in fact, it would appear he had got worse. The fleeting images he remembered of a thin, pale figure haunting the house like an unwanted spirit were not entirely of his imagination. He recalled the Friday nights he would stumble in and insist he sat on a bony knee and inhaled the lethal cocktail of whiskey and bullshit and he knew, even at that young age, he had poisoned him. But, not long after, he returned the favour and poured his own brand of poison into the drunken head with its hairy, unclean ears. God, why didn't he just die and fulfil the part he had made in life.

"Well, you can tell your boss you can take that job now." He felt compelled to say to kick-start the optimism that had waned inside of him.

"Yes, I will. First thing on Monday," Una brightened immediately, " look Brendan, I'm going to have to change my dress. I won't be long. I promise. We've plenty of time, the bar's got a late licence." She informed him, getting up from the table to leave the kitchen.

"Yeah, sure go ahead." Brendan submitted.

Terence set the tray on the coffee table and watched the spectacle of his mother trying to revive his father. He assisted her on pulling him forward so she could remove his jumper. He was ordered from the room having placed his father back to his original position and telling his mother that Jesus Christ Himself would have difficulty raising that man up.

"Get yerself on out, go on." His mother told him.

He went into the hall and stood in front of the mirror idly picking his nose and pulling faces to suit the grotesque nature to his actions. He had hoped to speak to Una about what women meant by 'we need to talk'. He knew it wasn't good and he thought back to the last week when the silences between them had grown more protracted and her eyes never stayed on him for very long, but Una was in no mood to be asked. He had a finger up each nostril when there was a knock on the door, followed by a rap on the letter box. He unplugged his nose and before answering the door wiped his fingers on the overcoat lying by the gloryhole.

"Hello big fella." Terence greeted the large dewy eyes staring at him from the security of his mother's arms.

"Here Terence, hold him for a moment please." The mother handed over the struggling bundle.

"And where's Martin eh? Where's your daddy?" Terence questioned the bemused face of the baby as he tried to subdue the child struggling to get back to the arms of his mother. The child nor his mother answered his question, she kept her back to Terence, her breath evaporating in the evening chill. She rubbed her hands to generate heat into her frozen body, but her small face did not stir from its vigil.

"At least it's stopped raining. Yes, yes it has." Terence smiled, returning to the child to carry on his conversation.

"And who's this then? A wee visitor, eh?" The child's grandmother addressed her grandson with a broad, welcoming smile. "Here Terence, go in and take the tray back to the kitchen and put it in the oven. We'll heat it up later for your father."

Terence gladly exchanged the child for the tray and went into the living room to return the untouched meal to the oven.

"There we are, that's better eh?" The child settled into the bosom of his grandmother. "Marie love, come in off the doorstep, you'll catch your death of cold." She went to the threshold. "Come on in." She pressed. "Where's that Martin one got to, eh?" She directed her question to the child's face, hoping her daughter-in-law would answer.

"He's over at Rory's house." Marie answered without turning.

"Come on in love, you'll catch your death." Her mother-in-law insisted.

Marie finally turned to her mother-in-law unable to ignore the inhibiting hospitality without appearing rude. She stepped back into the house craning her neck to grab a last look over to the house across the street. She was prevailed upon by her mother-in-law to take her child on into the living room so she and the child could get warmed up. Marie took her child from her mother-in-laws arms and followed her instruction to go into the living room to warm up.

Deirdre waited at the door impatiently. It had been almost a week since she last saw him. He had given Terence a lift home on Monday evening after work, normally Terence would walk or cycle home but they had worked late as a favour to one of Martin's friends who had got a MOT retest the following day. Terence had gone to get a bath before his dinner and she asked Martin to come into the kitchen for a cup of tea which he refused, but accepted a glass of orange juice. He appeared preoccupied and evasive when she asked if everything was alright. Just busy with work mum, he replied and he had to get home as Marie was waiting for him. She did not tell him she had rung several times during the week at his home and there had been no answer. She despised the telephone and the long distance protection it afforded.

She had reconciled herself to the many sleights and indignities since his marriage.

She had thought at thirty-nine he would never leave, certainly not to get married, he was too old, too set in his ways, preferring the company of his mates, the GAA club, his developing garage business set up with *her* financial help. Then Marie arrived to have her father's car serviced. She lived several miles from town at the foot of the Temple hills, but her father's illness meant she had returned home to look after him using her nursing skills to ease the man's final months. Four months after her father's death, Martin announced their engagement and that they would be married the following year and moving into her deceased father's house. It was too rushed, too hasty, they had both panicked, Marie could not be thinking straight so soon after her father's death. Her son told her she was wrong, so wrong and angrily denounced her as selfish and caring only for what she wanted.

She still felt those words levelled at her as keenly as a fresh cut. He loved Marie and she loved him, they wanted a family and they could not wait any longer. Don't make me choose mum, he said. She felt her breath stop. He told her he would visit as much as he could and that she could come and visit them. You can be our babysitter, he said winking, trying to make a joke of the whole thing. You shouldn't feel you have to do all that son. I'm just being silly, she told him. I don't, he told her, I want this and so does Marie, she needs a mother-in-law, she has no-one now.

Only his regular visits that eased her sense of betrayal; but they remained a poor substitute and now even they were becoming more like whistle stops on his way between work and his new-found home. He had dishonoured their contract and she felt deceived.

She felt the tightened muscles relax in her face as she saw him emerge from Rory Farran's house and watch him shake Rory's hand before turning to walk towards his home. Rory was the local community worker, an ex-prisoner, leaving prison with a degree in humanities and had begun his new life working tirelessly around the area for proper street lighting, a park and a community garden for the elderly and young children to work alongside in maintaining it. There should be no barriers between peoples, colour, creed, political or religious affiliation, or age, he told the assembled crowd in the community hall. Some said he came out of prison a communist and that's why he threw his wife out. But, the real story, Rory had confided to Martin, was he had got Janet help because of her drinking, he didn't want her near the kids when she was drunk, which by then, was most of the time. He had hoped it would sort her out, but she signed herself out days later and the last that he had heard she was living with a fella in some hostel in Strabane.

That was another reason she missed Martin, he or his friends knew so much of what was going in, not the gossip or rumour that her friends were content to trade in; and she was careful to keep good consul and not break the many trusts he had placed in her.

She returned his wave and broke into a girlish giggle as he tripped slightly on a discarded beer can as he crossed the road. She had to check her forgiving nature, quickly reproaching herself and assuming a look of disapproval as he strode up the path; but her stoicism melted as he drew close. "What is it love? You look worried. Did Rory say anything?" She asked of her eldest child towering over her, his frame eclipsing hers in the doorway. His face looked troubled, the eyelids half-drawn defending his own against the searching eyes of his mother. She pulled his arms away from his sides towards her. "Tell me son." She pleaded.

"It's nothing mum, honest. And no, Rory didn't say anything, it was just a friendly call." He pulled a smile releasing the creases knotting his mouth and forehead.

"Now son, you can't fool me." His mother chided, not at all convinced her own conclusions were wide of the mark. She drew his calloused hands inwards towards her bosom and using the full force her position could command, she asked again if anything was wrong. She detested her need to resort to tactics with her son, but her desire to share in and be involved in his problems proved much stronger.

"Let's close this door mum and get in from the cold." He said stepping over the threshold and positioning her back into the hall.

Marie had gone to the living room window to avoid the sight, sound and smell of her snoring father-in-law locked in a lover's embrace with the armchair by the fire. Thank God, Cornelius had fallen into a deep sleep; the drive down to the house had worked him into a deep sleep. She checked her child's face, slapped red on either side by the first sign of teeth. His plump face was a picture of peace and contentment in contrast to the evening of confusion and argument since her husband arrived home from work throwing his overalls into the washing machine she had already filled with the whites. She looked to her child's face again for reassurance and wished to God, her father, whom the child had been named after, were alive. How she missed him and his strong love and sound advice. She was so proud of him and his small business selling and fixing watches, jewellery, mending shoes; anything that required patience and delicacy. She would spend hours watching him examine those intricate metal insides, his long, artistic hands, intelligent and strong. His strange looking glasses enlarging his green eyes would search out the problems. She loved the smell of leather and polish, the musty smell of the large collection of old books, books on history, car manuals, geography, science and medicine.

Contrast to Cornelius's surviving grandfather, her father did not drink and devoted his life to his young daughter after their mother died and he had spoilt her, sending her to the grammar school and paying for her to train in nursing at college in Dublin.

She studied her child's face looking for signs of her father, clasping him as close to her body as much as she dared to without waking him. Here was her hope, her investment in a better, brighter future. The thought of the future raised her annoyance level up a notch, the happiness she had envisaged was being jeopardised by something outside the family unit they had created; something seen as important by her husband, important enough to see her son deprived of sleep. She smarted with rage at being herded down to this house and her countless demands for an explanation dismissed out of concerns for their security. Security! The doors were double bolted, all the windows were double-glazed and made with toughened glass, they had an alarm and security lighting at the front and back of the house and she would not be stupid enough to answer the door to anyone at night. However, they were remote, not a house for a quarter of a mile radius and there had been a couple of break-ins involving a despicable physical attack on an elderly pair of brothers that had made headline news.

It was her husband's look of bewilderment that she should even argue for staying in the house that she found so infuriating, that he would not even listen to her point of view, that the decision had been made in their best interests and she was left no choice. If she were to stand her ground and God forbid, their worst nightmare occurred... She could not now take that risk and she joined him in the car, the quiet determination of her hurt set and embedded as they travelled. His apologising made it worse, the weak, implausible manner of it was indicative of his triumph for his common sense over her irrational, reckless point of view. She kept her silence, chained to it by the loyalty he kept to this family and the priority it held, at times, over her. She knew it would not be easy for Martin to let go, that wasn't what she wanted. She wanted some distance, a marking, a distinction between the family he had made and the one he had been given. The employing of Terence at the garage against her argument, based purely on business, for a trained employee was still a daily embodiment of her resentment.

"Marie." The living room swung open and Una stood by it, her face flushed with anger. "Will you come out and speak to that husband of yours."

Brendan sat in the kitchen after Terence had called out Una to the hall. He would wait for whatever domestic crisis there was to unfold. His presence would have only hindered the transition to a full-blown drama. He smiled sadly on hearing Una's outburst, followed by their mother's appeal for calm. He noticed the bastard's absence; the loss of his pragmatism was all the more conspicuous given the revolt on his mother's hands. Brendan appealed for his voice to hear the bastard complimenting the mothers, the two unified, interlocked in a formidable alliance.

Una ranted ineffectually, steam from the boil, loud and alarming at first, but just so much hot air. And poor Terence, in the losing corner, unable and unwilling to fight, in the pay of his opponent; in the losing corner.

It sounded like the beginning of 'fuck' but it was shelved under tightened lips. Brendan stopped figure skating with his finger on the tabletop and made a fist. Martin said nothing as he went to the sink, ran the water loudly into the steel basin, and poured himself a glass of water. He had changed little, his hair was cut short, still dark but duller, its lustre lost to the years. He looked strong and fit, no middle age paunch, no grey, he leaned forward over the sink and doused his face, his back broadened inside his jacket, thick wrists rested on the sink. He snatched a piece of kitchen roll and dabbed his face dry.

Brendan had imagined his demon, saw him so many times, so long ago, all in the same guise, but here, now, he looked just like a man, a married man with a child and a business to run. The body was larger, older, but it was the demon's body. Brendan's words were flattened by the dryness of his mouth when he asked if everything was all right.

"What's it to you?" Martin fired back. There was ferocity in his use of the word 'you' that ignited the hatred Brendan held for him.

"Fuck all." He replied with a ferocity and candour that equalled The Bastards.

"No change there, then." Martin shot back, rubbing his hand around his wet face, his green eyes piercing through the wall above Brendan's head.

"No change here either. Still running a tight little ship." Brendan remarked sharply, rising to challenge the self-appointed authority and morality of the beast.

His revolt was met swiftly by the weight of his brother's hand; he felt his head propelled back striking the unforgiving surface of the wall. Instinctively he held both arms up to protect himself from a further assault.

However, it never came. Brendan heard the kitchen door slam shut leaving him alone to deal with the lights popping in and out of his head. He heard the sound of blood pumping through a thousand arteries and somewhere the blood deserted him. He could feel it now, trickling down over his top lip and onto the floor. He allowed it to drip and fall in thick tears onto the floor. He rested his head between both hands. Drip, drip, drip it fell falling onto the tiling like sealing wax. He made a game of it; he was bombing behind enemy lines staked out in yellow, ravaging the blue landscape. He attempted one straight line of devastating fire on the railway line, a hospital, airfield and the enemy's centre of worship. He grew bored now having destroyed his enemy and without thinking wiped his nose with the cuff of his shirt. "Fucksake fuck!" He seethed savagely at his stupidity and dismayed by the dark maroon patch he had made on the material. He got up, went to the sink, and spat out the sickly mix of blood and saliva. The taste of it forced him into re-inventing the scene where he choreographed every move, leaving his the wretch in a bloody, pummelled heap.

He turned from the sink and looked at the floor where his blood had spilt leaving him with a gnawing sense of humiliation. He tore strips of kitchen roll and gingerly dabbed his nose and saw that the blood had diluted to a light crimson. Satisfied that he would not bleed to death he wedded the strips of kitchen roll together and got down to wipe the floor of his blood engraving. As he knelt over the blood, he was swept by a fresh wave of revulsion at his muted response to the bastard's action. He wiped vigorously trying to clean away the memory. He got up, threw it into the bin by the back door, and looked at his cuff. He went to the cupboards beneath the sink and looked for some stain remover. He pulled out the cheap washing up liquid bottles, the weed killer, carpet cleaner and there behind the cans of air freshener he recognised the box containing half a bar of stain-removing soap. He wet the cuff under the tap and rubbed the soap into the material until he had a rich creamy lather and grabbing a dishcloth he wiped it off and washed the cuff again. He inspected the mark and was satisfied that it had definitely become less marked and would not be discernable except if you were looking for it.

"Brendan, Brendan." Terence crept into the kitchen hissing . "What a palaver over nothing that was, Una's upstairs with Marie, the both of them gurning over nothing." Terence snorted derisively. Terence walked to the end of the kitchen and checked the lock. "All because Martin said there might be trouble in the town. Might be," he repeated for emphasis. "He was just trying to warn us to be careful, he didn't say we couldn't go out, you'd think we were being chained to the walls the way Una's carried on."

Brendan walked to the bin, lifted the lid, and placed in the kitchen roll in the bin pressing it down beneath some teabags and a foil dish so it would not be seen at first glance.

"Martin said there was a row outside Hegartys about an hour ago and the boys piled out to get stuck into a foot patrol, real John Wayne stuff, then the cops came and arrested two of them and gave them a real battering in the barracks. Martin says there could be some trouble because of it. There's always trouble at that bar, it's full of hardliners. We just have to avoid that bar and the street, that's easy done I wouldn't go in there for a pension."

Brendan continued to say nothing; he walked to the kitchen table, sat down and lit up a cigarette.

"Well I'm heading off, I'll nip out the back here, I don't want a lecture from me ma about watching myself. Brendan, lock the door after me, will ya?"

"Yeah, sure, go on." Brendan prompted, getting up to accelerate his brother's departure.

Terence opened the door and gave his brother a thumbs up sign before closing the door behind him. Brendan got to the door, pulled aside the net curtain, and watched through the pane of glass his brother break the lines and shapes of the outside as he progressed through the maze of wooden fencing that marked the perimeter of the back gardens. What a prick, he thought, the poor bastard, there he went enjoying a unique, taunting moment of triumph. He hoped she was worth it, he really did.

Martin stared out across the estate from his parent's bedroom. Only the dull yellow glare of the streetlights alleviated the tightening, dense shadows. He ran a finger down the glass, the waiting had become senseless to him and he had grown annoyed. He waited unable, unwilling to do anything else as he knew how stubborn she could be. He willed the door to open and they would find the words to talk to each other, even though he was at a loss as to what to say. He was angered at his impotency and the anger made him feel positive, but it did not ease his sense of uncertainty. He would argue his stated case that he was only acting in the best interests of his family, his loved ones.

However, he felt beset by complexities that he could not control nor arrest and he needed assurance that what he did, he did for the best. He would not think on the other matter that troubled him, he could do nothing to assuage or resolve it. It was best left alone and it died of its much-needed neglect.

"Well? I'm here as you ordered." Her tone was forbidding and uncompromising. He turned to find her silhouetted in the door frame.

"It wasn't an order." He told her thinking back to his knock on Una's door and asking if Marie would join him in his parent's room.

"Sounded like one." She said, not moving from the doorway.

"Please Marie, I was only trying to warn them to be careful, that's all. I didn't know anything about it until Rory called me over." He explained.

"So we're to be stuck here and you go out, are you not running the same risk?" His wife asked.

"No," he began pleadingly, "I'm going to the club for the treasury meeting. I have told you, I can't miss it, thanks to you and the help you gave me doing the books. The club's never been so well-managed. I'd love to take you and Con, but its closed-door policy tonight in the lounge. Do you want to sit in the bar with Con? With all the old men? Look," he said taking a step towards her, "you know its two miles from here and I don't have to go anywhere near the town, there and back. I'm going with Cathal he's to collect me in ten minutes." He told her, finding a note of defiance in his voice. He checked his watch, the watch she had bought him for his fortieth, and glanced out the window wishing Cathal would be early for a change.

"Why don't you just go outside and wait for him. Better still, go down to your mammy and wait with her. You've really upset Una, you've ruined her night."

"Come on I haven't." He opined. "I told her she could a taxi out to McShanes , I offered to pay for it myself, she doesn't have to go into town, anyway when has Una liked the town?" He argued, remaining by the window, fixed to the spot by the rigidity and sarcasm in her tone. He could see her body was closed to any advances he might make and he stood by the window, the unease he felt resting awkwardly on his broad shoulders "Let's not argue love, I'll be back in a couple of hours and then we'll go home and watch that film you were looking forward to seeing on TV. Here's the car keys. I'll leave them with you. " He said placing them on his parents' dresser. "The books are with Cathal, he's taking a look at them before the meeting."

Martin moved purposefully towards her, afraid of words piling up in the gulf between them. He grew disturbed by what might be said or unsaid. He pulled her close, exerting his greater physical strength to impose closeness. He yearned for her touch; the gentle sound of her voice, his body ached for the feel of hers. He longed to feel the swell of her hips, anticipate the feel of her small tear-shaped breasts. But they were withheld in flat resistance. He buried his head in her strands of fragrant brown hair inducing in him an uncommonly strong desire to be touched. "Please." He asked, longing to look into her hazel eyes. Yet her body stiffened and resisted his desperate attempts to overcome her defences and find himself alone with her. "Marie." His voice implored, betraying his fear and anxiety, but the conflict of wills persisted, she avoided his lips, and her eyes remained shut tight against him. She summoned the strength to fight the impulse to fall tearful and afraid into his arms, to do so was to surrender the higher moral ground she had staked for herself. Her desire to punish him was compelling and the ugliness of it nurtured her. Almost immediately, she found herself released. Her body immediately relaxed, and she found herself grasping for air, sucking in the tight warm atmosphere, startled to find she had been withholding her breath from her husband too.

She allowed the bedroom door to close, unable to stop the assault on her husband's feelings; she closed her eyes picturing his face a riot of mixed emotions. She remained frozen, suspended by the demanding impulse to hurt. Suddenly, seized by a frenzied need to see him, hold him, to squeeze out the fear, the anger, the inconsistencies that plagued her mind all these things sent her rushing to the door and onto the landing only to hear him speaking to his mother in a hushed voice in the hall. She froze. She stood motionless, afraid to make sound in case she were discovered.

Brendan heard the mother in a series of rushed whispers to her beloved and then the front door close. Brendan lifted his hand and made a gun and pointed out towards the mother in the hall and the son walking up the path and blam, blam, blam into their respective heads and blam, blam, blam into the lying mouths, and blam into the Bastards crotch blowing his heinous bollocks off. Sure that both fuckers were dead he sat back against the chair and lit up a celebratory cigarette.

Minutes later, he heard footsteps thunder down the stairs and the kitchen door was flung open. "Can you believe that man?" Una's open-mouthed outburst intruded upon Brendan's moment of glory of burying his victims in lime. "Gobshite." She walked over to the kettle and filled it. "I'm going to make Marie a cup of tea, and then we'll order a taxi and go to McShane's Inn, just to keep them quiet, ok?" She did not wait for his answer. "Marie'll stay in my room with the baby until Martin gets back. I think Niambh and some others from the salon will be at the Inn, you'll like Niambh, she's great craic." Una continued, she flicked the kettle on and got the cups out of the cupboard.

Brendan viewed her little performance with increasing contempt and loathing, the little woman had re-emerged, her innate domesticity, her concerns for family, the emphasis on the puerile galled him. He saw for her a future a similar sink somewhere in the estate. Despite her protestations, her ambitions and independence of spirit, she was her mother's daughter...

"Where's our Terence?" She asked, turning her attention to what she would serve for the tea. She set out biscuits and several slices of chocolate roll on a plate.

"I don't know maw." He drew out the nasty little hate he had for our Terence, our Martin, our ma and our bleedin' father. He despised her implications of family and his inclusiveness implicit in her performance. "He's gone out." He told her, testing his theory of regression in his sister.

"What! Where to?" her question was made all the more extraordinary by the open-gaped exclamation. She barely held onto the plate, exhibiting a manual dexterity rarely seen outside of a circus act. "Typical of that stupid wee shite. He'd better not be near the centre of town." She returned to her chore using it as an outlet for the busy anxiety pulsating through her. Cups were slammed onto the kitchen top and the cups hastily force-fed milk, spoons rattled in a translation of her annoyance.

Brendan my boy, you were right, for all her bleating she was her mother's little help. There would be no metamorphosis, just a slow inevitable assimilation and inexorable decline.

Una composed four cups in a tight formation; her father could make his own if he wanted a cup. She turned to ask Brendan how many sugars he took her mouth opened and a thunderclap of sound emanated, a dreadful rumble synchronised with her mouth and plunged both of them into a twilight world of excruciating shocked sensibilities. Automatic gunfire peppered the air and raped the senses in a rehearsal of blistering sound that contained a ruthless and indiscriminate danger.

Brendan blindly found the floor his hands held over his head in some absurd hope of protecting himself. It was shooting alright; he knew its clapperboard sound, aimed and directed; the blank, blank, blank of oblivion calling.

Una had fallen heavily on her knees; the fall, neither planned nor calculated wrought an awful retribution on skin and bone. Brendan called out to her on hearing her cry out, she didn't answer, he shouted at her if she was alright, but Una was lying on one side in a foetal position wrapped up in considerable pain. Cautioned by a second burst of gunfire he crawled on all fours and laid a hand on her ankle. "Una, are you alright? Let me see your knees." He struggled to prise open her arms, sewn together with clasped fingers. "Una let me see, your not bleeding." Una kept her eyes tightly shut breathing in slow, considered breaths in an attempt to control the pain. "Come on, try to sit up and I'll get a damp cloth for them, come on, please sit up and we'll attend to those knees." She slowly allowed her body to unwrap; she kept her hands attached to her knees as he led her gently to rest against the fridge door. He could her see lips tremble just like a child before the onset of a squealing fit. He stood up, leaving her for a moment to go to the sink and doused a tea towel in cold water. He squeezed out the residue and kneeled down facing her. "Here, this should help. Put this over your knees."

"Oh God." She issued, squeezing out the words in agonised monosyllables. Her performance rendered her brother helpless with spasmodic belly laughter, the build up of nervous tension ensured it continued even after sister's outburst of pain and anger.

"I'm sorry; I didn't mean to laugh. I know it's not funny." He laughed out his apology.

"We'd better see if Mum and Marie are alright." She said determinedly, making a poor show of attempting to get up.

"Stay there." He instructed." If there's any moving about to be done, I'll do it."

Just then, there was a knock on the kitchen door and it opened to allow their mother to ask if they were all right. Una hurriedly assured her that they were and they would be making tea. "We'll bring it in mum; don't worry everyone's fine, no damage done to the front of the house?"

"No love." She answered her child.

"Look we'll go and see how Marie and wee Con are." Una told her, feeling a swell of emotion rise up in her throat as she realised how scared she was that she might never have heard her voice again. She felt she was about to cry but she did not want to add to her mothers worry. She would act.

"Ok love." And the door gently closed.

"Brendan would you go up and see how Marie and the child is, will ya? And I'll get up and put the tea on. I think everyone's gonna need one."

Brendan helped her to her feet. "Are you ok?

"Yes, just a bit sore but I don't want to be climbing those stairs just yet." She said.

"Where do you think that was?" Brendan asked, he was growing concerned about

Terence and his whereabouts.

"It didn't sound like the town, sounded like it happened next door. But it's hard to tell with these things." He replied.

"The only place it could've been in the estate is at Miller's Mound, that's the only open ground around here." Una told him. The mound was a large hill of open ground that was used for scrambling, but more often by local youths to build fires and drink. It sat at the end of Cores road and was a ritual site for recreational riots. The only reason the security forces did not raze it to the ground is that it kept the rioters tied to a small area within the estate where damage was limited to the estate itself.

Una got out the bread and opened the fridge to get out cheese and ham. "Would you like a toastie?" She asked, trying to discipline the urge to purge the fear that resonated in her being. A fear fertilised by the awful violence and its sound had quickly resumed the air of normality but it made the normality appear abnormal and alien and made to be broken. It was not the time to succumb, not the time of betrayal, it would come though, ready to erupt at the wrong time and the wrong occasion.

Overhead they could hear the mechanised nocturnal bug clap heavily above the estate and the sound of distant sirens all marked the seriousness of what had just occurred. Brendan, concerned that these sounds and what they could mean, would alarm his sister into a session of morbid family concern and tears. He asked her again how her knees were and that he would like a ham and cheese toastie, in fact he'd like a couple, he was starving and he would need some lining if they were heading out for a drink.

"We couldn't go out now, not after this. I can't leave mammy and Marie, not now. Look Brendan; please let's see how the next hour or so goes, ok? I'll put the radio on and see if there's any news coming in."

"Sure." He said sourly, knowing very well that the idea of them getting out for the night was now impossible. "Look I'll get up and see how Marie and her child is." He said, conscious that the lead male role had fallen to him and he was determined that he would not be cast in the same mould as his da. "You're sure those knees are alright?" Una nodded that she was ok. "If you're sure, I'll get up and see them and you make yourself busy with the tea. I'm sure everyone could do with a strong cup." He told her ,becoming increasingly conscious of the mantle he had adopted.

He made his way to the kitchen door, he prised the door open and cautiously peered out into the unlit hall. This time it was Una who vented her fear and nervousness in a burst of laughter. "For God sake Brendan, don't be so melodramatic."

Brendan turned to his sister joining in her laughing at what his performance must have looked like. "Aye, aye captain. I'll get on upstairs." He saluted her and opened the door to carry out her instruction. He peered into the unlit hall fighting an insane impulse to switch on the hall light and advertise his presence. He pulled the door behind him mindful not to close it completely. He felt completely alone and wondered if he should try and get eh John? to stir from his hideaway. Outside, excited voices charged the air with the darkened hall vastly amplifying an indiscernible importance. He stood at the door listening to the magnified pastiche of calls, shouts, cheers, whistles and running feet that brewed in the quietened hall. It was as if the air itself had been revolutionised and the voices of the oppressed were in uprising.

He looked to the living room door fearful of it opening. He looked to the stairs and he felt incarcerated. He missed Francis. He missed Gerry for fucksake. He had never felt so far away from her and she had never felt so far from him. It was at that moment, in a spark of recognition, he knew she was truly lost to him. There would be no tearful reunion, or fateful meeting, no miraculous reconciliation he could conjure up his mind and want made real. A meeting where they would talk quietly, tentatively, then laugh as they recalled the good times they shared. Then they would find a coffee shop so they could prolong their meeting. He would tell her of his enrolment at university and how his stories going to be published and he was buying a house now; he'd applied for other jobs that would lead to a meaningful career and she would be delighted for him. She would tell him that her life was much the same, her career in psychology had been kick started with a post working with those dependent on drugs and alcohol, but her life was missing something and it had become functional, forced. He would joke that it was because she missed him and she would look at him and tell him earnestly that it was. He would tell her that he missed her too.

"Jesus, I'm losing the plot, eh John?" But eh John was not to be enticed, he was sulking at the paddies dishing out some of what they had received. Fuck him. He began climbing the stairs, moving stealthily, keeping the noise to his movements to a minimum. He enjoyed the predatorial nature to the execution of his task and on the top landing; he again had to suppress a dangerous impulse to look out of the window. It seemed absurd to be so conscious of his security, judging from the sound of the voices singing to an orchestra of alarms and sirens that ripped the night air like technological banshees. However, he remembered how a classmate, back in Belfast, had lost his mother when she went to the window to see into her street after a blast bomb was set off as a foot patrol passed and a trigger-happy soldier shot her dead.

He straightened up from his crouched position and looked to the door to Una's bedroom and he became hesitant. The wedding invite embossed in tacky gold lettering requesting the pleasure of his company and guest suddenly flashed before him. He tore it up, binned it without thinking, and thought no more of it. Now the thought of it and his lack of a RSVP haunted his every step as he inched his way to the door.

He knocked once, a light tap, conscious not to alarm. "Hello, Marie, it's Brendan." He said to the door. *Remember me? The one who couldn't go to your wedding because he had viral conjunctivitis.* Yes, that twat, now we established who we are and where we stand, he pushed down the handle and slowly opened the door.

A single bedside table lamp lighted the room, the curtains were drawn and he could see Marie sat on the bed with her back to him. He could see the soft top of the child's head with long strands of blonde hair brushed down to the forehead. With a tilt of his head, he could see that Marie's blouse was undone exposing the curved forbidden flesh of a breast. She folded the blouse quickly over covering her nakedness and shaming him for his stare.

She brought the child up to rest against her chest and she looked to down upon her child to see if he still slept he imagined. She turned her head and nodded to him in that peculiar way that intimated that he could speak now. Even though moments later, he regretted that she had.

"And all I got was a Farley's Rusk." He snorted out his small laugh as the still born atmosphere begged to be broken and he had to inject some space in which he could breathe; but his remark sounded crass and inappropriate and the faint smile on her lips fractured and disappeared and looked gone forever.

A terror ravaged her face, draining it of colour to point of translucence. He glanced away looking into the farthest corner of the room unable to bear witness to the remorseless show of concern for the husband she took.

He always imagined her to be fucking simple or a troglodyte, desperate to have married the Bastard, but he saw the photographs of the smiling bride that granny proudly produced after copies were sent to her and were now adorning the front sitting room. She said it was a real pity he had missed it, as he flicked through the set of photographs. He grimaced at the smiling, happy face of the bastard and was surprised and intrigued by the bride's attractive face; no missing features, arms and legs no apparent psychological or pathological deficiencies. She was lovely, nice, his granny told him, a trained critical care nurse; so she wasn't stupid either. All this confounded him. He readjusted his view of her and thought her gullible, easily duped and he forgave her crime as she was the innocent party and he hated the Bastard even more for this corruption.

He waited an age before he looked at her again from the corner of his eye, he remained motionless afraid that any movement might provoke a reaction from her; but she concentrated on her child who made a tiny sneeze in his sleep. A strong, angular jaw line and a fine long nose that lent an intelligence and refinement to her face tilted in towards her child and she kissed his head tenderly. He could only look on unable to move, he now required her dispensation to leave, and he needed her to expel him from the room.

He was struck by the vibrancy of colour in the room, the strong deep richness of the terra cotta walls, the yellow skirting, the radiator painted in both colours, the matching duvet and curtains with its isometric patterns.

A neat, compact, capsule.

Then he realised where he had seen it before. He was standing in a replication of the bedroom in the flat.

It was a magpie's nest of contraband and ideas, planned and engineered to act as a buffer, a haven from the outside world.

He felt his anxiousness rise at his confinement and mushroom in the heat and silence. The child sneezed again and his mother there there'd him, shushing him in a low comforting voice as she gently rocked him.

It was his first glimpse of the child's face, there had been an informal invite to the christening over the phone, using granny as a conduit to sound him out. Not able to cite another case of conjunctivitis he used a holiday break he and some friends had pre-booked. They would lose the deposit if they cancelled at such short notice he wailed to his granny from his bedroom. She said that was all right, they'd understand. He could hear the excuses reverberate around the room, in, and around his ears like spectres. The child let out a tiny sneeze. He felt compelled to speak. "How's the little one? He doesn't have a cold has he?" He asked brightly hoping to dispel the flourishing silence.

"No, he's fine. It's most likely the change in environment for him." Her voice was flat and unemotional and gave nothing of her personality or character or of her opinion of him. It served to impress a real sense of detachment between them.

"The tea will probably be ready by now." He had gone to the window and peered through the gap onto the back of the estate. He could see the helicopter hover over what he knew to be the town centre, bearing down a great bale of light. He noticed she didn't seize to warn him to be careful; it would probably have made her day to see a hail of bullets rip his bloody head off. "No-ones injured or anything, that's the main thing." He said, very aware of the glaring holes in his analysis. "I'll get down and see if Una has the tea made."

Yes, you do that and get the fuck out of my sight he imagined lay behind her simple '

'Ok.'

"Well I'll get down, is there anything you need brought up? For the child?"

A simple 'No' was all he heard from the movement of her blonde head.

He made for the door and got outside the room where he could breathe. He told himself that he did not care what she thought, but he had to stop on the landing to check the irregular breathing spawned by the crass ineptitude of his performance and he could not understand the gnawing sense of failure that followed him downstairs and into the kitchen.

Marie shifted her body as quietly as she could and as quickly as she dared to settle her back against the head of the bed and slipped into a train of thought provoked by the blast and its snapping cousins. Thank God, she had cushioned her son from the worst effects by drawing him deep into her, surrounding him with her body. She saw with clarity that she had kept dulled by excuse and indecision; that if they were now to survive as a family they would have to cut the suffocating links with Deirdre. She had bit her tongue and held her point of view, kept it subdued, fearing she would be seen as going too far, too demanding, a caricature of 'er indoors, the woman who made the lives of men one of quiet desperation spawning, the trouble and strife that men loved to propagandise in a thousand bar jokes.

She had been blown, literally out of her stupor, a stupor induced over time by her husband's obduracy. She had been shown that the grasp on life that they all had was short and at all times tenuous and it emphasised her treachery of the life she was making of hers and her son.

"Well, how are they?" Gushed the anxious voice.

"Shaken, not stirred." He replied facing down his sister's urgent enquiry with laconic delivery. He needed to lance this particular boil before becoming subsumed by family concerns.

"Mum's distracted, she's glued to the box and she has the radio on in there. It was a car bomb and they're saying that nobody's been injured thank God." Una said, having completed her domestic chores, she was now preparing to leave with the tray. She stopped, the milk carton suspended in her left hand not quite at an acute angle for its contents to spill. "I had to tell mum Terence was upstairs in his room with you. Mind you," she said, "I don't think she believed a word." Her conclusion brought to an end the miserable wait for the milk. "Shite." She said stepping back from the small amount she spilt onto the kitchen top.

"Don't worry about it. I'll wipe it up. You get on up to Marie and the child."

"Ok, God," she said, pausing setting the milk carton on the tray, "Brendan, Martin and Terence are still out there."

"It'll be alright, don't worry, as you said, there's no reports of injuries let alone fatalities, so it'll be alright, there probably having trouble getting back to the estate because of security. You got more injured than anyone" He said smiling, trying not to sound agitated or bored, but like a brother. It was not something he had practised. Her frenetic energy filled the kitchen fed by spoonfuls of nervous emotion that went off in a series of implosions that her voice gave vent to. You could see it working on her in the way she busied herself. Here was life sponsored by the fear and exhilaration of imminent change that was enticingly close.

"I'd better bring a jug of hot water for the baby's bottle." Una explained clicking on the kettle.

"I don't think that'll be necessary, he's using something much better." Brendan told her and slumped into the chair. He sat up re-establishing his shape from the slump he had consciously allowed his body to fall into to express his depressed state of mind. He wondered if he would ever get out for a pint, he felt at one with his separateness, detached from Una's little dramas; he saw the glory of a triumphant loneliness and the beauty of his redundant soul. He took the mug that Una had brought to him prompting him to sit up "Thanks. Do you think we'll get out for something slightly stronger later?" He asked attempting a jovial tone.

"As soon as they both get back and it's safe, we'll get a taxi out to McShanes, it's open to all hours. I need to get pissed after all thus" Una told him and smiled a smile that Brendan found completely disarming. Jesus, my sister is one heartbreaker, he thought proudly. "I'd better get up to them; it'd be a sin to leave them alone any longer."

Brendan paused before saying 'I know you should' but for a moment, he did not want to speak; he wondered if he ever wanted to again. He wanted Frances, he wanted Granny, he wanted the pub with their persiflage, drinking at the bar, on the bar even, peppering their conversations with words like transubstantiation, logorrhoea and sobriquet; though quite how they could fit those into a stream of bullshit had him conquered now. However, he felt exhausted by his selective use of language and tone since he had arrived, seeking appropriate words and sentiment, to acclimatise to the situations as they arose.

"Ok." He barely managed. He got up and opened the door for Ulna to pass through and on up the stairs to attend to Marie and her child with hot tea and her pre-occupationary talk.

He sat back in the chair and pulled out another cigarette, looking into the box he had only nine left and knew he would have to get out soon to get another pack. His first drag was a long, deep inhalation of thankfulness for being on his own and using his feet he tippy-toed the chair back to rest against the wall. He did not want to think of the bastards strike, his head throbbed slightly, but there was no bump or obvious damage except for the bit lip on the inside of his mouth. He did not want to think of Frances, how it was her who had been the catalyst for this journey and therefore responsible for his miserable incarceration. She would deny it of course, telling him it was entirely his own fault, if he had thought of her more than being the punch line to a joke, to be the centre of whatever attention there was to be had. Just this, instead of going to University or college or making an effort to be someone to do something with the potential he clearly had. Why do they do that? Why can't they leave you the way they found you. He grew alarmed as her voice was growing fainter, she was sounding further and further away from him.

They meet you in a bar, you're drinking with your mates, you're talking shite, probably. Nevertheless, its funnee shite and they see enough to want to go out with you and then down the road somewhere they want you to change completely, to cast off that person they first wanted to be with and with a metamorphosis, change into somebody you're not. Is it true that all girls are in love with their fathers? That's whom they want their partners' husbands to be like. If that's the case, stop clipping your nose and ear hair, get your head shaved all around the top, leaving some at the sides of course, you could dye that grey later, get out the tank tops and hey presto you're Woody Allen and with the sexual magnetism that all women secretly yearned for. The love that cannot remember its name!

He was jolted out of his indulgent thought process by a noise to the right of him, just to his right. It was a regular noise, persistent in its pattern with several lapses between its resumption. He tried to decipher its meaning between the local radio station, the helicopter, the dulled alarms whining, the noise from the radio and he held fast in his chair listening for it to go away.

Someone was at the back door. Jeezus, it could be Martin, you mean the bastard he quickly corrected. He was outside on the run from the old bill and the three bob bits, a breathless fugitive dressed in battle fatigues, gun in hand, ready to blow away his pursuers; ready to blow you away, if you open that fucking door.

"Open the door for Godsake! Brendan, open the door it's me, Terence."

The voice startled him into a high state of alarm. Brendan pushed forward to regain the four legs of the chair on the ground and jumped up ready to confront whatever lay behind the net curtain and the glass blackboard of the kitchen door. Contained within the flat darkness he saw a figure move, but he couldn't identify the figure.

"Hurry up Brendan; it's freezing out here."

Brendan stood up and walked hesitantly towards the door watching the darkness move like it had an unnatural life force.

"Hurry." Brendan moved at the hissed command coming from the outside, twisting the key and pushing against the locking mechanism that snapped open the lock to allow what was outside, in.

"God, it's a nightmare out there." Terence gushed; spilling into the kitchen accompanied by a fresh late evening chill and a companion whose hand he clasped. "We've been stopped at nearly every corner, haven't we Dervla?"

Brendan stepped back to allow the both of them into the kitchen. "This is Brendan, my much older brother." He smiled and gestured with one hand his stage introduction of his brother. "And this is Dervla." He said, repeating his gesture this time with the other hand. Brendan gave brief 'hi' to her nod. The introductions concluded, Terence guided Dervla past Brendan to the table. "Come on let's get seated and warmed up." He ushered her into the chair Brendan had just vacated.

Brendan went to the door and stared out over the roofs and aerials of the houses unable to see anything of the incident that had aroused such technological screams to be unleashed into the night air. He shut the door and turned facing the pair now seated at the table. He could see that Terence held his hands out onto the kitchen table in search of hers. But Dervla kept her hands clamped firmly between her legs close to her knees to give the impression of seeking much needed warmth. Brendan felt acutely aware of his displacement by the two new entrants. He walked to the cooker in search of something for him to do.

"I'm sure you could both be doing with something to warm you up, would you like tea?" He directed the question to Dervla but Terence hastily accepted his offer. "Or coffee? If you prefer coffee." Terence added, looking earnestly at Dervla's face.

"There's hot chocolate there to, if you'd like that." Terence said encouragingly to Dervla. She shook her head in such a manner that did not express a preference for anything offered. "Tea'll do." Terence told him flatly.

Brendan filled the kettle, plugged it in, and pressed the switch on ready for his shift at café O'Donnell, the newest recruit in generations dedicated to domestic servitude. Have the special, cup of tea, fag and a sympathetic ear. He emptied the teapot of its sodden kidneys into the sink and rinsed the teapot, humming to himself; conscious of the role he had taken, exaggerating his movements and purpose in a calculated insult to the generations of charwomen whose blood ran through his veins.

Terence sat with Dervla staring at the zip running down the centre of her torso, watching the slight drizzle of rain glisten the black leather; the same rain they had ran from when they had met in the square; the same rain they had embraced each other when the world they took for granted appeared to crumbling around them. Only minutes before he had stood by the side of the post-box smoking a cigarette, waiting for her; staring at the face of his watch as it passed the scratch marked above the number four several times. Before the second hand got to seven on its fourth orbit her taxi pulled up to the pavement. Michael, her brother, brought the car to Newry for all its servicing as part of the warranty. He had pretended to take offence that her brother wouldn't use their garage and Dervla stroked his forearm telling him not to be too upset and that when she got her Lamborghini he could change the water for the window wipers. He smiled into himself at the memory.

Feathers of excitement fluttered in his throat and floated to his stomach as she stepped form the car. Frustratingly, she stopped as she closed the door, leaning in through the window for a final word with the taxi driver as if she couldn't have said everything needed to be said in the taxi. Cheeky bastards them taxi drivers, he concluded. Come on Dervla, he demanded impatiently. But the waiting only served to increase his sense of anticipation and excitement and gave him the chance to chew down several fruit pastilles to hide his smoking.

This was their meeting place; he was heartened she had agreed to meet there tonight. It told him that she must have attached some importance to what they had, central, neutral, with people going and coming in cars, buses vans and on foot; it felt like a crossroads. 'Their brief encounter,' only with buses she said. He didn't understand the joke but laughed anyway, he always felt the compulsion to laugh in her company. He loved the idea that she concealed to her family about coming into town to meet him, as she should be studying most nights if she were to become a dentist like her father. He was convinced it was a testament to the strength of feelings she held for him. He concealed his relationship from his family for very different reasons.

Terence reached out to her across the kitchen table; he drew out her hands, clasped as if in prayer. They were warm to the touch, soft, fleshy and clean. He held them reluctant to ever let go of those hands he loved. He looked at the polished shells of her fingernails; those would never change, no matter where she went. There was longevity and continuity encased in those small, manicured half-moons; a longevity and continuity he longed to share. Yet he knew in his heart his tenure was less assured, extended by her failure in one of her A levels last year and now the re-sit which had taken place and had gone, for him, unnervingly well.

"Terence." Brendan said at last staring into the panoramic view of the kitchen filmed on the roundness of the stainless steel kettle. "I think it would be a good idea for you to show your face in the living room." He watched his brother linger at the table still holding onto Dervla's hand. It felt like voyeurism at its lowest, with him standing at the sides, without company, without a ticket.

"Yes, you're right. I'll go and show my face, let mum know I'm ok." Terence complied, resigned with relinquishing Dervla's hand to the uncertain future. "After that, we'll get you home." He told her in a promise and slowly and gently released her hand.

"Don't go in with your jacket on." Brendan pointed out as his brother got up from the table and reached for the door. Terence quietly took his advice, unbuttoned his jacket, and placed it over his chair.

"Won't be long." He assured her.

"Ok." She smiled back up at him, the smile disappearing as soon as he left the kitchen.

Brendan watched in the widescreen of the stainless steel teapot and a serrated stab of envy attacked him for the closeness and affection intimated in their exchange.

Dervla retracted her feet and hands as Terence left the room, the hard rubber of her soles scraped the floor below the seat of her chair. She lowered her hands into the bowl of her crotch to make herself invisible to Brendan until Terence returned to the room.

"Do you take sugar Dervla?" Brendan asked with his back to her, he took out three cups and waited over the kettle to boil. He turned down the volume on the radio fearing it's constant updates were intrusive and unsettling making the incident never far from their consciousness.

"No, none thank you, just some milk." She answered him in a voice subdued by politeness.

"Dieting eh?" Brendan said, immediately regretting the remark. "Would you like anything with your tea? Biscuit? Sandwich?" He quickly followed up. Box of buns, family bucket of Kentucky fry, ha, ha, he countered to evade the sense of embarrassment he felt and may have caused.

"No, nothing thanks" She submitted without looking up from her hands.

"I think we have semi-skimmed." He teased, opening the fridge door, hoping she would be receptive to his playfulness.

"Just a drop, please."

"A drop it is." He took the carton of milk and put in the drop she asked for. The kettle boiled he poured the water into the teapot where he had placed three teabags and lifted the pot to swirl it around and then poured out the tea for him and Dervla. He placed it back on the electric ring and turned the heat on to its lowest. He took her cup, placed it on the table, and returned to his post at the cooker. Dervla made no move to drink from the cup; she remained perfectly still, only a slight pulse move on the small belly of skin under her chin.

She had not bothered to sweep away the long loose strands of her dark hair that bound her pale, round cheeks. Using the cover of his mug of tea, he watched her breath being pushed through the flared nostrils of her sculpted, upturned nose.

He sipped at his tea, enjoying the quiet moments spent alone with her. He imagined his brother's discomfort in the living room as he fought his mother's line of questioning. His mind operating on two fronts, worrying what his brother was saying, wondering if he had talked her knickers off and they were both at it on the kitchen table making little fuck faces whilst he was trying to fend off his mother's questions. Brendan took a bite out of the digestive biscuit and pondered on the incongruity of the relationship.

Although he knew nothing of Dervla, her clothes strongly suggested a disposable income, her boots were real leather and looked brand new, her jeans were new and probably designer as was her leather jacket;and her hair had been cut professionally and coloured slightly. A tampax girl, modern symbol of the freedom and choice of a new generation of women emancipated from their enslavement of their bodies. He guessed there was most likely a social and intellectual chasm too. Terence was good-natured and funny, largely unintentional, he granted; but he wasn't too far up the evolutionary scale, no wot I mean?

"Tea alright?" He asked.

"Yes, it's fine." And she placed a hand around the cup.

"It must have been pretty traumatic being caught up in what happened." He said.

"Yes." She said quietly and lifted the cup up to her mouth. "It was." She confessed.

"Look have you had a chance to contact your family, to let them know your ok?" He asked.

"No not yet. Dad's away on business and my brother is in Edinburgh." She recited it as if it was a resume. Dervla knew her sister would have been miles from the town, she had left them in the centre of town and sped off to be with her boyfriend and it was at least half an hour before the explosion. Dad was in Waterford. But she would have to get home soon in case they saw the news or heard it on the radio. But dad would be at a late dinner no doubt. Business came first and this trip was as important as all the rest. Michael was just the same about work, although he did find time to go horse riding with her when he was home; but there was no substitute for her mum. When she were alive they were the female force in the house, the boys would be their own alliance against their womanly machinations to get them to make meals, to clean up, to stop watching sports on tv all the time, to agree that they knew best when it came to the décor of the house. It was so much more fun then.

"Sorry, I didn't mean to pry." Brendan said. However, something gnawed at him; he did not want her to believe that he lived in this house amongst them. His ego demanded that.

"It's ok." She replied simply. "Do you think Terence will be long? I'll have to get home soon."

"Of course. Look I'll go in and see what's taking him, if you like" Brendan set his cup and biscuit down.

The kitchen door opened and Terence walked into the kitchen producing a broad smile for Dervla. "Is there tea left in that pot Brendan?" He asked.

"Sure. I'll get you a cup." Brendan turned the cooker off and got a cup and milk from the fridge. "Is everything ok in there?" Brendan asked as he poured the milk into the cup.

"Yeah, fine, mum's a bit worried about Martin being out, but I told her, he's wasn't anywhere near the town. He's at the club, miles away. Mum's been in touch with the club, it's closed, only wee Dannys there closing up, everyone's left to get home after what happened. Won't be long 'til he's home." He answered, smiling at Dervla.

"Terence, how much sugar do you take?"

"None." Terence affirmed sitting down opposite Dervla.

"Here you go." Brendan said, walking to the table with both cups. "Just the way you like it I believe. He remarked, smiling at his brother as he set the cups down on the table.

"Cheers." Terence said.

Brendan knew the charitable thing to do would be to leave the two of them alone, but he was more than intrigued to see them interact, to see for himself where and how the attraction manifested. Moreover, his ego had developed a nasty little ambition to show his character and personality in comparison to his brothers. After several agonisingly quiet moments Brendan spoke.

"Cigarette anyone?" He asked fishing in his breast pocket for the pack, remembering now he had an emergency ten pack secreted in his travel bag. The contingency planning of an addict, you had to be proud.

"No, not for me." Terence hastily declined.

"Dervla?"

"No, I don't smoke. Thanks."

"Dreadful habit I know, been trying to cut them out altogether myself." Terence you crafty old sod, he thought, so Dervla doesn't think you smoke. Well, wait until you need one later fatboy. Most likely, you don't swear or tap yer ma either. To be high on moral fibre and low on self-esteem is a self-delusion that will explode in the face you have manufactured. Brendan knew only too well. His brother had retrained his voice, his deliberate enunciation had ironed out the sharper tone of his countrified accent, but it groaned under the weight of his constant vigilance, but the first time you let slip, you're fucked.

Brendan decided he too would play in the game and added his own voice to the charade. "What exactly happened out there, did you see anything? Terence?" He saw Terence hesitate and look to Dervla who kept faith with her mug of tea.

" I think they attacked the police station." Terence faltered and looked down at the table inviting Brendan's interjection.

"Good grief. Is that station manned? Not that that matters." The disapproving tone in his voice was mocking.

"They had used a digger and drove up to the back of the station and blew it up. That's what we heard on our way back here. We were a coupla streets away thank God. That's all we know. Once it went off we headed straight to the house." Terence stumbled to join the dots of what he knew and what he thought he knew to give a picture to his brother. He returned to his tea that was uncomforting liquid after his enforced admissions.

"That's absolutely terrible and pointless; they'll have wrecked a good part of the town and for what. There's probably no-one in it. Not that that matters." Brendan had conveyed his elaborate and false dismay and condemnation and returned to his tea to wait for Terence's reply.

"Terence, I'll have to get home soon." Dervla spoke up.

"Yes, I know." Terence said sympathetically. "I'll ring for a taxi, Area will work through the Apocalypse, they can go out through the back of the estate and park out at Corcoran square where we've just come from" He turned to tell his brother.

"Right. I'll leave you two to it, finish this upstairs." Brendan said, raising his unlit cigarette. "Wouldn't want to be the cause of any passive smoking." Brendan said, directing his comment towards his brother. "Nice to have met you Dervla, sorry it was in these circumstances. Get home safe and sound, the both of you. Terence, be especially careful coming back on your own" He told him. Before leaving them, he asked: "Do you need any money, for the taxi?"

"No, we're fine thanks." Terence replied tersely.

He had to resist the urge to say it was nice to have met the non-smoking, sugar-free Terence too "If you two ever have the inclination or the chance to come up to Belfast you're more than welcome to come and stay." He took his leave with a wave, took his cup and cigarettes and left the kitchen, leaving his brother to reclaim centre stage with an adopted character and an assumed personality.

He climbed the stairs quietly, slowly, not wanting to find himself in that bedroom on his own. Outside a large cheer went up into the air. He reached the landing and peered out of the window, careful not to disturb the lace curtain. People had ventured out on to their doorsteps, others had congregated at certain doors where the information was perhaps more readily available, the gossip more speculative. His eyes grew accustomed to the obstruction of the curtain, the poor lighting and the wet glass; dark, shifting figures, became groups of people, became pot-bellied mothers, their arms folded, uniformed in dark skirts and cheap figure-hugging fleece tops. All of them smoked. It made him wonder why she was not out amongst them making up the numbers. But then, she would be fastened to her chair by the measure of her concern for her beloved. He was still out there somewhere and not at home. He peered further up the road to where the laundrette of his youth used to be and was now a small off-licence. It was closed, but youths stood outside to trade insults with soldiers entrenched in and around garden walls. There appeared to be a checkpoint set up as the one car on the road slowed down dramatically as it approached Bell's junction where the road into town met the road circling the estate. Darkened green faces, wary of everything that moved, poked out rifles and scanned their hostile environment. He could see one soldier encamped at what used to be old Jimmy's house. Jimmy ('I'll put me toe up yer arses) end parentheses, McGuikian.

"Jesus." Brendan gasped. The front door had opened sending a shaft of light across the path and diminutive figure emerged, looking exactly the way Brendan had remembered him from years before. The scourge of all football, hopscotch, skipping, running, walking, cycling or sitting child on the estate. He saw the bald head look up and imagine his toothless twisted mouth, purpose-built for the filth that spewed forth from it. He was a nasty, ill-tempered, soiled-in-the trousers old bastard, who put the fear of God into every child, but in memory, he never raised a hand to them, his blood curdling threats were enough. Beside his left leg was a bucket and with Brendan imagined must have been an enormous last gasp effort was hoisted to waist level. Those vital seconds of raising the bucket had given the soldier the time to escape over the wall. Jimmy was not to be denied his moment to strike out. He would never allow himself to be outdone or out manoeuvred. He tilted the bucket and with what could only have been with a Herculean effort from every sinew, every flaccid muscle, and every rotten impulse that coursed through his decomposing body he flung the contents in a move and aim of perfect precision to where the soldier had been. The water, if that's what it was, you could never be sure with Jimmy, splashed harmlessly at the wall and he gesticulated wildly at the laughing soldiers, ignoring the encouragement of the cheering youths. He turned, bucket in one hand and with his free hand bid them all a goodnight with two fingers and closed his door to all of them.

Brendan was jolted from his memories of old Jimmy and the scene he had created as an expensive-looking, silver car drew up to the house parking behind Martins car. The lights and engine went off and two figures emerged from the front doors, the passenger leaned in to release the front seat and help a third figure emerge from the back seat. Brendan recoiled from the window and shrank back into the darkness of the landing. He felt his heart pound, pumping blood to his head, which was now awash with thoughts regarding the men and their arrival. He knew the last to emerge was a priest, he knew from the clothing and the deferential way his front seat companion escorted him safely to his feet.

Brendan crouched down onto his knees and lit another cigarette. He opened his pack to use an ashtray, knowing he would remain there until they had entered the house. He knew they would. He felt it deep in his chest and he became crippled by his desire to listen to whatever was to unfold. He felt he was about to witness a self-fulfilling prophecy he had waited and wished for. Now he prayed, fervently, to be wrong.

The doorbell sounded. Ding, ding. The ring suggested that they did not want to appear be in haste or urgent need in their business. Oh what the hell, let's get out of this weather.

Ding, ding.

Brendan's desire to meet whatever was to come was satisfied almost immediately. The sobbing reached him as reverberating rings, open, loud sobbing that had signalled the owner had given up on maintaining any vestige of dignity or resoluteness. Terence, Brendan thought, it has to be. He could listen now to the crying and recognise the intonation; cocooned in his dark shell, surrounded by his own calmness, the cries acted like primeval urges that called upon him to embrace or repel. However, he was removed from his being;

he was without, he was void. He knew instantly that the beast was dead. But it didn't make sense the latest reports had confirmed that there were no fatalities or serious injuries; a few people had to be treated for shock, mostly elderly folk in sheltered housing some distance from the attack. How could it have happened? A stray silver bullet? But Terence's utter abandonment to his grief confirmed that clearly something as serious as death had occurred. Did he die in the aftermath of the attack? There had been a warning and the surrounding area had just been cleared before the bomb went off. Was he in a getaway car, injured, dying and then placed in open ground by his comrades?

The voices moved invading the hall, the door closed, trapping and fusing the grief that would now swarm each room and each room would contribute to the avalanche that would engulf them all, except him. He would have to act quickly, think about his response to the grief. He could wail and join the chorus and competition of the most grieved or he could try to be admirably stoic. He chose the latter as he could assume this in his new role as eldest child. He would have to improvise, respond to each situation as it arose; for him there was no guidelines, no conventional structure for him to follow.

The voices were on the move again, they were on their quest to seek out those within the house. He felt himself forced to get up and make his way quietly to the bedroom where he could prepare. He closed the bedroom door, knowing his respite would be too brief before the incalculable force arrived. He sought out the best place to be when they would finally arrive, somewhere where he could be found unknowing and unprepared. He positioned himself at the dresser and waited, trying to find which role he could assume. He could be Terence, burst into a flood of expectant tears, and receive the communion of comfort and understanding; or he could try Una, but all would be eclipsed by Marie's greater demand on the limited resources as chief- mourner- in- residence. The rest would be handicapped in the race for the most grieving; he wasn't even in the starting blocks. No matter, the one hundred meters was not his kind of race, he favoured the marathon; this would be his mother's race with her grief and energies tied in with the long term implications to her empire.

The voices were uncomfortably close; he could hear their feet squeezing out small, muffled cries on the stairs. He could hear a waterfall of whispered codes on the landing and then outside the bedroom door. He kept very still, feeling heated exhilaration in every suck of smoke he took from the cigarette.

He sought help from the reflection in the mirror. Fuck it, why did he care, just tell them to get lost, it was of no concern to him. But the eyes told a different story. It did mean something, more than he dared contemplate. His nemesis had gone, no longer there to sustain and nourish his failings, weaknesses and faults. The rationale behind all this was gone, rendered it meaningless, and left him with the reflected truth of his being.

He felt cheated, robbed and he stubbed out his cigarette on the base of the crucified One. He pulled out another waiting for the door to open before he would light up. He stood waiting cigarette and lighter in hand, Holmes without his Moriarty. "Or Tom without his Gerry." He laughed; the descent into self-mocking released him from the self-analysis.

Bare knuckles on the wood announced an end to his isolation. Unthinking, he rose from the dresser and moved towards the sound. He stopped himself, sat back on the dresser, and lit his cigarette. The door opened slowly brushing a whisper over the carpet.

"Brendan? It's Brendan isn't it?" The low subservient tone matched the tilting cower of the priests head glancing furtively into the room. He emerged into the room looking remarkably fresh, young, crease-free, only a sheet of lead-coloured hair gave a true indication of his true age. "Sorry to disturb you. I'm father Kieran." His apology gave him full access to the room, yet he remained at the door a long immaculately white hand clutching the door handle. To Brendan, his show of piety was a touch too theatrical.

"Yes father, what is it?" Confessions-at-home service?" The priest closed his eyes as an act of visible forgiveness, leaving Brendan to smile mechanically at the tasteless flippancy of his sacrilegious remark.

"If needs must." The priest replied at some length vainly searching for a dignified response to move smoothly and quickly into the role he had rehearsed since Father Peter had answered the call at the door and taken in the two callers who had informed him of the accident and the death of the passenger and the driver's minor injuries. Father Peter had baptised Martin, knew the family well, and had given him a run down of the family line on their way to the house. He had not told him of Brendan; it was only at the house that his brother, Terence, had told them who was upstairs. He was relieved that father Peter was anxious to go to the parents and Martin's wife. Father Peter took control, as he explained in the car journey over to the house, he felt that Father Kieran would have a greater affinity to the younger members of the family. He knew the parents well and he had baptised the child, it make sense Father Peter said and Father Kieran quietly acquiesced.

Father Kieran had arrived in the Parish a year and a half ago, and had seen his faith sorely tested by the spiritual squalor he encountered. From the youths who sniggered as he greeted them and made little show of the drink and drugs they were using to the despondency and caustic attitude that Father Peter had developed over the years of serving in such a parish. Unemployment, years of bad governance, little amenities had sapped the humanity from these people Father Peter had explained .This after a particularly nasty robbery in which two elderly brothers were badly beaten in their home for the princely sum of thirty-five pounds and a bottle of whiskey. They both remained in hospital for several weeks and he would visit them on a regular basis as their priest, but more importantly as he grew to know the two unmarried men, as their friend. He wanted them to know that there was kindness and friendship in the world. When they were released from hospital, the two men retired to their home and rarely left it. Within weeks Charles, the youngest of the two by four years died, and one month later, a day after the month's mind for his brother, David died from an overdose of the prescription drugs he had been taking for his bruised ribs.

The words of Father Peter now seemed like the bleatings of a defeated man, a shepherd who had no interest in the flock let alone the lost sheep; and in a small recess of his heart he despised him for it. He recalled the bitter laugh Father Peter made, as he informed him of the graffito painted on the cemetery wall. 'Is there life before death' it was a question he had more than once asked of himself. If ever there was a place in need of Christ's message, it was here. The people were dispossessed of their own souls, they needed the ministry of Christ to be restored, the hopeless would be given hope. He would see to it. He had spoken to Father Peter about trading in the car for a cruiser so they could collect the house-bound to celebrate mass or just to visit and look in on them. That was still under review.

"Smoke Father?" Brendan asked, holding out his pack to the priest.

"No, thank you." Father Kieran declined quietly with a wave of his hand and he gently closed the door behind him. "I'm sorry to be the bearer of such news." He began to rock on his feet inside his shoes. His voice trailed off in anticipation of an interruption. It was method of address he had quickly adopted over time to a point where it had become second nature. It gave the recipient the opportunity to spell it out for themselves, to draw their own conclusion and he hoped, lessen the shock. He found it especially helpful during those interminable confessions that had him wishing the confessor would tell the truth or invent an entertaining lie. God knew he needed every weapon, every trick in the ecclesiastical book available in this place heavily veiled in benign indifference and agnosticism. "I'm terribly sorry but there is no easy way to say this, but your brother, Martin." He paused momentarily over the name, "has been killed in a road accident."

Brendan thought it a strange qualification for the priest to make, "your brother Martin" as if it were required, was he not sure that he was his biological brother or that he had the correct house? Was it meant to have a greater impact, if so, he was going to be bloody disappointed.

"I'm truly sorry. It's a loathsome business." Father Kieran lowered his eyes in an act of respect interpreting Brendan's silence for shock and grief. Father Kieran gave him a few moments to absorb the news and gave his trousers a self-conscious wipe, making a mental note to iron his trousers inside out, just as his mother had done. He did not like Mrs McConville to carry out any of the menial chores that she was always only to willing to do. "Brendan, are you alright?" He asked, quickly returning to the business at hand, feeling his tangential thinking had bordered on a dereliction of duty. He was ever mindful of the need to maintain a reverential demeanour. All too often delicate situations, particularly tragic deaths could bring the priest into the world of passion and feeling that lost the priest the authority and objectivity they needed to truly help their parishioners. He had to comfort and communicate to them God's love through His church. "The car he was in was hit by a rapid response unit on their way to the to the police station . Apparently, from what we've been told, Martin was changing a tyre on the car and was struck by the lead vehicle." Father Kieran hoped an outline of what had happened would somehow help to make sense of the loss. "Father Peter will going with your father and mother to the hospital. You're the eldest I believe."

"I am now." Brendan found irresistible to say, fighting the urge to smile. How ironic, he thought, killed in an accident doing his job, but the catalyst for the events that led up to his death was the violence he had so endorsed years ago and more than likely up to his death. He who lives by the sword and all that, eh?

"Sorry. I meant within the home." Father Kieran added, to demonstrate that he had meant no disrespect or that he had not cared enough to know the family structure. He trained his eyes on the young man trying to gauge how he must be feeling, recapturing the pain and loss he experienced at his mother's death. But he had to dismiss those thoughts, as he needed to be acutely aware and responsive to his function and responsibilities. "You're going to have to be strong for everyone now Brendan." He added, attempting to find the right thing to say. "Your family will need you, your younger brother and sister, your parents and Mary."

"Marie." Brendan said to correct the priest, not in spite for he had no claim to do so in her name.

"I'm sorry." The priest said puzzled.

"Martin's wife. Her names Marie, Father."

"I'm terribly sorry, Marie, of course." The floor creaked in a lazy late evening stretch as the priest stepped back slightly on his heels as if he were distancing himself from his error. "Marie," and this time the priest emphasised the name, "your mother, father and myself, Father Peter and Councillor O'Kane will be going to the hospital shortly I believe.

We would hope you would remain and look after your sister and brother, if that's what you want. Your sister will stay with Marie and the baby. She's understandably in a deep state of shock. God be kind "

"I'll stay." Brendan said simply.

"Good man. I think Councillor O'Kane has contacted certain relatives so you won't have to hold everything to-gether on your own."

"Fine." Brendan said, unable to infuse his voice with any emotion. He stubbed out his cigarette to prepare to leave the room and fulfil the job description outlined by the priest.

"Grand so." Father Kieran replied, feeling he was now no longer required and if he stayed he would be seen as posturing, as procrastinating and unsure. He had to demonstrate that he, as the church's representative, could provide comfort and guidance even in the most difficult of circumstances. Now he felt the need to leave the room, he felt himself flounder in the face of the younger brother's abject paralysis of emotion, word and deed. The news he had brought to him had been received with a constipation of quantitative or qualitative emotion which he found disheartening and unsettling.

It wasn't just the emotional rectitude, which could be forgiven for shock or resilience, it appeared to go deeper, there was an almost palpable feeling of release surrounded the body language; regret and sadness, yes, but a relief also as when someone dies after a long illness. God forgive him, but he wanted to leave this house; tears, anger, even words of revenge and anger were all within his understanding. He sensed something deeper, beyond the normalcy of grief , there was loss but as to what that loss meant, was beyond his grasp.

"Well, we must get on. You'll be fine. Stay strong. God bless and take care now." Father Kieran was prompted to say as he heard the silent murmurs of succour and comfort glide along the corridor and towards the landing.

Brendan barely noticed his departure, head lowered, chin resting down on his chest, he had returned to a place he had not gone to since his childhood.

A small cluster of trees grouped at the bottom of a steep slope of a privately owned field. The children of the estate called it a forest, their forest; such was the magnitude of their imaginations. In reality, it consisted of about eighty trees, huddled against the neglect of their owner and a stream of unruly visitors' blind indifference. Its primary function was straightforward enough, it was an essential hide for persistent truants escaping the boredom of the classroom; trading it for a life on the high seas, a world brimming with cutthroat pirates, of injuns hiding in every pass planning bloodthirsty raids on heroic cowboys. That was before the 'troubles' came to the estate through the death of a local man. With the backdrop of the riots that erupted in Belfast and Derry the attack was viewed in the social and political context of the time. The death of the man shot outside The Hibernian club at the hands of the police during a fracas was seen as an attack on the entire community. Given the treatment of Catholic people in those turbulent times, that death was anyone of them. The arrival of British soldiers had re-opened ancient grievances and general hatreds had focused on the soldiers whose attitude and behaviour seemed hell-bent on renewing it with vigour. Those with longest memories fed the youngest minds and made the bitterest of hearts. Hatred flourished as people came to the realisation of their diminished status within their own country and saw it played it out on their televisions and newspapers.

Then one day it arrived at their doorstep. Martin was eighteen, serving his apprenticeship as a car mechanic, walking home from work one evening he encountered a joint police and soldier foot patrol which were routine for Nationalists. The local newspaper described it as an unprovoked attack when they had interviewed him. When he came home from the hospital to have his wrist put in a sling for heavy bruising and stitches put in the inside of his mouth. There was nothing they could do about his black eye. He said nothing to the reporter he allowed his mother to recount the story from the fragments he had told her. He refused to have his photograph taken, but relented when his mother insisted that the police 'couldn't get away with this, beating up wee lads in the street, whenever they felt like it, if they get away with this, they'll get away with murder. And they're supposed to be protecting people' Martin was adamant that he would not take steps to have the police prosecuted. The story in the paper was headlined: 'Is this the face of law and order?" With Brendan's swollen mouth, black eye and arm in a sling; he looked like a pirate. He became quieter, secretive and shunning of the family meals, coming home late at nights and roll into bed smelling like his father, dragging the bedclothes from him. He'd remove his trousers and leave his socks and shirt on, sucking in breath and blowing out a stench to fill the bed. He'd be drawn in his shoulders rubbing the fabric of the bed sheet, the buttons of his brother's shirt tearing at his chest and throat.

One night the shouting came and strange sounding voices he knew from TV came and despite his mother's shouting and fearful cries, he saw his nightmare end. He heard his father's coughing being led downstairs and the body in his bed was dragged cursing from the room while he watched the event being shadow played on the wall, cold and guilty that the hated enemy had answered his prayers.

His father came back several days later, his coughing worsened and he was admitted to hospital with pneumonia, while he waited for the return of the monster. He woke up in the cold damp most mornings, getting up early to sneak downstairs and dry the bed sheet and his underpants by the electric fire in the living room. He had learnt to leave his pyjama bottoms off so he could wear them on his trek down to the living room.

Outside the games had changed, cowboys and injuns, pirates and the high seas were forsaken for the real heroes and villains they had in their own country and in their own town; Ra men, Brits, peelars and prods. They drilled in earnest, sides were picked on the basis of size and aggression, his pedigree of having a brother arrested put him on the side of the angels; he was bomber, sniper and frontline rioter. The enemy were given time to establish their HQ, then armed with an arsenal tore from the trees and ground they'd attack. The chase was on down the slopes and in and around the trees, stumbling and hollering blood-curdling threats infused with passion and hate; they dodged sniper fire as they sprinted towards the invader who was, due to natural selection expected to put up fierce, but futile resistance. Nothing. They scoured the edge of the wood only to see that their enemy had made a hasty and tactical retreat across O'Hara's field having discarded their weapons, which had impeded their escape.

They gave chase, infuriated by their cowardice, their denial of a battle royale, the enemy were unmasked to be the cowards they knew them to be and only in a mood to fight when the odds were heavily in their favour. They had killed and battered their men, terrorised their women and denied the children a future of equal citizenship in their own country! They quickened the pace, excitedly jumping and hollering abuse and threats at Ireland's enemy who had thought her sons would not rise up to defend her honour. Yella bastards!

The captured were dragged back, made to stand spread-eagled against the trees, legs kicked apart; arms extended, their weight supported by their fingertips; protests slapped down. They were searched roughly, then frog marched to a clearing for interrogation. The prisoners shouted at, hit with branches about their legs and arses until some kind of information that humiliated the prisoner and their family divulged. Before their release the vanquished would have to denounce the Queen as an 'oul hoor' and that the Ra ruled ok. He had become interrogator in chief; employing the techniques he had learnt from the bogger and carried out with the excited enthusiasm and viciousness of a coward and a fraud. A most wanted list was drawn up on those who had evaded justice and a fire was made of the enemy's weapons.

He sat on the butchered torso of a tree caressing his weapon feeling cold, despite the heat from the blazing weaponry. He felt his face heat up and the sweat rise out of his scalp listening to his comrades free and ambiguous talk about girls and who fancied who and what they'd like to do given a tin of beer and a game of spin the bottle. He listened to their sniggers gang up on him as the war was left behind. He sat by the fire as the pirates and cowboys turned Irish Republican Army burned their weapons and made for the warmth and comfort of home. He remained under the soft, sombre, darkening clouds where the trees bore witness to his young agonies.

Sheltered beneath their many arms, feeling guilty for his part in their mistreatment, his cries unheard and carried off by the growing wind, from tree to tree like a malicious whisper and on out to the empty fields and towards the heavens.

Fuck, this succulent slice of mother's pride, this rainbow of substantive joy, mute and monstrous in unfeeling; he was left to shoulder all the blame, all the guilt that was theirs, not his. Words he remembered came to his mind. My words fly up, my thoughts remain below. Words without thoughts never to heaven go. Jeezus, how pretentious, how meaningless; the big fatuous nothingness, this was the contents to his redundant soul. He had denied to him the most basic of human instincts and the comfort that could be drawn upon. He knew the tears tickling down his face on a race down to his chin were only for him.

"Brendan." Terence was already in the room before his quiet call registered. Brendan looked up his vision blurred by the tears, he didn't care how it looked; his brother could mistake it for grief, it would be a natural assumption to make. Then again it was grief, grief for the caricature of self and his redundant soul. Now that was something to mourn.

"Yeah Terence, what is it?" He asked, wiping his eyes, surprised at how compassionate he felt towards him.

"Sorry for...ahmm, but Dervla needs to get home. And I was wondering,... if you could drive us." He paused searching the surface of the door for the next words. "We can use our Martin's car, its outside and the keys are now in the kitchen. Mum got them for me.Mum," he said tearfully, "God love her, and Marie, she handed them over and said to get Dervla home safely." His voice rippled and broke in a paroxysm of sobbing. "Sorry." He managed between deep sobs reaching for the door handle. For a dreadful moment Brendan thought Terence was about to collapse to the floor. An eon passed as Terence fought to suppress his cries, his body convulsing, still arched over, his head down.

"It's alright Terence, let it out." Brendan said kindly to him, still standing at the dresser, unable to move and physically console his brother. He remained motionless, fearful that he too would break down and would involve his truth in the hope to save his brother from his grief. But he could not do it, he could not subject his brother to the purgatory between two hells that he existed in. "I'm sorry Terence." He said, full of compassion for the heartfelt and innocent grief his brother was enduring.

"Oh," Terence exclaimed, raising his head and straightening up. "I'll be alright," he said quietly, "I'd better get to the bathroom and freshen up, make meself presentable. Big boys don't cry." He smiled sadly. "Would it be okay for you to take Dervla?" He asked, his face flushed and his eyes hidden behind a pool of shimmering tears.

"Yes, of course I'll take Dervla, give me a couple of minutes to get my coat and stuff and wash me face." He timidly joked.

"I'll see you downstairs then. Thanks Brendan." At that, he fell forward and embraced his brother, whose arms were trapped at the sides. "Oh Brendan." Terence sobbed into the cup formed in his shoulder, the cries warming him. "Poor Marie, mum…"Terence leaned his head into gentle contact with the nape of his brother's neck and gently rocked him for several moments.

Suddenly Terence broke away leaving Brendan to vault forward and seek support of the dresser.

"I better go, get Dervla, see you downstairs." Terence told as he rushed from the room shielding his face.

"I'll be down shortly." Brendan replied and watched as his brother turn and slowly closed the door behind him. Should he have offered him some morsel of comfort? After all, it wasn't any of Terence's fault, poor sod. But he couldn't, he stood ostracised from his brother's grief, here was a sacred moment in life denied to him, moments to which he had no claim. Now his brother's death and funeral and the inevitable cherished memories would galvanise and compound his isolation. He was a body now, death reduces you to that, immediately death stripped you of personality and character as those left behind try to exert some form of control over the incomprehensible concept of death and its eternity.

Oh fuck, he thought, Granny, had someone told her? Who would've? It should be him, he could do it right, use the right words and tone and be as comforting and loving as needed. Oh Gran, you're in your wee house on your own and he began to cry again. She would never be alone again he swore, never. He had the urge to race out after Terence and ask him, but instead he got his jacket, put his cigarettes and lighter in a pocket, checked that he had his wallet and wiped his face. He waited in the bedroom for Terence to finish in the bathroom using the time to rub his eyes dry.

The house felt eerily quiet and empty when he left the bathroom and walked down the stairs. Death had entered the home. Even though he knew Una, Marie and the baby were upstairs and Terence and Dervla were in the kitchen waiting for him to drive her home; he could not hear a human sound. It was if those harbingers of the news of the death had taken all life with them as they left. He could hear outside voices and noises and quickened his step downstairs.

Brendan knocked on the kitchen door and walked in. "Terence, I'll go out and start the car. Do you have the car keys?"

"Yes, I have them here." Terence said and lifted the keys from the kitchen table. Dervla stood close to Terence and Brendan could tell that she had been crying. They were to leave both their coats either zipped or buttoned up.

"Terence, has anyone been in touch with Gran?"

"Dad rang her." Terence said pulling up the collar of his jacket.

"And? How is she? Someone should be with her. She can't be left alone in the house." Brendan felt his voice rise to breaking level.

"It's ok Brendan. Cousin Sheila is going over. Dad rang her first."

"Cousin Sheila, that's good." Brendan said he had forgotten about Sheila, not surprising, given that she rarely visited because of her job as the personal secretary for some CEO of a major industry. Brendan had seen him on TV once during his opening of a new plant for manufacturing the casings for some Japanese company dealing in microprocessors. God, she had to hear it from the ghost, wonder how delicately he had broken the news to her. 'Here ma, thing is Martin's dead, you know.' That'd be more like him. She deserved so much more, so much better and he was gripped by a wave of determination that he would make her life so much happier when he got back. Standing there with the car keys in his hand he just wished it was him there to comfort his granny.

Brendan sat gripping the steering wheel to his dead brother's car, having adjusted the seat and rear view mirror to his size. He had left Terence and Dervla in the kitchen on the excuse that he would start the car and get it warmed up for them; he didn't need to be told that they needed a few moments alone together. An opened packet of mints rested on the dashboard. "Won't be needing these any longer." He commented, and took several from the packet and crunched down on them, releasing a mint freshness in his mouth and nostrils. The light from the hall and the sound of the front door handle rattle as it opened and closed alerted him. He used the mirror to watch Terence and Dervla approach, it was clear Dervla was anxious to leave she was several feet ahead of Terence. Brendan turned the ignition and the engine rumbled into life and purred like an awakened beast that had been carefully and lovingly looked after.

Terence quickened his pace and reached the rear passenger door before Dervla opening it for her. He waited until she was seated in the back, before closing the door and joining Brendan in the front, muttering his thanks as he snapped in his seatbelt. Brendan turned the arm of the steering wheel and the headlights shot into life, he checked the mirror and indicated to move off.

The car moved smoothly, it handled well, responding to his every touch. You would expect that kind of smoothness from a mechanic's car he supposed. He slowed down as he approached the junction to the main road out of the estate. "Which way do we go, right or left?" He asked.

"Left." Terence told him.

The security checkpoint had been set up some hundred yards up the road and was examining a small Hi-ace van. The driver was standing away from his van giving a soldier his details. Brendan drew up very slowly and stopped yards behind, another soldier with black Labrador jumped from the back of the van and motioned them closer with his hand. The soldier pulled the van door down revealing the legend P.D.McAleer Glazier. Jeezus, a jamboree for him tonight Brendan thought. Windows and cars shredded, the material world humbled before the destructive power of the blast and P.D. McAleer was in like Flynn to collect the bonanza.

"Brendan." He heard Terence and looked ahead to where the dog handler beckoned him forward with and up and down movement of his red torch. Brendan drove up slowly until he was almost parallel to a gargantuan armoured vehicle; that looked like a recreation of a rhino layered in steel muscular skin.

"Evening sir." The soldier greeted him warmly, taking the smile he had given the dog into the occupants of the car. "Just a few questions." He said, flicking open his notebook.

"So long as they're not on geography." Brendan got in, thankful for a respite from the silence of his two passengers.

"And you are sir." He asked, staring straight at Brendan who was left to assume that the barrage of alarms screeching needlessly into the night air had drowned out his joke, as it was funnee. Brendan unlocked his seatbelt, ready to produce his drivers licence.

"Brendan McConnell. Here's my licence." The soldier took the licence and noted the details on his pad.

"You're from Belfast?" He asked in a professional, soldierly tone examining the licence.

"Yes, back home for the weekend, leaving my brother's girlfriend home." Brendan told him trying to be helpful to expedite the security transaction.

"And what is your home address here?" The soldier asked, his pen poised to take the answer down.

"19 Manse Road." Brendan answered.

"Down from Belfast." The soldier said absently to himself as he wrote the information down.

Yes. Down for weekend see the family and set off a bloody big bomb, Brendan said to himself, as if to paraphrase what the tone in the soldier's voice seemed to be implying.

"You must feel quite at home with all this tonight." The soldier smiled, but there was no trace of humour in his voice. He bent down and leaned in to look at the occupants; oily stripes blighted his young face, you could hear his breath escaping through his nose. The upturned fruit bowl on his head looked far too big for his head as it turned to focus on Terence. "And your name sir?"

"His brother." Terence replied unhelpfully, looking away from the soldier and out his window. Brendan could have laughed at that one, but felt it prudent to remain still and say nothing.

"And you are, sir?" The soldier asked in a composed voice that suggested he was well versed to these cat and mouse strategies.

"Terence." He replied flatly.

"And you live at the same address?"

"Yes."

Brendan felt a nervous bubble of laughter mercifully implode in his mouth.

The white van was allowed to move off and P.D.McAleer went to town where the streets where quite literally, littered with gold. The soldier stood up and motioned for a policeman to come over. "Excuse me, just a moment." He left the car and met the policeman halfway to consult. The policeman walked over to car and peered in, his large puritan face robust with health loomed in; his features as flat and featureless as the land that had forged him. He returned to the soldier and they consulted again. The soldier scribbled down some notes and returned to the car. Brendan had quickly glanced at the notepad reading off what the soldier had written. He noticed he had spelt Terence with an 'a' and 'McConnell with one 'n, he had spelt Manse correctly and had safely abbreviated road to 'rd'. Come on hurry up, it's bloody freezing, he thought, shuddering involuntarily.

"Ok sir, that's fine. Drive safe." The soldier said, slapping his notepad shut, to prevent Brendan viewing anymore. The chekky basturd, ha, ha.

"I will."

"Take this road on the way back, avoid the town." The soldier advised.

Brendan had to fight the urge to ask why, but he thanked the soldier for his advice and drove off slowly.

The road, barely wide enough for two cars and chiselled by the side of the mountain, rose steeply to meet them and Brendan worked the gears to make the drive as smooth and quick without appearing to be in haste. The road required concentration that he was grateful for, which naturally precluded him from conversation so he was not in any way culpable for the silence which had embedded within the car. Dervla sat in the shoulder corner of the backseat, performing her I'm invisible act. Brendan wished he could turn the radio on, but the winding road with its large bends ensured that both hands remained on the wheel.

Terence's gaze remained fixed out of the passenger side window his arms rested tentatively in his lap, Brendan imagined, the road was akin to the future Terence could see for himself; bleak, dark, long and with twists and turns. Fuck, what was his, if not the same?

Ahead of them, with the full beam on, some distance up the road, Brendan could see something on the road, something that was on fire. "What the hell." He said, to startle his passengers into life. He slowed the car down to give them time to examine what lay in front of them and to give them a fighting chance of escape should it come to that.

Strewn across the road from one end to the other, a makeshift barricade consisting plastic crates, shopping trolleys, half-burnt tyres, branches and from somewhere the architect's had found an old gas cooker. From the right side of the road behind large rocks behind the crash barrier, small figures emerged. They had a good vantage point the bend was acute and vehicles would have to slow down considerably or run the risk of plummeting down the steep rise that led to the back of the Moyle Road and into the estate. More and more appeared, their faces concealed by a variety of scarves, caps and handkerchiefs; armed with bottles, rocks and ugly-looking poles. Three of them cautiously approached the car.

"They should be in their bloody beds." Brendan thundered as he snapped the release on his seatbelt and wound down the window.

"Alright there?" The taller, leaner one of the trio greeted, leaning to peer in at the occupants. " Seen any Brits or peelars on the road?" He asked, blowing out the words through a green and white scarf.

"What?" Brendan asked with true incredulity. "Get that cleared; you could have someone off the road with that." He demanded, deepening the tone of his voice and mustering all the authority he could summon. He looked at the barricade again, the guts of a burnt out waste bin had been spilt out over the road and the stench from the burning waste was fouling the crisp night air. The smell infuriated him even further as did their dumb stance in the middle of the road. "Are you deaf? Are them ears painted on?" He shouted. Above him the helicopter kept its rhythmic clatter, the air was undeniably charged with adrenalin, it was exciting because of the potential for danger, he remembered it all too well.

"Look there's Terry." The smallest one of the three shouted, his face completely covered by a hooded top and a scarf. Brendan heard Terence open the door and get out, he glanced over to see Terence stand outside of the car and ask that the lads clear enough of the barricade to let the car through. His word was enough to have the young men scamper towards the barricade and wave to the others to come out from behind the boulders and bushes to assist. The tallest fought hard to keep pace with the dismantling shouting out instructions that had already been carried out. They were methodical, removing the heart of the barricade as if by numbers wheeled the giant metal waste bin wheeled to one side; leaving Brendan wondering where on earth they had got it. The bin had not yet been set alight, presumably so the bin could be removed then restored to the centrepiece of their barricade. There was method in this madness.

Brendan wasted little time in purposely revving up the engine until Terence got back in the car and the car screeched off through the gap in the barricade to the yells and salutes from the tiny apostles of terror. Either of his fellow travellers did not miss Terence's indiscreet acknowledgement in a show of support.

The journey continued in resumed silence, groaning under the weight of an old argument that no one could remember. Only the sound of the engine and concentrating on the road kept Brendan occupied. He grew angry at Dervla, he could see her silence as a form of punishment, the withdrawal into a tight-lipped defiance, condemned Terence to his fears and insecurity. And the poor sod wasn't equipped to deal with it. The way they would retreat into their own world you cannot comprehend and therefore engage. His grip on the steering wheel tightened this was just the type of strategy Frances would adopt. How would she take the news, would she feel for him, would she say he did not like his family anyway and he was using the tragedy to gain sympathy and comfort from her. He chose the latter and the tiny hatred that grew inside his mind engulfed the car to include his passengers who had brought it all to mind. Frances' family would heave a collective sigh of relief around the The Royal Doulton and give thanks for their daughter's escape. The fuckers.

"Slow down."

"Huh?"

"Slow down Brendan. We were nearly off the road there." Terence told him.

Brendan eased his foot from the accelerator, watching the needle on the dashboard dip from forty down to thirty. "Sorry about that." He said as the road stopped winding and straightened out before him and the drive became a comfortable cruise.

"Here, just on the right." Terence directed him moments later. Brendan approached the small, unmarked junction.

"Where to now?" He asked looking left and right for any sign of traffic.

""Go right and it's about four hundred yards, and then turn left at the sign, you'll see it." Terence told him. Brendan indicated and took a right and drove, moments later; they were approaching two large stone columns that stood sentinel on either side of a large black gate that marked the entrance to a long, winding driveway.

"This is it." Terence said. "Just stop here, thanks."

Brendan stopped the car metres from the gates which were set back from the lane. His eyes traced the driveway that tongued its way up to large house that sat on the top of a hill. He imagined the lane itself was seventy to eighty metres long. Atop this driveway sat the house; large round bay windows on either side of double-doors fronted the house. At its side a large garage. Dervla's hand was already on the handle before they had rolled up to the gates.

"Thank you Brendan, for the lift." She said, pulling down on the handle. She slid across the seat and got out shutting the door. Terence waited in the front and watched her go to the gates and search through her bag.

"Give me a minute Brendan." Terence said, releasing the seatbelt and opening his door.

"Sure, of course." Brendan said, waiting for Terence to join Dervla before switching on the radio. Terence walked over to Dervla as she had unlocked the gate and was about to enter the grounds of the house. Behind Dervla lay the grassy well-cut lawn with bushes dotting the length of the driveway up to the house. Brendan thought the scene was ludicrously symbolic, Terence just outside the gates, with Dervla moving behind them, her hand on one side of the gate ready to shut him out. Brendan took out several mints from the packet and concentrated on finding a radio station he could listen to. He looked up again as he found radio two, his eyes tracing the leisurely rise of the driveway that appeared as if it were newly laid. A large, stand-alone lampost, similar to those you see in films set in Victorian England lit the path to the front of the house and he could see that all the curtains were drawn and that lights had been left on inside the house. Then he noticed a 'Beware of the dogs' sign on the left hand column of the gate and wondered if it were for show only. His scepticism was soon answered; two large dogs appeared from the side of the house and bounded down the drive. They both circled Dervla affectionately, nudging their large heads at her legs for attention. Terence crouched down to stroke both of the dogs them, but they returned quickly to the object of their affection.

Brendan calculated that there must be at least eight to ten rooms in the house, two front rooms, the dining room, the kitchen, four bedrooms and bathroom upstairs. It was symptomatic of the Noveau riche, the emancipated Catholic, professional, landed, free to pursue the wealth and influence their protestant counterparts had enjoyed for generations. Terrence's plight was beyond redemption, the sight of that house daunted even him for God sake. It exuded wealth, its pursuit and above all its maintenance. He returned to the radio, the news had just ended thankfully. Some night-time DJ he had never heard of began inanely spouting about some band he had never heard of proving to the world that his lobotomy had been a complete success. The DJ then introduced a singularly unpleasant thrash of cacophony from a 'band that was the future of rock'. God help us. He took out a cigarette and saw that he had only four left. The song involved a good hookline, but lacked the subtleties to co-join its parts, it lacked a story and interconnectedness between its good parts, it sounded laboured and lazy at the same time. His music had gone. There were to be no more compositions, no more narratives, just the cannibalistic instinct to plunder the past. Come on Terence, let's go, you're blown out. he said, lighting up a cigarette. He rolled down the window unable to hear the words, if any, were being spoken by the two.

Moments later Terence walked back towards the car, his movement slower than when he left, hands in his pockets. Brendan watched Dervla lock her gate and walk up the drive with a large black dog skipping happily on either side of her, both nuzzling their necks against her legs for attention.

"Come on, let's get out of here." Terence said, as he got into the car, his voice like stone. He slammed the door shut and if it had been Brendan's car, he would have told him to be careful with the car. But as it wasn't and as much as his curiosity had piqued, he said nothing, checked the mirror, and indicated to turn on the road. "What way?" He asked.

"The way we came." Terence said flatly.

"Nice house. What's Dervla's father do?" Brendan asked, checking the rear-view mirror to turn the car.

"Dentist." Terence swore. "Big house, big money, just like the prods. He's a big cheese in the stoop down low party too, so he'll have plenty to say about tonight, talking a load of bollocks as usual." Terence fired his remark up at the ascending figure on the drive. "Come on; let's get the fuck out of here. We don't belong."

Brendan felt a burn of resentment by the inference that had included him, but said nothing and turned the car back onto the road. Perhaps he didn't, but he didn't like the implication that he was excluded to anything and included in the family.

"What's up?" Brendan asked.

"Story of my fucking life," Terence replied tersely, "she's applied to University."

"That's good isn't it?" Brendan said, looking to his left for any sign of traffic.

"Not in Edinburgh it's not. Tonight, of all nights, she decides to tell me." Terence glared out of the passenger window up at the house. "What a bitch, when your down they kick you in the balls."

"It's not the ends of the earth." Brendan said, trying to be helpful.

"It's not that, not the distance. I might not be university material, but I'm not fuckin' stupid. She wants away, to broaden her horizons as she says, but its more than that." He said, and then turning to Brendan. "And she said she'll be with me for the funeral, like it was fuckin' charity." He spat out bitterly.

"What did you say?" Brendan asked.

"I gave her directions." Terence replied harshly.

Silence returned to the inside of the car, Brendan noticed that Terence had dispensed with the need for his seatbelt and he reminded him to put it on out of a moment of empathy with his situation. Terence slammed in his seatbelt and sat in continued silence. Brendan drove on thinking that the scenario his brother had sketched out seemed uncannily and uncomfortably close to his own. But he dismissed it instantly, his had been a proper, real relationship and the breakdown had involved a battle of wills and more importantly a battle of minds. What Terence was experiencing was akin to teenage infatuation, puppy love, nothing that seriously risked his heart, mind and soul.

Minutes later they approached the bend where they had encountered the youngsters and their barricade. The youngsters had gone and the barricade had been driven to the left side of the road only a small fire was left to man the remnants of the barricade. Brendan accelerated and the car bobbled slightly, snapping branches as if they were bones, that lay strewn across the road. Yards in front a solitary tyre, half-eaten by fire smouldered in the centre of the road and Brendan had to swerve to the right to avoid it completely.

"Rebellion's over then." Brendan observed dryly.

"What's up with you?" Terence rounded viciously, startling Brendan and causing him to swerve involuntarily this time. "Everything's a big joke to you; us small-town hicks must be give you a right laugh."

"For fucksake have a day off, will ya?" Brendan returned." Those kids could have seriously injured someone or themselves, someone like Martin." He shouted back. " What would that prove? What point would have been made?"

"Same one we've been making for years; that we're not going to be treated as second-class citizens." Terence argued back his voice rose to an intimidating level.

"Shite. Heroes and martyrs eh? Churned out by old men, beardy 'oul bastards, licking their lips at the prospect, the anticipation, to turn young impressionable minds with their two or three words of Gaelic, just so they can be a part of something. Something that they can't find in their lives when they're sober and thanking their sacred hearts that it wasn't them or theirs getting buried, literally, up to their necks in it. They've put too many people in their graves long before their time."

Terence did not respond, he sat in angry silence, his arms folded tightly, his eyes fixed straight ahead. Brendan sat back in the seat, the argument had not been fair, he had rehearsed that speech many times, but until now did not have the opportunity or courage to use it. They drove under a laboured silence laden with the weight of the said and the unsaid until they reached the estate.

"Let me out at this corner." Terence snapped. Brendan pulled the car to the side of the road where two young men of Terence's age sat on the front wall of a house. Terence opened the door.

"Terry, a chara, c'mon over, grab yourself a beer. Bring your mate." One of them shouted raising a can of beer to greet him, his companion jumped from the wall and delved into a large blue that bulged with cans of beer. Brendan laughed in delightful recognition that the point he had just made could be borne out so quickly and graphically by Terence's own friends, he hoped the irony wasn't lost on him. Terence turned to look at him before leaving the car.

"Aye, we're all numpties to you." He spat. He pushed the door open and got out. "That's no mate, that's the brother." He told the two without a trace of humour and slammed the door behind him. The young man who had delved into the bag threw a can high up into the air which Terence caught with both hands to a roar of approval from his two companions.

Brendan checked the mirror and without indicating drove off. As he got closer to the house he saw dark pools of people materialise and gather; they appeared to be gravitating towards the house. They were vague, indiscernible blobs of humanity, some accompanied by smaller figures. The theatregoers, descending to take active part in the drama, everyone would get a role; well-wisher, sincere, the not so sincere, the curious, the bored, and those who would remain outside the theatre content to be part of the chorus. The main parts already assigned, with some supporting roles up for grabs amongst the flourishing mob.

Brendan drove past his foot edging down on the pedal, his need to escape the the set and flee the role he had been signed up for.

"A lorry load of volunteers went out for a packet of crisps. " He sang out in a gravelly mock falsetto, trembling with Oirishness. "They came across a mudder hung on a gallows tree, the cruel wind whistling through her bare fannee." He broke off; laughing at the ridiculousness and crudeness of the travesty he thought of everything he was encircled by. Fuck, how he needed this to counter the culture of death and deification he would soon be engulfed by. " Me grandadee, shot like a dog, in some forsaken bog. Me fadder taken by the blight and the heroes of ole Oirland put to flight, oooohhhh." He sang at the top of his voice. "Oh, the whole things a pile of shite." He burst into a coughing fit of laughter.

He knew the gradual rise of the road leading out of the estate towards the old quarry where the grey and white wall of mountain peered anxiously into a vast chasm dug into its heart. The razor sharp jaw-line of the mountain cut a jagged tear into the night sky; the merging synthesis of cramped colour darkened the evening as it squeezed out the last vestiges of light. There was something terribly familiar about the scene, too familiar, for he felt a stab of cold recognition and he acknowledged it by turning left at the unmarked fork in the road.

The car grounded to a halt, he remained in his seat, staring straight ahead past his knuckles, past a myriad of disjointed reflections super-imposed on the windscreen. He fixed his gaze to the beams of light penetrating deep into the grey nothingness and watched them disappear.

He switched off the rhythmic chugging of the engine, listening to it fall into a rumbling sleep, feeling an immediate loss for its company. He longed to be home, resting on the sofa with her, just out of the shower, wrapped in a large towel; her freshness and fragrance charging the air with anticipated love-making.

He reached for the glove compartment; feeling a conscientious driver, especially a mechanic, might well have kept a torch there. He was right. Among the usual paraphernalia peculiar to drivers, cloths, maps, spare bulbs, lay a black heavy duty torch. He placed the torch beneath his chin and pressed down on the on off button and stared at the grisly, macabre image the light made; dark, sunken eye sockets, jutting cheekbones and a large block of a forehead. He thought he looked like his corpse would. He took the polo mints and cigarettes, switching off the torch; he took the car keys and got out of the car.

He stood by the car locked the doors and took a deep breath of the cold night air and the fresh greenery of the grass and trees. Invigorated by the air and the memories that blew and swirled around him, he walked to the place where he had found sanctuary as a child.

PERSIFLAGE

A car drew up alongside Martin's car and stopped. The passenger got out and signalled to the driver to move off. The driver hesitated and waited as the figure broke the beams of the headlights, walked to the ridge of the steep bump of land, and began to descend.

The figure moved carefully, listening to the sound of the car reversing, dispersing gravel in its wake; the sound keeping company on the downhill negotiation of the treacherous surface. Balls of muscle at the back of the legs tightened in complaint as they dug in for grip.

A full stop of light opened up yards from the figure illuminating the last few yards she had to negotiate.

"Not up to this anymore." She would wheeze, attempting to engender conversation and embrace the familial. She would reach deep in the pockets of her long coat. "I had an idea you would come here." She would say, lighting up her cigarette, shielding the flame of the cheap lighter from the stiff breeze that swirled and blew in and around them. Again, he would say nothing. She would offer him a cigarette and despite his wanting one, he would decline. That was when he would turn from her and to the trees, his co-conspirators; they would share their common hatred of her and sneer with him at her pathetic attempts to strike up a conversation, however trite.

Then, as if she had been reading his mind, she would make an indiscreet show of tears. Her wrinkled fingers would rise up to clasp her face, her cigarette eaten away by the wind. She looked old, ragged and small, as if the years were driving her inch by inch into the earth. She was no longer the indestructible woman of his youth. She would apologise in a general way, not knowing if it was for the tears, the hurt, the abandonment. She would call you son. He would stare at the trees, the autumn leaving them bare and he would tell her not to call him that. He would sit on waiting, wanting another chance to hurt. He would like to tell her how he had to hide here after his place of refuge under the stairs had been discovered. The glory hole beneath the stairs where he would sit buried in her overcoat smelling in her smells; the smells of a mother, the best there is. He would wait for her to pull open the door and wrap her arms around him and tell him everything will be alright. And with those magic words he knew that it would. But he no longer believed in magic.

He stared out at the landscape, out over a patchwork quilt of fields to another town, its lights radiating out signals of despair. Small hopes and ardent prayers all went unanswered as the town's beacons glittered to a multitude of shattered dreams, damned to eke out some form of existence while a ponderous universe looked on.

"There's only about thirty left." He said, referring to the remaining trees." I used to have names for some of them." He laughed, feeling self-conscious and vulnerable.

"Here son." She again offered him a cigarette and this time he accepted it. Only the glow of their cigarette tips was visible between the two silent figures. Their smoke lifted by the wind, was carried on its swirling dance up and around the trees and on out to the rolling hills and fields and up to experience the emptiness of the heavens.

APORIA

The Scene: Three characters in a small room, all seated. Two characters dressed in white shirts, a blue tie and a red tie. One character sat in centre of room facing the other two sat behind a desk. On the desk is a manila folder containing a large number of pages.

"Well, quite a tale, wouldn't you say? Compelling in parts, imaginative, putting it mildly, in places, pompous, derivative, conceited, vague and feeble in others. Wouldn't you say? Let's check it against what we do know, shall we?"

(Character in centre of room shrugs his shoulders)

"The facts, (opens folder), let's see what we do know. The facts, family, let's see. Mother, father, sister, and two brothers. That much is established. All living in Belfast. All at the same residence. Except fro the older brother, who is married and with...yes two children, a boy and a girl. You agree so far? No? Yes?"

"All at the same address, yeah guvnor that's true." (Character in centre of room smiles)

"And further investigation reveals, the mother, a care assistant, having worked a lifetime in the RVH as a cleaner, a good lady, solid, maternal, loving. A mother any boy would be proud of. And he vilifies her. Why is that? Never mind, we'll get to that. His father, not a shambolic drunk, but a hard-working store man with thirty-two years at the same company, now medically retired, through angina and diabetes. Brother…"

(Character in chair moves)

"Uncomfortable?"

"Bored, mate."

"Younger brother, Michael, a CAD technician, in a highly skilled field, highly qualified and a bit of a sportsman with the cycling, done a few charity treks, Cuba, even Africa. Is that why he has tried to destroy him? Plain old jealousy? Well, let's continue, it's becoming clear, his raison detre."

(Character in centre of room sniggers)

"Sister, Bronagh, a personal secretary with Architects Dott and Wilson, designed that new hotel by the Lagan and the Shopping Mall just outside Bangor."

"Yes, lovely one that is too, me and the wife have been to that, great cinema complex." (Character in blue tie confirms)

"Well, what an odious collection of lies, half-truths, deceit, heinous character assassination, just pure malice, drivel from a nasty, petty-minded. You know what this sounds like to me? (slaps folder) "What all of this about. Nothing sinister, far from it. All this is down to plain old jealously. The middle son. Not the first born or the youngest. The middle, starved of all that affection he sees given to the other two. There he is, not getting mummykins' full attention."

(Blue tie sniggers)

"Yes, I believe it's that simple, quiet boring really."

"You don't 'alf talk some crap." (character in centre of room says)

"Shut up." (Character with blue tells him)

"Correct, they all live at home, not in this, this…"

"Moneyduff." (character in blue tie informs his colleague in the red tie)

"Thank you, yes. Moneyduff, fashioned like some urban Brigadoon, the figment of a diseased imagination. Why the need to place them some distance from himself? To push them away some…?"

"Forty odd miles."

"Indeed, forty odd miles away. This re-location, you know the reason why. He himself lives away from home with his granny, one of the few honest details he has given. Why the need for it, why the need to dump you there?"

"fack orf, no-body dumped me anywhere. Unlike you two muppets, he can't get rid of me."

"Can't get rid of you (sneers), he's determined to get rid of you. What possible need does he have for you? What on earth can you provide for him? This need for manifestations, your just another, probably in a long line of them in his flight from the truth."

"The trufh, the trufh won't 'elp 'im. I know the truth, more that he knows it. I know who I am, more importantly, I know why I am. Do you?" (Stands up)

"Sit down. And shut up." (Blue tie orders)

"Thank you. Why does he need you? You seem sure of that, but explain it to me. You really think so, don't you, even when, quite clearly, he is panning to leave you in a fictional place far, far from himself."

"Lissen, this routine's getting' tiresome, no matter wot 'appens I'll be there to the

most likely, bitter end. The trufh can't 'arm me, but it will spell the end to the likes of you."

"Will it? It would be a small price to pay, to be rid of you. Let's see, shall we?"

AN EPILOGUE OF SORTS

He got a good funeral. Well organised, well attended, thanks to a tv crew, choreographed, menacing in numbers, swollen with counterfeit emotion dealt out in large swathes as the cortege passed. His feet shuffling behind the coffin, hemmed in by an assortment of cousins, feeling and looking every inch the rain-soaked imposter. Head down, moving with the tide of people, a mass of badly dressed androgyny, feeling nothing but the rain and the cold; emphasising his sense of isolation and sense of dislocation.

Gran was there in the big black car, he was glad she was travelling in style and warmth. He had told her that when he returned he would come back to live with her. She smiled which was deeply gratifying to him. He did not mind her tears at the funeral it was understandable, natural. He told her he would come back to the house, so she could look after him, and they both smiled. This would prove to be the impetus he needed. He would go back to studying and he would get up earlier for work and they both smiled at that. Things would be much different, much better he promised. He held her, breathed in her wet coat smell, and told her he loved her. She told him that she loved him and this time, he meant it.

I'm wearing one of me da's old coats, a pair of donated black trousers and tie. I looked a right bleedin' mess, no wot I mean? That's what I told Mickey, Una's recently installed ex, as we were asked to do another lift of the coffin.

Mickey and me carried the coffin at the back with two other smaller family members, Terence and the Da at the front, I wondered what Frances was doing at that moment, probably shopping or shagging. Now, now stop that.

He wondered what Bumpkin would say, she'd be genuinely sorry and sympathetic and The Case For Spontaneous Human Combustion would worry what effect it would have on his work and time-keeping, he wondered what Brian would say, 'So..so..sorry, your bro..bro…brother's dead'. Pro.. pro…probably, ho ho. Or Jimmy, he would put it less sympathetically 'he's dead, so he is."

He did not ask eh John what he thought. He had prepared to bury him with the coffin, into the Irish earth that would forever be a part cockney and beyond the sound of the Bow Bells. Anyway, he would have said something out of place, like about him not belonging there among these good people, what with his monstrous feet plodding behind the coffin.

He was determined to get better.

No wot I mean?

ENDS

© Laurence Todd

XXX

Printed in Great Britain
by Amazon